CANYONS OF NIGHT

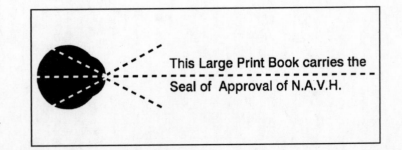

AN ARCANE SOCIETY NOVEL:
THE LOOKING GLASS TRILOGY, BOOK 3

CANYONS OF NIGHT

JAYNE CASTLE

THORNDIKE PRESS
A part of Gale, Cengage Learning

Detroit • New York • San Francisco • New Haven, Conn • Waterville, Maine • London

LIBRARY OF CONGRESS CATALOGING-IN-PUBLICATION DATA

Castle, Jayne.
  Canyons of night : an Arcade Society novel : book III of the looking glass trilogy / by Jayne Castle. — Large print ed.
    p. cm. — (Thorndike Press large print basic)
  ISBN-13: 978-1-4104-3897-3 (hardcover)
  ISBN-10: 1-4104-3897-X (hardcover)
  1. Large type books. I. Title.
PS3561.R44C39 2011
813'.54—dc22   2011030921

Published in 2011 by arrangement with The Berkley Publishing Group, a member of Penguin Group (USA) Inc.

Printed in the United States of America
1 2 3 4 5 6 7 15 14 13 12 11

This one is for Rex.
Your sense of style is classic.

A NOTE FROM JAYNE

Welcome to Rainshadow Island. You are about to discover a whole new aspect of the world of Harmony and learn some of the future secrets of the Arcane Society.

In the Rainshadow novels you will meet the passionate men and women who are drawn to this remote island in the Amber Sea. You will also get to know their friends and neighbors in the community of Shadow Bay. You are invited to be a part of their lives; lives which are deeply entwined with the island's dark and mysterious history.

I hope you will enjoy the Rainshadow novels.

Sincerely,
Jayne

PROLOGUE

Rainshadow Island

The small vehicle was traveling too fast on the narrow, twisted road that snaked along the top of the cliffs. Charlotte Enright heard the insectlike whine of the tiny flash-rock engine behind her and hastily stepped off the pavement onto the relative safety of the shoulder. A moment later one of the familiar low-powered Vibes that visitors rented to get around on the island careened out of the turn.

The driver hit the brakes, bringing the open-sided buggy to a halt beside her.

"Hey, look what we have here," the man behind the wheel said to his two passengers. "It's that weird girl with the glasses who works for that crazy old lady in the antiques store. What are you doing out here all by yourself, Weird Girl?"

There was enough light left in the late summer sky to illuminate the three young men in the car. Charlotte recognized them immediately. They had wandered into Looking Glass Antiques earlier in the day, drawn into the shop not because of an interest in antiques but by the rumors that swirled around her aunt.

"Didn't anyone ever tell you it's dangerous to hang out on empty roads like this late at night?" the man in the passenger seat asked.

His voice echoed along the lonely stretch of road that led to the Preserve. The laughter of his two companions sent icy chills through Charlotte. She started walking. She did not look back. Maybe if she ignored the three they would leave her alone. She quickened her pace, walking faster into the rapidly deepening twilight.

That weird girl with the glasses who works for that crazy old lady in the antiques store. The words might just as well have been emblazoned on her T-shirt, she thought. She was pretty sure that just about everyone on the island, with the exception of her friend Rachel, thought of her in exactly those words.

The driver took his foot off the brake and let the Vibe coast slowly alongside Charlotte.

"Don't run off, Weird Girl," the one in

the passenger seat called out. "We've heard that it gets a little strange out here after dark. Guy back at the bar guaranteed us that if we could get into the Preserve on a moonlit night like this we would see ghosts. You're from around here. Why don't you show us the sights?"

"Yeah, come on now, be friendly, Weird Girl," the driver wheedled. "You're supposed to be nice to tourists."

Charlotte clutched the flashlight very tightly and kept her gaze fixed on the dark woods at the end of Merton Road.

"We'll give you a ride," the driver said, mockingly lecherous. "Come on, get in the car."

"All we want you to do is show us this place they call the Preserve," the one in the backseat urged. "From what we've seen today, there sure as hell isn't anything else of interest on this rock."

Charlotte wondered how the three in the car had found their way all the way out to Merton Road. Only the locals and the summer regulars were aware that the old strip of pavement dead-ended at the border of the private nature conservancy known as the Rainshadow Preserve.

The trio in the Vibe was a familiar species on Rainshadow during the summer months.

11

The type typically arrived on the private yachts and sailboats that crowded the marina on the weekends. They partied heavily all night long in the dockside taverns and restaurants, and when the bars closed down they moved the parties to their boats.

"Come back here, damn it," the driver ordered. He wore a pastel polo shirt that probably had a designer label stitched inside. His light brown hair had obviously been cut in an expensive salon. "We won't hurt you. We just want you to give us a tour of the spooky places the guy in the bar told us about."

"Forget the ugly little bitch, Derek," the man in the backseat said. "No boobs on her, anyway. Trying to get into this Preserve is a waste of time. Let's go back to town. I need a drink and some weed."

"We came all the way out here to see the Preserve," Derek insisted, his tone turning surly. "I'm not going back until this bitch shows us where it is." He raised his voice. "You hear me, weird bitch?"

"Yeah," the man in the passenger seat said. "I want to see the place, too. Let's make the bitch show us."

Charlotte's pulse pounded. She was walking as swiftly as she could. Any faster and she would be running. She was very frightened but her feminine intuition warned her that if she ran the three men would be out of the Vibe in an instant, pursuing her like a pack of wild animals.

"Is she ignoring us?" the man in the passenger seat asked. "Yeah, I think she's ignoring us. That's just flat-out rude. Someone needs to teach her some manners."

"Damn right, Garrett," Derek said. "Let's get her."

"This is stupid," the man in the backseat said. But the other two paid no attention to him.

Derek brought the Vibe to a stop and jumped out. Garrett followed, and so did the man in the rear seat, albeit with obvious reluctance. Charlotte knew that she had no choice now but to run. She fled toward the woods at the end of Merton Road.

Derek and Garrett laughed and gave chase. Her only hope was to reach the dark trees up ahead. If she could get even a short distance into the Preserve she might be able to lose the three behind her. It was common knowledge on the island that things got very strange inside the Preserve.

There were risks to the strategy. She might get lost, herself. It could be days before she was found or managed to stumble out on her own, if ever. According to the local residents it was not unheard of for people to disappear for good inside the Preserve.

The pounding footsteps got louder. Derek and Garrett were gaining on her. She could hear their harsh, angry breathing. She knew then that she probably would not be able to outrun them.

She was almost at the end of the pavement, thinking she just might make it after all, when a hand closed around her arm and dragged her to a halt.

She whirled, all of her still-developing para-senses hitting the upper limits of her talent in response to the adrenaline and fear flooding through her. The driver, Derek, was the one who had grabbed her. Garrett hovered nearby. The third man hung back, clearly uneasy about the way the violence was escalating.

With her senses at full sail, she could see the dark paranormal rainbows cast by the auras of the three men. For all the good that did her, she thought bitterly. She did not need to see the flaring bands of ultralight to know that, of the three, Derek was the most unstable and, therefore, the most dangerous. Why couldn't she have been born with something flashier and more useful in the way of a talent? The ability to deliver a psychic hypnotic command or a freezing blast of energy that would stop Derek cold would have been nice.

She had no choice now but to fight. She flailed wildly with the flashlight. A brief flicker of satisfaction swept through her when the metal barrel struck Derek on his upper arm. She hauled back for another blow.

"Who do you think you are?" Derek snarled. "I'll teach you to hit me."

His face twisted into a vicious mask. He shook her furiously. The flashlight fell from her hand. Her glasses went flying.

Garrett laughed nervously. "That's enough, Derek. She's just a kid."

"Garrett's right," the man from the backseat said. "Come on, Derek, let's get out of here. We've got a lot of drinking left to do tonight. I need my weed, man."

"We're not leaving yet," Derek said. "We're just starting to have some fun."

He drew back a clenched fist, preparing to deliver a punch. Charlotte raised both arms in a desperate attempt to ward off the blow. At the same time she kicked Derek in the knee.

Derek howled.

"Are you crazy?" Garrett said.

"Bitch," Derek screamed. He shook her again.

A shadowy figure materialized out of the woods. Charlotte did not need her glasses to see the obsidian-dark hues of a familiar ultralight rainbow. Slade Attridge.

Slade moved toward the driver with the speed and lethal intent of an attacking specter-cat.

"What the hell?" Garrett yelped, startled.

"Shit," the man from the backseat yelped. "I told you this was a bad idea."

Derek was oblivious to the danger. In his rage, he was obsessed only with punishing Charlotte. He did not realize what was happening until a powerful hand locked on his shoulder.

"Let her go," Slade said. He wrenched Derek away from Charlotte.

Derek screamed. He released Charlotte and frantically tried to scramble out of reach. Slade used one booted foot to swipe Derek's legs out from under him. Derek landed hard on the pavement, shrieking with rage and pain.

"You can't do this to me," he screeched. "You don't know who you're messing with. My dad will have you arrested. He'll sue your ass."

"That should be interesting," Slade said. He looked at the other two. "Get him in the Vibe and get out of here. Come anywhere

16

near her again and you will all wake up in an ICU or maybe just plain dead, depending on my mood at the time. Is that understood?"

"Shit, this guy's crazy," the man from the backseat whispered. He ran for the vehicle. "You guys do what you want. I'm out of here."

He hopped into the driver's seat, rezzed the little engine, and put the Vibe in gear.

"Wait up, damn it." Garrett raced toward the Vibe and jumped into the front seat.

Derek staggered to his feet. "Don't leave me, you bastards. He'll kill me."

"It's a thought," Slade said, as if the idea held great appeal. "Better run."

Derek fled toward the Vibe, which was now halfway through a U-turn.

He lunged forward and managed to dive into the back of the buggy.

The Vibe whined away into the night and vanished around a turn.

A hushed silence fell. The eerie quiet was broken only by the sound of labored breathing. Charlotte realized that she was the one trying to catch her breath. She was shivering but not because she was cold. It was all she could do to stand upright. Great. She was having another stupid panic attack. And in front of Slade Attridge of all people. Just her rotten luck.

"You okay?" Slade asked. He picked up the flashlight and put it in her hand.

"Y-yes. Thanks." She struggled with the deep, square breathing exercise the parapsychologist had taught her and tried to compose herself. "My glasses." She looked around but everything except Slade's darkly luminous rainbow was indistinct. "They fell off."

"I see them," Slade said. He started across the pavement.

"You m-must have really g-good eyes," she said. Geez. Now she was stuttering because of the panic attack. It was all so humiliating.

"Good night vision," Slade said. "Side effect of my talent."

"You're a h-hunter, aren't you? Not a g-ghost hunter but a true hunter-talent. I thought so. I've got a c-cousin who is a hunter. You move the same way he does. Like a b-big specter-cat. Arcane?"

"My mother was Arcane but she never registered me with the Society," Slade said. "She died when I was twelve."

"What about your father?"

"He was a ghost hunter. Died in the tunnels when I was two."

"Geez." She wrapped her arms around

18

herself and forced herself to breathe in the slow, controlled rhythm she had been taught. "Wh-who raised you?"

"The system."

She went blank for a moment. "What system?"

"Foster care."

"Geez."

She could not think of anything else to say. She had never actually met anyone who had been raised in the foster-care system. The stern legal measures set down by the First Generation colonists had been designed to secure the institutions of marriage and the family in stone and they had been very successful. During the two hundred years since the closing of the Curtain, the laws had eased somewhat but not much. The result was that it was rare for a child to be completely orphaned. There was almost always *someone* who had to take you in.

Slade seemed amused. "It wasn't that bad. I wasn't in the system long. I bailed four years ago when I turned fifteen. Figured I'd do better on the streets."

"Geez." No wonder he seemed so much older, she thought. She was fifteen and she could not imagine what it would be like trying to survive on her own.

At least her pulse was starting to slow

19

down a little. The breathing exercises were finally kicking in.

"You're Arcane, aren't you?" Slade asked.

"Yeah, the whole family has been Arcane for generations." She made a face. "Mostly high-end talents. I'm the underachiever in the clan. I'm just a rainbow-reader."

"What's that?"

"I see aura rainbows. Totally useless, trust me." She tried to focus on Slade as he reached down to pick up her glasses. "They're probably smashed, huh?"

"The frames are a little bent and the lenses are scratched up."

"Figures." She took the glasses from him and put them on.

The twisted frames sat askew on her nose. The scratched lenses made it difficult to see Slade's face clearly. She knew exactly what he looked like, though, because she had seen him often in town and down at the marina where he worked. He was nineteen but there was something about his sharply etched features and unreadable gray-blue eyes that made him seem so much older and infinitely more experienced. Other boys his age were still boys. Slade was a man.

She and Rachel had speculated endlessly about where he had come from and, more important, whether he had a girlfriend. If he was dating anyone they were very sure that she was not a local girl. In a town as small as Shadow Bay everyone would know if the stranger who worked at the marina was seeing an island girl.

He had shown up in the Bay at the start of the tourist season that summer, looking for work. Ben Murphy at the marina had given him a job. Slade rented a room above a dockside shop by the week. He was polite and hardworking but he kept to himself. Occasionally he caught the Friday afternoon ferry and disappeared for the weekend. It was assumed that he went to a larger town on one of the other nearby islands — Thursday Harbor, maybe, or maybe he went all the way to Frequency City. No one knew for sure. But he was always back at work at the marina on Monday morning.

"Luckily I've got a backup pair of glasses at my aunt's house," Charlotte said.

She was immediately mortified. She felt like an idiot talking about her glasses to the man who currently featured so vividly in her fantasies. Not that Slade knew about his role in her dreams. She was pretty sure that to him she was just the weird girl who worked for her crazy old aunt in the antiques shop.

"What are you doing out here at this time

of night?" Slade asked.

"What do you think I'm doing out here? I wanted to see the Preserve. My aunt talks about it sometimes but she won't take me inside."

"For good reason. It's beautiful in places but it's dangerous in some parts. Easy to get lost inside. The Foundation that controls the Preserve put up those no-trespassing signs and the fence for a reason."

"You were inside just a few minutes ago. I saw you come out through the trees."

"I'm a hunter, remember? I can see where I'm going."

"Oh, yeah, the night-vision thing."

"Are you sure you're okay? Your breathing sounds funny."

"Actually, I'm getting over a panic attack. I'm doing a breathing exercise. This is so embarrassing."

"Panic attack, huh? Well, you had good reason to have one tonight. Getting assaulted by three jerks on a lonely road would be enough to scare the daylights out of anyone."

"The attacks are linked to my stupid talent. I started getting them when I came into my para-senses two years ago. At first everyone assumed that I was just reacting to the stress of high school. But finally my mom sent me to a para-shrink who said it appeared to be a side effect of my new senses."

Great. Now she was babbling about her personal problems.

"That's gotta be tough," Slade said.

"Tell me about it. If I run hot for any length of time, I start shaking and it gets hard to breathe. I was really jacked a few minutes ago so I'm paying for it now. I'll be okay in a couple of minutes, honest."

"You should go home now," Slade said. "I'll walk with you and make sure those guys don't come back."

"They won't return," she said, very certain. She finally managed to take a deep breath. Her jangled senses and her nerves were finally calming. "I don't want to go home yet. I came all the way out here to see the Preserve."

"Does your aunt know where you are?"

"No. Aunt Beatrix took the ferry to Frequency City today to check out some antiques at an estate sale. She won't return until tomorrow."

Slade looked toward the dark woods. He seemed to hesitate and then he shrugged. "I'll take you inside but just for a few minutes."

Delight snapped through her.

"Will you? That would be wonderful. Thanks."

He started walking back along the road toward the woods. She switched on the flashlight and hurried to catch up with him.

"I heard someone at the grocery store say that you're going to leave Rainshadow for good tomorrow," she said tentatively. "Is it true?"

"That's the plan. I've been accepted at the academy of the FBPI."

"You're joining the Federal Bureau of Psi Investigation? Wow. That is so high-rez. Congratulations."

"Thanks. I'm packed. I'll catch the morning ferry."

She tried to think of what to say next. Nothing brilliant came to mind.

"Do you think those three guys will try to have you arrested?" she asked.

"No."

"How can you be sure? They might remember you from the marina."

"Even if they do, those three aren't going to go to the local cops. If they did they'd have to explain why they stopped you on the road."

"Oh, right." Her spirits lightened at that realization. "And I'd tell everyone how they attacked me. Chief Halstead knows me and

24

he's known Aunt Beatrix forever. He would believe me long before he took the word of a bunch of off-islanders."

"Yes," Slade said. "He would."

She was surprised to hear the respect in Slade's voice. She glanced at his profile.

"I saw the two of you talking together a lot this summer," she ventured.

"Halstead is the one who suggested I apply to the academy. He even wrote a recommendation."

That evening Slade gave her a brief glimpse of the paranormal wonderland that was the Preserve by night. And then he walked her home, saw her inside the cottage on the bluff, and waited until she locked the door. She listened to his footsteps going down the front porch steps; listened until he was gone and the only sound was that of the wind sighing in the trees.

The following morning she went down to the ferry dock. Slade didn't see her at first. He lounged against the railing, a duffel bag slung over his shoulder. He was alone. There were a handful of other passengers waiting for the ferry but no one was there to see him off to his new life in the Federal Bureau of Psi Investigation.

She approached him cautiously, not certain how he would react. She knew that as far as he was concerned she was just a kid he had helped out of a jam and then humored with a short trip into the forbidden territory of the Preserve.

"Slade?" She stopped a short distance away.

He had been watching the ferry pull into the dock. At the sound of her voice he turned his head and saw her. He smiled.

"I see you found your backup glasses," he said.

"Yes." She felt the heat rise in her cheeks. Her second pair of frames was even nerdier than the new pair that had gotten busted last night. "I came to say good-bye."

"Yeah?"

"And to tell you to be careful, okay?" she added very earnestly. "The FBPI goes after some very dangerous people. Serial killers and drug traffickers."

"I've heard that." His eyes glittered with amusement. "I'll be careful."

She was feeling more awkward by the second. At this rate she would have a panic attack without even raising her dumb talent.

She held out the small box she had brought with her. "I also wanted to give you this. Sort of a thank-you gift for what you

26

did for me last night."

He eyed the box as if not sure what to make of it. It dawned on her that a man who didn't have a family of his own probably didn't get many gifts. He reached out and took the box.

"Thanks," he said. "What is it?"

"Nothing important," she assured him. "Just an old pocketknife."

He got the lid off the oblong box and took out the narrow black crystal object inside. He studied it with interest. "How does it work? I don't see the blade."

She smiled. "Well, that's the unusual thing about that knife. It was made by a master craftsman named Vegas Takashima. He died about forty years ago. He was Arcane and he made each knife by hand so his pieces are infused with a lot of his creative psi. Whatever he did made the blades almost indestructible. You'll eventually figure out how it works and when you do, you'll see it's still good. It will last for decades, maybe another century or two."

"Thank you."

She hesitated. "I tuned it for you."

Slade raised his brows. "You can tune objects that are hot?"

She shrugged. "Provided there's enough energy in them. It's a rainbow-reader thing."

"What does tuning a para-antique do?"

"Nothing very useful," she admitted. "But people seem to like it when I find the right object and manipulate the frequencies to resonate harmoniously with their auras. Just a trick."

He hefted the Takashima knife on his palm and smiled slowly. "It does feel good." He closed his fingers around the black crystal knife. "Like it belongs to me."

"That's how the tuning thing works," she said earnestly. "It's not a real spectacular talent but my family feels I may have a career selling art and antiques."

"Is that what you want to do?"

"No." She brightened. "I want to get a degree in para-archaeology and work for one of the Arcane museums. Or maybe go underground with some of the academic and research people who explore the alien ruins."

"Sounds exciting."

"Not as exciting as the FBPI but I'd really like to do it."

"Good luck."

"Thanks."

He slipped the knife into the pocket of his jacket. The ferry was docked now. The three other people who had been waiting for it started down the ramp. Slade hitched the duffel bag higher on his shoulder.

"Time to go," he said.

"Good-bye. Thanks for last night. And remember to be careful, okay?"

"Sure."

He leaned forward slightly and kissed her lightly on the forehead. Before she could decide how to handle the situation, he was walking away from her, boarding the ferry.

She stood on the dock until the ferry sailed out of the harbor and out of sight. Just before it disappeared she waved. She thought she saw Slade lift a hand in farewell but she couldn't be sure. Her backup glasses were fitted with an old prescription and her distance vision was blurry. Or maybe the problem was the tears in her eyes.

She made a promise to herself that morning. When she went home to Frequency City at the end of the month she was going to get a trendy new haircut and a pair of contact lenses. Common sense told her that she was highly unlikely to ever meet Slade Attridge again. But just in case she did get lucky, she was going to do her best to make certain that, whatever else happened, he didn't kiss her as if she were his kid sister.

CHAPTER 1

Rainshadow Island, fifteen years later . . .

Charlotte folded her arms on the glass-topped sales counter and watched the two feral beasts come through the door of Looking Glass Antiques. One was definitely human, definitely male, and definitely dangerous. The second was a scruffy-looking ball of gray fluff with two bright blue eyes, six small paws, and an attitude. The dust bunny rode on Slade Attridge's shoulder and Charlotte was quite sure that in his own miniature way he could be just as dangerous as his human companion. They were both born to hunt, she thought.

"Welcome to Looking Glass Antiques, Chief Attridge," Charlotte said. "You might want to keep an eye on Rex. I have a strict you-break-it-you-buy-it policy."

Slade stopped just inside the doorway. He quartered the shop's cluttered front room with a swift, assessing glance, cold, mag-

31

steel eyes faintly narrowed. Rex sleeked out a little, revealing a ragged ear that appeared to have been badly mangled in a fight at some point in the past. His second set of eyes, the ones he used for night hunts, popped open. At least he wasn't showing any teeth, Charlotte thought. They said that with dust bunnies, by the time you saw the teeth it was too late. The bunnies were cute when they were fluffed up but under all that fur lay the ruthless heart of a small predator.

"This shop is even hotter than it was fifteen years ago when your aunt ran it," Slade said.

Charlotte was amused. "You remember, hmm?"

Slade looked straight at her. "Oh, yeah."

Small thrills flashed across Charlotte's senses. *I had it bad for him fifteen years ago and this time around it's going to be a million times worse.*

Her fantasies about Slade had been dormant for so long that she had been convinced that she had outgrown them. But when he had walked off the morning ferry five days ago to take over the position of police chief on Rainshadow Island, she'd had a shocking revelation. The Arcane matchmakers had given up on her, labeled her unmatchable and blamed it on the nature of her talent. But one look at Slade and she knew why she had never been content with any of the other men she had met. Some part of her had always insisted on comparing her dates to the man of her dreams. It was not fair, it was not wise, but that was how it had been. And now Dream Man was here, standing right in front of her.

She was saved from having to come up with a snappy response by Rex. The dust bunny chortled and bounded down from Slade's shoulder. Charlotte watched uneasily as he fluttered through the cluttered space and vanished behind a pile of vintage purses and handbags.

Slade surveyed the room. "Coming in here was always a bit like walking into a mild lightning storm but the sensation has gotten stronger. There's more energy now."

"Most people aren't aware of all the psi in this shop," she said. "At least not on a conscious level. But strong sensitives usually pick up on it. The reason it feels hotter now is because my aunt acquired a lot more stock during the last fifteen years before she died. In addition, I brought most of the objects from my store in Frequency City with me a few weeks ago when I closed my business there and moved to the island."

"Hard to believe fifteen years have gone by."

"Yes," she said.

Trying not to be obvious, she raised her talent a little and studied Slade's aura rainbow. He was not running hot so the bands of dark ultralight were faint, but that was enough to tell her Slade hadn't changed much in those fifteen years. He had simply become a purer, more intense version of what he had been at nineteen: hard, tough, self-contained, and self-controlled. His eyes were colder now, as cold and bleak as the mag-steel they resembled.

Slade hadn't smiled a lot fifteen years ago and she was pretty sure he'd never been prone to frequent displays of lightheartedness. But from what she had seen of him during the past five days he had evidently lost what little he had once possessed in the way of a sense of humor or cheerful spirits.

"Out of curiosity," Slade said, "didn't your aunt ever sell anything? This place looks like someone's attic, a two-hundred-year-old attic, at that."

She laughed and pushed her glasses higher on her nose. "All Aunt Beatrix cared about was collecting hot antiques. But I did a lot of business back in Frequency and I expect to make money with Looking Glass, as well. Trust me, I won't starve. I'm good at this."

To her shock his mouth kicked up a bit at the corner in the barest hint of a smile. "So it turned out you did have a career in art and antiques sales, just like your family thought?"

"Yes. Aunt Beatrix left her shop and the entire collection to me when she died a while back. I decided to operate from here instead of Frequency. It took a while to process my aunt's will so this place has been locked up for some time. I just got the doors open again a couple of weeks ago. I'm still taking inventory and trying to get the paperwork straightened out. Aunt Beatrix was not much for organization."

"I can see that."

"Weird that we both wound up back here on Rainshadow, isn't it? I mean, what are the odds?"

"Damned if I know," he said. "Returning to Rainshadow wasn't in my plans until recently."

"Oh?"

"I'm making a career change. Turns out I need a short-term job to pay the bills while I get things going in a new direction. A friend told me that the chief's job here on the island was open so I took it."

"I see." It was as if all the energy in the room had gone suddenly flat. So much for the little frissons of excitement and anticipation that had been flickering through her over the course of the past five days. Slade had no intention of hanging around Shadow Bay for long. She cleared her throat. "This isn't a permanent move for you, then?"

"Not if I can help it," he said. "I figure I'll be here six months at most. I'll need that much time to get my new project up and running. You?"

"After Aunt Beatrix died, I had planned to close Looking Glass and ship the stock to my Frequency City store but I changed my mind. I sold that store and moved here, instead."

"What made you do that? Weren't things going well for you in Frequency City?"

"Very well," she said. She wasn't boasting. It was a fact. "I made a lot of money with that store. But I'll make money with this one, too. The power of online marketing, you know. In addition, I plan to turn Looking Glass into a destination antiques shop. In my line it's all about reputation, and when it comes to paranormal antiques, I'm one of the best in the business."

"I believe you," he said. "I always knew

you'd be successful at whatever you decided to do."

"Really? No one in my family had a lot of hope. Whatever gave you that impression?"

He moved one hand slightly. "Probably the way you tried to fight off that bastard who manhandled you that night out on Merton Road."

"Wasn't like I had a lot of options that night."

"Most people freeze when they face serious violence. They can't function. You were fighting."

"And losing," she pointed out dryly.

"But you weren't going down without a fight. That's what counts. That's why I agreed to take you into the Preserve that night. Figured you were owed that much after what you'd gone through."

"Oh," she said. "I was scared to death that night, you know."

"It was the logical response to the situation."

There was a muffled clunk from the far side of the shop. Charlotte heard a faint, ominous buzzing noise. She realized that she could no longer see Rex.

"Your dust bunny," she yelped. Alarmed, she rushed out from behind the counter. "Where is he? What's he doing?"

"Rex is not my dust bunny. We're buddies, that's all."

"Yeah, yeah, I understand. That's not the point. The point is that you are responsible for him while he is in this shop. Now where is he?"

"He may have gone behind that fancy little table with the mirror."

The buzzing sound continued. Charlotte heard more thumps and thuds.

"That dressing table is a genuine First Century Pre–Era of Discord piece," she snapped. She hurried across the room to the exquisitely inlaid dressing table. "It was designed by Fenwick LeMasters, himself. The inlays are green amber and obsidian. The mirror and frame are original, for goodness' sake."

"Who is Fenwick LeMasters?"

"Just one of the finest furniture craftsman of his time. Also a very powerful talent who could work green amber. Collectors pay thousands for his pieces. Oh, never mind."

She peered over the top of the dressing table and saw Rex. The dust bunny had trapped a vintage action figure in the corner between a First Generation cabinet that reeked of the old-Earth para-antiquities it had once contained and a Second Generation floor lamp. Rex was batting the toy unmercifully with his paw as if tormenting a mouse or some other prey. The foot-high plastic figure wore long, flowing plastic robes marked with alchemical signs. The toy was armed with a small, fist-sized crystal.

The unprovoked assault had activated whatever energy was left in the old, run-down amber battery inside the figure. The action doll repeatedly raised and lowered one arm as though to ward off Rex. The buzzing noise came from the odd little crystal weapon. Each time the arm shifted, the toy weapon flashed and sparked with weak, violet-hued light.

"Stop that," Charlotte said to Rex. "Sylvester is a very valuable collectible. Fewer than five hundred of them were made."

Rex ignored her. He took another swipe at the figure.

She started to reach down to retrieve the action figure but common sense made her hesitate. Dust bunnies could be dangerous when provoked.

She rounded on Slade, instead. "Do something about Rex. I'm serious. That figure is worth at least a thousand dollars to certain Arcane collectors."

Slade came to stand beside her. He looked down at Rex and the hapless Sylvester doll.

"That's enough, Rex," Slade said quietly. "You don't want to mess with Sylvester Jones. According to the legends the old bastard could take care of himself."

To Charlotte's relief Rex stopped batting the figure. He sat back on his rear legs and fixed Slade with what Charlotte concluded was the dust bunny equivalent of a disgusted eye-roll. He sauntered off to investigate a pile of vintage stuffed animals.

"Whew." Charlotte scooped up the action figure and examined it closely. "Luckily I don't think he did any damage."

Slade looked at the toy. "Never saw one of those. When were they made?"

"About thirty years ago. The designer was Arcane, obviously. Most of the customers who bought the original Sylvester Jones action figures for their kids assumed the character was supposed to be an Old World sorcerer. But everyone who was connected to the Society recognized him at once. Sort of an inside marketing joke." Satisfied that the action figure was unharmed, Charlotte set it on top of the dressing table. "Luckily Sylvester seems to have survived."

"Sure. This is Sylvester Jones, we're talking about."

Charlotte smiled. "True. Legend has it he was a hard man to kill."

"Tell me about the break-in," Slade said.

"Right." She dusted off her hands. "As I explained to Myrna when I called the station this morning, I *think* I had a break-in. The problem is that I don't know if anything was stolen."

"I can understand why it would be hard to tell if something was missing. This place is crammed with junk."

Charlotte glared. "That's antiques and collectibles to you."

"Right. Antiques and collectibles. Tell me about the break-in you think you had," he said.

"He came through the back door. I'm positive I locked it last night when I closed up."

"No one locks their doors here in Shadow Bay."

"I do. I'm from the city, remember? At any rate, the door was unlocked this morning when I arrived. And there are what look like muddy prints on the floor."

"Oh, good," Slade said. "Actual clues. That should be interesting."

"You're not taking this seriously, are you?"

"In the five days that I have been chief of police here the most serious crime I've had to deal with involved the supposed theft of Hoyt Wilkins's bicycle. It turned up the fol-

41

lowing day. Astonishingly, it was still leaning against the tree where Hoyt had left it when he realized he was too drunk to ride it home from the Driftwood Tavern."

"I heard that two nights ago you also had to break up a fight at the Driftwood."

"Breaking up a bar fight is not the same thing as conducting an investigation. Mostly it involves trying not to get slugged while you separate the drunken idiots involved."

"But wait, there's more," she announced triumphantly. "Yesterday you arrested those two hot-weed runners who anchored their boat in the marina in order to hide from the Coast Guard."

"Both of those guys were too stoned on their own product to notice that they'd been arrested. All I did was throw them in jail until the authorities from Frequency could get here to collect them and the weed," Slade said.

"Still, it sounds like a busy first week on the job. Why am I getting the feeling that you're already bored?"

"Is it that obvious?" Slade asked.

"If you didn't want to be a small-town police chief, why on earth did you take the job here on Rainshadow?"

"I told you, I needed something to tide me over until I can get my project up and running."

"Things didn't work out in the FBPI?"

"Let's just say I'm ready for a change. Now, about your break-in."

"Follow me."

She led the way through the crowded, shadowed space and into the back room of the shop. She was very aware of Slade following close behind her. *Face it,* she thought, *he's the sexiest man you've ever met in your entire life and you are alone with him on an island.*

Okay, not alone, exactly. She and Slade shared Rainshadow with the other residents, but an island was an island, and given that a ferry that operated twice a day was the only regular link to the outside world, there was a very real sense of remoteness and isolation.

The back room of Looking Glass was even more crowded than the front sales room. It was jammed almost to the ceiling with packing crates and shipping boxes full of antiques and collectibles that her aunt had never bothered to unpack. The containers formed a narrow canyon that led to the rear door. There were also several new crates stacked around the room. They contained the objects that she had elected to bring with her when she closed down her Frequency shop.

"I don't envy you trying to take an inventory," Slade said. "Some of these crates look as if they've been sitting here for decades."

"Like I said, Aunt Beatrix wasn't big on organizing stuff."

"This goes beyond a lack of organizational skills. There's a word for folks with this kind of psychological problem, you know."

"Hoarder? Yes, I know." Charlotte stopped. "What can I say? It's no secret that my aunt was a little weird." She gestured down the narrow path created by the towering walls of crates. "That's the door that was unlocked this morning when I arrived."

Slade walked forward and crouched on the floor directly in front of the door. "Huh," he said.

"What do you think?" she asked.

"Looks like the print of a running shoe." Slade got to his feet. "Judging by the muddled footprints, he spent some time in this room and then went into the front of the shop. Turned around and came back here. Left the same way he got in. Through the back door."

"Believe it or not, I figured that much out all by myself."

"Yeah?" Slade raised his brows. "You ever

think of pursuing a career in crime fighting?"

"Very funny. What do you think happened here?"

"I think someone found the door open last night, walked into the shop, took a look around and then left."

"I told you, I locked up last night," she said firmly.

Slade glanced at the lock on the back door. "Even if you did, all anyone would need to get through that door is a credit card."

"I intend to order new locks. But there's been so much else to do that I haven't gotten around to it yet."

"Good plan."

She frowned. "Shouldn't you be dusting for fingerprints or something?"

"Oh, yeah, and maybe swab for DNA while I'm at it. Thanks for reminding me."

"You really are not going to treat this seriously, are you?"

He looked at her. "If you were in Frequency City and your shop got robbed what do you think the cops would do?"

She wrinkled her nose. "Not much. Probably just ask for a list of stolen goods in case any of the objects turned up in a pawn shop."

"Since nothing appears to have been stolen here and there are no pawn shops on Rainshadow, the scope of this investigation is somewhat limited."

"Cripes. You're really not into your job, are you?"

Slade shrugged. "It's just a temporary detour."

"It strikes me that you have a very poor attitude, Chief Attridge."

"Okay, okay. Here's the most likely scenario. Last night after closing up someone noticed that the door of your shop was open. He came inside, took a quick look around to make sure everything was okay, and then he left. How's that for a theory of the crime?"

"Absolutely pitiful. But it's obviously all I'm going to get in the way of law enforcement so I'll take it." She turned and went into the front room. "Would you like a cup of coffee?"

"Depends. Is that a bribe? If it is, I think you're supposed to include a doughnut."

"Sorry, no doughnuts. Something tells me bribery would be useless with you, anyway."

"What makes you so sure of that?"

"My intuition. You are in luck, however. I happen to have half a loaf of leftover zucchini bread that my neighbor, Thelma Duncan, made for me."

"Thelma Duncan's zucchini bread seems to be everywhere at the moment. Myrna brought a loaf to the station this morning. Rex ate it."

"The whole loaf?"

"Well, he and Officer Willis split it. Turns out Rex loves Mrs. Duncan's zucchini bread."

"That's good, because I'm told it will be around for a while. Mrs. Duncan is an incredible gardener and as it happens zucchini season just hit. I'll cut a slice for Rex."

She went behind the counter and unwrapped the zucchini bread. She was very aware of Slade watching her as she cut a slice and set it on a small paper plate. She set the plate on the counter.

Slade looked over his shoulder. "Come and get it, Rex. Zucchini bread."

There was a muffled chortle from the vicinity of the vintage purses and bags. Rex appeared. He scampered across the room and bounded up onto the counter. He rushed to the plate of zucchini bread and fell to it with evident enthusiasm.

"Amazing," Charlotte said. "You'd think after the loaf he shared with Willis this morning he would have had his fill of zucchini bread."

"Not yet," Slade said.

Rex polished off the slice of zucchini bread and bounded back down to the floor. He disappeared amid the array of antiques.

Charlotte ladled coffee into the filter. "Keep an eye on him, please."

"That's hard to do in this place."

"I'm warning you —"

"I know. Your you-break-it-you-buy-it policy."

"Right." Charlotte poured water into the coffeemaker and started the machine.

There was a short silence behind her. She watched coffee drip into the glass pot.

"You never went for a full Covenant Marriage," Slade said after a while.

Startled, she swung around. "No." She took a deep breath. "No, I haven't. Not yet." She turned back to the coffee machine. "I take it you never went for a CM, either."

"No. Tried a Marriage of Convenience somewhere along the line but it didn't work out."

The legally recognized Marriage of Convenience had been designed by the First Generation settlers as a short-term arrangement that allowed couples to experiment with commitment before moving into a full-blown Covenant Marriage. Young people were encouraged to try an MC before taking the plunge into a Covenant Marriage. An MC could be dissolved by either party for any reason, no harm, no foul. Unless there was a baby. A baby changed everything. In legal terms it transformed an MC into a full Covenant Marriage.

The legal and social bonds of a Covenant Marriage were as solid as alien quartz. There was a move afoot to make divorce easier but for now it was extremely rare largely because it was a legal and financial nightmare, not to mention social and political suicide.

Only the very wealthy and well-connected could afford a divorce, but they usually avoided it because the repercussions were major. Politicians could expect to be kicked out of office if they dared to break free of a CM. CEOs got fired by their boards of directors. Exclusive clubs canceled memberships. Invitations to important social functions dried up.

Most sensible people who found themselves in an untenable marriage simply agreed to live separate lives. But their social and legal responsibilities toward each other and their offspring were not affected. Family came first. Always.

The downside of making a poor choice when it came to a spouse ensured the stability of one profession in particular, that of matchmaking. Families did their utmost to make certain that couples were well matched by certified marriage consultants.

"You know," Slade said, "I always figured you'd be matched by now. Maybe even have a few kids."

"Did you?" She smiled over her shoulder. "I'm amazed you even remembered me, let alone thought about me during the past fifteen years."

He reached into the pocket of his trousers and took out the black crystal pocketknife she had given him the morning he had sailed off to his new career in the FBPI.

"I thought about you every time I used this," he said.

Delight sparkled through her. "You kept it all these years."

"It's a good knife." He dropped it back into his pocket. "You were right about the blade. Still sharp and still strong. It saved my ass more than once."

"Really?"

"Really."

She smiled, ridiculously pleased. "Nothing like a Takashima knife. How long did it take you to figure out how to open it?"

"I had it down by the time the ferry reached Frequency City. Takes a little talent to rez it."

"Yes," she said. "It does."

"Since we seem to find ourselves stuck together on this rock for a while, would you be interested in having dinner with me tonight?" Slade asked quietly.

Although she had been fantasizing about him since she had watched him walk off the ferry last week, the invitation nonetheless caught her by surprise. She had to work hard to keep her response calm and light.

"Sounds great," she said. "There are not a lot of options when it comes to restaurants around here. How about the Marina View?"

"I was thinking my place," Slade said. "I'll pick up some fresh salmon at Hank's."

"All right," she said. "What can I bring?"

He pondered that briefly. "You'll probably want something green to go with the salmon."

"A few veggies on the plate is always good. In addition to the zucchini bread, Mrs. Duncan has been inundating me with tomatoes and basil. I'll make a salad."

"My keen cop intuition tells me you probably drink white wine, right?"

"I drink red, too," she assured him. "It's not like I'm inflexible. But white goes better with fish."

"I'll pick up a bottle on the way home,"

51

he said. "All I've got in the refrigerator is beer."

There was a faint thump from the back room.

"Rex." Charlotte rushed back out from behind the counter. She shot Slade a glowering look. "I told you to keep an eye on him."

"Sorry."

Rex appeared in the opening between the two rooms. He carried a small black evening bag studded with glittering black beads. The dainty purse was barely large enough to hold a lipstick and a compact.

Charlotte confronted him, her hands planted on her hips. "Step away from the clutch."

To her amazement, Rex dropped the object at her feet.

"I think he likes you," Slade said. "Usually he ignores commands like that. What is that thing?"

"A very nice Claudia Lockwood evening clutch bag. It's worth several hundred dollars in good condition and this purse is mint."

Rex sat back on his haunches and fixed her with an expectant expression.

"He wants you to throw the purse," Slade said.

"Forget it. This thing is too valuable to be used as a dust bunny toy." She hesitated. "I didn't know dust bunnies liked to play fetch."

"Rex doesn't exactly play fetch," Slade said. "Not like a dog, at any rate. But if you throw an object he goes after it."

"What does he do with it?"

"He kills it," Slade said.

"Obviously you want to be careful what you throw for him."

"Very careful," Slade agreed.

She looked down at Rex. "Sorry, Rex. I can't let you rip this to pieces."

Rex's expression intensified. He was utterly still on his rear legs, a statue of a dust bunny.

Charlotte laughed. "Do you think he's trying to use psychic power to make me do what he wants?"

"Wouldn't put it past him."

"You can't have the purse," she said to Rex. "How about a duck?"

She went to the counter and picked up the small, yellow rubber duck sitting near the cash register. She squeezed the duck a couple of times. The duck squeaked. Rex was electrified with excitement.

She tossed the duck into the back room. Rex leaped to follow. There was a thump.

Several increasingly faint, desperate squeaks could be heard. Eventually there was silence followed by much gleeful chortling.

"Something tells me the duck didn't make it," Charlotte said. She went behind the counter and poured the coffee. She set the mug on the counter in front of Slade. She studied his cool cop eyes.

"You know who was inside my shop last night, don't you?" she said.

"Yes," Slade said. He picked up the coffee mug. "I'll talk to him. It won't happen again."

CHAPTER 2

Hank Levenson tossed the headless, tailless fish onto the scale. "Lot of expensive Amber River salmon for one person to eat. Planning on sharing with the dust bunny? I can always sell you a smaller piece of the salmon and give you some cheap bottom fish for Rex. Doubt if he'd know the difference."

Slade leaned one arm against the glass display case and contemplated his options. There was no point trying to finesse the situation. The news that he'd had dinner with the owner of Looking Glass Antiques would be all over Shadow Bay by tomorrow morning, no matter what he did.

"I'm not so sure that Rex wouldn't know the difference," he said. "He's damn picky. He'll get some of that salmon but I'm planning on sharing the rest with a dinner guest."

"A guest, hmm?" Hank swept the salmon off the scale and wrapped the silvery fish in

55

brown paper. "Would that be Charlotte En-right, by any chance?"

"What was your first clue?"

Hank snorted. "Saw you come out of her shop this morning. Had a feeling you and she might get on well together."

Hank was in his late sixties. He had grown up on Rainshadow and he was endowed with the tough, weathered features of a man who had spent his life on or around the water. When he reached for a strip of tape to seal the package of salmon, a portion of an old tattoo appeared beneath the rolled-back sleeve of his shirt. The image was that of a mythical sea serpent.

"Charlotte thought she had a break-in last night," Slade said. "I went to her shop to check it out."

"Yeah?" Hank looked up, eyes faintly narrowed in concern. "Anything stolen?"

"Who knows?"

Hank snorted. "Good point. That place is crammed with junk. Beatrix Enright was a very strange woman and she got more eccentric toward the end. She was obsessed with those antiques of hers."

Slade remembered the talk he had overheard that long-ago summer when he had worked at the marina. "I remember. Everyone thought she was a little weird fifteen years ago."

"She got even more odd as time went by, and that's saying something around here. Rainshadow attracts a lot of eccentrics. We know the type well. The thing about Beatrix was that she was always buying antiques from estate sales and the like but she never seemed to worry much about selling the stuff, leastways not as far as I could tell."

"She managed to keep the business going," Slade pointed out.

"That's a fact. Sometimes I got the feeling that she was searching for some particular object but whatever it was, I don't think she ever found it. What happened to make Charlotte think that she'd had an intruder?"

"She found the back door of the shop unlocked this morning. It made her nervous. But as far as she can tell, nothing is missing."

"City girl." Hank nodded in a knowing way. "Glad it was nothing serious. But then, we don't have a lot of trouble around here."

"I've noticed that," Slade said.

"Once in a while we have a few problems with some of the boating crowd on the long summer weekends. A little local drunk and disorderly stuff. And there are always a few hot-weed dealers operating in the islands, as you discovered this week."

"Right." Slade glanced at his watch.

"The Amber Sea Islands have always been popular with smugglers, drug runners, and pirates." There was a note of pride in Hank's voice. "Long history of that sort of thing around here. Fifty years ago, Captain Harry Sebastian himself sailed these waters. Legend has it he buried his treasure somewhere on Rainshadow."

"And then disappeared, presumably murdered by his former business partner who felt he had a claim to the treasure. I know the story. Heard it fifteen years ago."

Hank winked. "They say Sebastian's ghost walks the Preserve at night."

"If I see him, I'll arrest him."

Hank laughed. "You do that."

Slade took another look at the portion of the tattoo that was visible on Hank's arm. He'd seen similar tats, mostly on old smugglers.

"But generally speaking, the Bay is a real quiet place," Hank continued with satisfaction. "Yes, sir, I'd say it's the perfect little town for a man in your profession."

"So people keep telling me." Slade reached for his wallet. "What do I owe you?"

"Nineteen ninety-five. I gave you the local rate."

"Thanks. I appreciate that."

Hank handed over the package of fish and lounged against the counter. "No, sir, don't have any of the usual big-city-crime problems here on Rainshadow."

"I've noticed."

No rogue psychics to profile, Slade thought. No serial killers. No investigations of murder by paranormal means. And it was just as well because he was no longer able to handle that kind of work.

"Got to admit, I wasn't sure what to expect when that Reflections business opened up at the old lake lodge a few months back," Hank continued. "But so far the folks coming in for the retreats seem like a quiet, well-behaved bunch. They spend money in the shops. The chef at the lodge buys his fish from me, so I'm not complaining."

"Given what it costs to attend one of those flaky weekend meditation seminars, I doubt that Reflections will attract the kind of crowd that is prone to break into the local shops and businesses," Slade said.

Hank chuckled. "You're right about that." He glanced through the front window of the shop at Rex, who was perched on the railing outside, graciously accepting pats and coos from passersby.

"Where'd you pick up the dust bunny?"

59

Hank asked.

"He showed up a while back," Slade said.

"Didn't know they made good pets."

"They don't," Slade said. "Thanks for the fish. See you later."

"You bet." Hank beamed. "Have a good time tonight now, you hear?"

"I'll do my best."

Outside on the front porch, Rex examined the package of salmon with great interest.

"Forget it," Slade said. "This is dinner, not an afternoon snack. It's going into the refrigerator at the station and then it's going back to the cabin after work."

Rex appeared to lose interest in the salmon. Slade was not deceived. He went down the steps.

Cautiously he jacked up his other senses a couple of degrees. He knew better. The doctors at the clinic had warned him against pushing his talent beyond a very minimal range. But he was unable to resist. He had to know how much worse the damage was getting, had to know how much time he had left before his senses shut down altogether and he went psi-blind.

His other vision kicked in for a few seconds. Waterfront Street — with its weathered, wooden storefronts — the ferry landing, and the marina began to glow in eerie shades of ultralight. The footprints of the people strolling on the sidewalks heated with iridescent energy. But when he inched a little higher and tried to work his way into the zone, he sensed the seething storm of energy that was out there waiting to envelop him. The good news was that it did not seem to have grown any darker since he had last checked.

He still had some time left before his talent failed completely, but the psychic powers that had shaped his life and made him so good at what he did for the past fifteen years were slowly but surely being consumed by the storm at the end of the spectrum.

He clamped down on the useless tide of rage that threatened to well up inside. There was no point giving in to the anger. He had to keep moving forward because there was no alternative.

At least he was going to have dinner with an attractive, interesting woman tonight. It had been a long time since he'd had a date. Susan had left after the verdict had come down from the doctors and para-psychs. He didn't blame her. For a time it had looked like he was probably going to self-destruct. They had both known that there was nothing she could do to stop the slide. Even if he did not put a mag-rez pistol to his head or get permanently lost in a haze of drugs and alcohol as some expected, he would never again be the man she had planned to marry.

Susan had cut her losses and he had been relieved when she did. At least he no longer had to pretend that some day he might recover his talent; that some day he might be able to return to the Bureau.

But Charlotte Enright had never known him in what he now thought of as his other life. To her he was a clean slate. No baggage. And he would not be hanging around Shadow Bay long enough for her to get the wrong impression. He'd been straight up about that. She now knew that he planned to leave within six months. He was pleased that he'd gotten that issue out of the way before he'd asked her to dinner.

They were just two semi-strangers passing in the night, he thought. No reason they couldn't spend some time together. She wasn't a kid anymore. They were both adults.

He had been literally stunned to see her when he'd walked off the ferry five days ago. Most of the town had turned out to greet the new chief of police, but it had been the sight of Charlotte in the crowd that had sent the jolt of lightning across his senses and awakened sensations he could not identify.

The first thought that had slammed through him that day was completely irrational. *It's as if she's been here, waiting for me all these years.*

It made no sense but for the past five days he hadn't been able to shake the feeling that he had spent the last fifteen years trying to get back to Rainshadow to see if she was still here.

She had definitely grown up in the years they had been apart, but he would have recognized her anywhere. The elements of the woman she was meant to become had all been in place that summer, waiting to bloom. And the final result was everything he had sensed it would be. Intelligence, energy, and the promise of a passionate nature had illuminated her brilliant hazel eyes that year and those qualities were more luminous than ever now.

Some things had certainly changed, he thought. Gone was the awkward, shy, painfully vulnerable fifteen-year-old girl. In her place was a sleek, savvy, sophisticated woman. Her hair was cut in a shoulder-length style that framed her fine-boned face. She still wore glasses but the new ones were a trendy-looking pair that made a perfect frame for her spectacular eyes. Everything about her, including her energy, thrilled his senses.

He had known that day that he wanted her more than he had ever wanted anything in his life. He had also known that she was the one thing he could not have.

The Shadow Bay Police Station was located at the far end of the street in the town square. The headquarters of the volunteer fire department sat directly across the small park. The post office and the office of the part-time mayor, Fletcher Kane, completed the picture-perfect small-town scene.

It was enough to drive anyone who hated small towns as much as he did mad, Slade thought morosely. He really had to get moving on his new career path.

Devin Reed was sprawled on one of the stone benches in the park, legs shoved straight out in front of him. He was dressed in a pair of logo-splashed running shoes, jeans, a gray hoodie, and the new sunglasses he had invested in recently. In addition he wore the utterly bored, world-weary air that only a thirteen-year-old boy could pull off. The thing was, Slade thought, in Devin's case, he had a right to the attitude. The kid had gotten some tough breaks.

Rex bounded ahead and hopped up onto the bench seat.

"Hey, Rex." Devin patted the bunny and then peered at Slade through the new shades. "Hey, Chief Attridge."

"Dev." Slade stopped. "What are you doing this afternoon?"

"Nothing much."

"How about last night between midnight and dawn? Do anything much then?"

"Huh?" Devin jerked his hand away from Rex.

"You broke into the antiques shop."

"I didn't break anything, I swear it."

"You went inside."

"I found the door unlocked," Devin said quickly. "I just wanted to make sure everything was okay inside."

"Take anything?"

"No."

"That's good. I wouldn't want to have to arrest you. It would break your grandmother's heart."

Devin was stunned. "You wouldn't arrest me."

"In a heartbeat."

"I don't believe you."

"Try me."

Devin's expression closed down into a sullen scowl. "I was just doing Miss Enright a favor, that's all. I just checked to make sure there was nothing wrong inside the shop."

"Right. Next time you're out wandering around after midnight and you find an unlocked door, you call me or Officer Willis."

"Yeah, sure, whatever."

Rex moseyed off to investigate the stone-and-tile fountain. He liked to play in water.

Slade propped one booted foot on the bench and rested his forearm on his thigh. He was no guidance counselor, but Devin definitely needed some advice. Whether the kid took it or not was another problem.

"Does your grandmother know you snuck out of the house last night?" he said.

"No." Devin looked uneasy now. "She'd think I was doing drugs or something."

"I know why you went into the shop, Dev."

"I told you, I just —"

"You can sense the energy in there, can't you? I feel it, too. It hits you like a shower of small sparks of lightning, doesn't it? Jacks you up a little."

"Huh?" Devin went very still.

"What you pick up on in there are traces of paranormal energy."

"You mean like in the Old Quarters and in the Underworld? Alien psi?"

"Sort of, but what you sense in Looking Glass isn't alien energy. It's human psi."

"I don't understand."

66

"Miss Enright says there's a fair amount of it infused into most of the antiques in the shop. Evidently there are collectors who will pay big bucks for stuff like that. Go figure."

Devin looked first shocked and then hurt. "Come off it, you think I'm dumb enough to believe that? Why don't you try telling me that Santa Claus and the Tooth Fairy are real?"

"I think you're developing some serious psychic talent, Dev, not just the low-level kind that everyone uses to resonate with amber to start a car or switch on a washing machine. Something a lot stronger."

Dev brightened. "You think I might be a ghost hunter? That maybe I can join the Guild someday?"

"Ever rez any ghosts?"

Devin sank back into himself. "No. Tried a few times back in Frequency. Went down into the tunnels with some other kids. They pulled some small ghosts but I couldn't do it."

"Probably because your talent is different."

"Yeah?" Devin did not try to conceal his skepticism. "How?"

"It doesn't depend on amber, for one thing, although you'll probably be able to use amber to focus it more efficiently."

"Huh?"

"Look, it's common knowledge that something here on Harmony has speeded up the evolution of the latent psychic senses we all possess. That's why we can use amber in the first place, right?"

"Right. We learned that in science class. So what?"

"Here's what they didn't teach you in science class. Some of the First Generation colonists already possessed a lot of natural psychic talent when they arrived two hundred years ago. They kept a low profile because back on the Old World the paranormal wasn't accepted as normal. People who claimed to have psychic talent were considered weird or even dangerous."

"Yeah?"

"Things are better here on Harmony but a lot of folks still have a bone-deep fear of those who possess powerful talent of any kind, whether or not they use amber. And sometimes there's a good reason for them to be afraid of strong talents."

"Come on, nobody takes those movies and comic books about rogue psychics and paranormal killers seriously."

Slade thought about his last encounter with a rogue psychic. "You'd be surprised."

"Yeah?" Dev was starting to sound intrigued now.

"Natural talent, which I think you've got, takes a while to develop. It will be a few years before you find out how strong you are. That's good because you need the time to learn how to control and focus your new abilities."

"Huh."

"My advice is to keep quiet about what's happening to you unless you're sure you're talking to someone who understands and believes you."

Dev gave him a wary, uncertain look. "You think people would laugh at me?"

"Probably. Strong talent usually has a genetic component. Has your grandmother ever talked to you about the possibility that you might have some above-average psychic ability?"

"Are you kidding? No way. If I asked her about something like that she'd pack me off to a shrink. I'd wind up in the loony bin. She's already worried about me as it is. The last thing I want to do is make her think I'm going crazy, like my mom did."

It was no secret around the station or in town that Devin was the offspring of an illicit affair. His mother had taken her own life a year earlier. The kid's father, a married man who lived in Crystal City, met his

69

financial obligations but took no interest in the boy. What Devin had going for him was his grandmother, Myrna Reed. Myrna cared deeply about his well-being. But sometimes a boy needed a man's firm hand.

"Coming into a talent can be a little scary sometimes," Slade said. "You don't always understand what's happening to you. And other people will think you're strange. That's why I'm advising you not to talk to anyone else about it, at least not for a while."

"Can I talk to you?" Devin asked softly.

"Yeah, sure."

Having this conversation was probably a mistake, Slade thought, just like inviting Charlotte to dinner tonight. He had established a strict rule for himself when he took the job. The rule was simple. *Don't get personally involved with the locals.* He wanted no strings attached when he finally got his act together and boarded the ferry six months from now to leave for good. But today he had broken the rule twice. Not a good sign. He never broke his own rules.

"There's someone else you need to talk to, and soon," he said.

"Who?" Devin asked.

"Miss Enright."

Devin looked uneasy. "Why?"

"Why do you think?"

70

Devin's mouth tightened. "You want me to tell her that I was the one who went into her shop last night?"

"What I want doesn't matter here. What matters is that you need to do what's right."

"I told you, I didn't take anything," Devin insisted.

"She knows that. But how would you like it if someone you and your grandmother didn't know walked through your house sometime when neither of you was home."

Devin looked alarmed. "That would be illegal."

"Yes, it would. Even if all the guy did was look around."

Devin processed that for a moment. His mutinous expression morphed into tight-lipped resignation.

"Okay, okay, I'll tell her it was me," he grumbled.

"Good plan." Slade reached into the pocket of his shirt and took out the small, wire-bound notebook and a pen. He opened the notebook, clicked the pen, and wrote down a website and a password. "Next time you're on your computer, check out this address." He tore the page out of the notebook and handed it to Devin.

"Arcane?" Devin's brow furrowed. "Is it some kind of game site?"

71

"It's not a game. But if anyone asks you about the Society, it's okay to pretend that it's just some whack-job website. Lot of those online."

"How do you know all this stuff?"

"Because I've got a little talent, too."

"Yeah? Prove it. Tell me what I'm thinking. Or better yet, let's see you fly up into the air."

Slade smiled. "There's no such thing as mind-reading or levitation, although I know an illusion-talent who could make you believe that both are possible. We're not talking superhero abilities. We're talking psychic sensitivities and, sometimes, the ability to manipulate some of the energy in the ultralight regions of the spectrum."

"What's that mean?"

"Go do some research at that website. We'll talk about what you learn there some other time. I've got to get this fish into the refrigerator at the station."

He took his boot down off the bench and started toward the entrance of the station. Devin came up off the bench and fell into step beside him. Rex popped up out of the fountain. He hopped up onto the rim and fluffed the water out of his fur. Then he scampered across the lawn to follow Slade and Devin.

"Is the fish for Rex?" Devin asked.

"Not at this price. Rex can have the leftovers or go catch his own fish."

"Looks like a big salmon for one person."

"I've got a guest coming over for dinner."

"Yeah? Who?"

"Miss Enright."

"Holy crap." Devin slammed to a halt. "You've got a date with *her?*"

Slade kept walking. "You got a problem with that?"

"No way." Devin rushed to catch up. "It's just that Grandma and some other people have been saying that the two of you should date. And now you're doing it."

"Talk about a psychic intercept."

"Huh?"

"Never mind. Just a little inside joke." Slade went up the steps. "Why does everyone think that Charlotte and I should date? Because we're both new on the island?"

"I guess. I dunno. I overheard Grandma talking about it to Mrs. Murphy." Devin paused. "I think everyone's afraid you'll be leaving soon."

"Yeah?" *Everyone is right,* Slade thought, but he did not plan to say that out loud to anyone except Charlotte. She needed to know that he had no intention of getting involved in a long-term commitment of any

73

kind. "Why would they think that?"

"Because the guy who was the chief before you didn't last long, and neither did the guy before him. Grandma told me that after Chief Halstead died five years ago, no one has stayed more than a few months in the job."

"Small-town police departments often experience a high turnover."

"Maybe Grandma and the others figure that if you have a girlfriend here in town you'll stick around for a while," Devin offered.

"An interesting theory."

Slade opened the door and went inside the station. Rex and Devin followed. Automatically Slade removed his sunglasses and stuck them in the pocket of his shirt. Devin did the same.

Rex fluttered across the room and bounded up onto his favorite perch, a waist-high file cabinet. He settled down with a lordly air and proceeded to observe what he evidently considered his territory.

Myrna Reed was at her desk, gazing deeply into her computer screen. She jumped a little when Slade and Devin came through the door. Slade caught a glimpse of a screen full of what looked like women's sweaters and the words *Free Shipping* before

Myrna got to her mouse and clicked off. The clothes disappeared and a screensaver appeared in its place.

"Hi, Chief." Myrna swiveled around in her chair.

She was a good-looking woman in her early fifties who kept herself in shape. Her blonde hair was in a twist at the back of her head. She looked at Slade over the rims of a pair of reading glasses balanced on her nose.

Slade knew something of her history. When he had taken the job, the first thing he had done was run background checks on Officer Willis and Myrna Reed. Old habits died hard. He liked to know who he was working with. He knew that Myrna could not have been more than seventeen or eighteen when she had gotten pregnant with Devin's mother, who had, in turn, also gotten pregnant in her teens. Myrna had never married. Now she found herself raising her thirteen-year-old grandson. She clearly loved Devin and was determined to do her best. As far as Slade was concerned, that was all that mattered.

"How did things go down at Looking Glass?" Myrna asked.

Slade was aware of a sudden silence behind him. He knew Devin was holding his breath.

"There was no problem at the shop," Slade said. "Charlotte found her back door unlocked but she says nothing is missing."

Myrna laughed. "I've seen the inside of that shop. How would she know if anything had been taken?"

"It's a little crowded in there," he agreed.

"Beatrix seemed to buy a lot more than she sold," Myrna said. "We could never understand how she made any money, but she always had the cash to buy antiques for the shop."

"Guess she made enough on the few pieces that she did sell to keep going."

Myrna shook her head. "The woman was obsessed, that's for sure."

Devin spoke up. "I'm gonna go to the grocery store and get a soda and then maybe see if Nate is hanging out at the marina. We've gotta make some plans for our hike to Hidden Beach."

Slade looked at him. "Later."

Devin took his sunglasses out of his pocket and set them on his nose with a practiced movement.

"Later," he said. He headed for the door.

"Be home by six for dinner," Myrna called after him.

"Sure," Devin said over his shoulder.

In the next moment he was gone with a

lightning-quick speed that any hunter-talent would envy. Nobody could move faster than a teenage boy on his way to hang out with a buddy. The door closed behind him.

Myrna exhaled slowly. "I suppose you noticed the sunglasses?"

"I noticed," Slade said.

"Same brand you wear. He found them online. He even puts them on and takes them off the way you do. With both hands, not one."

"I do it that way because they last longer. Less wear and tear on the itty bitty hinges."

"Nice to know there's sound engineering logic behind your method, but I don't think that's the reason Devin is imitating you," Myrna said.

"He thinks I'm making a fashion statement?"

"No. He thinks you look stone cold when you take the glasses on and off. Very ice-rez, as the kids say."

"I'm telling you, it's all about saving the hinges." He hefted the package in his hand. "Anything I need to know before I go put this fish in the refrigerator?"

"All is calm on the streets of the Big City." Myrna studied the packet of fish. "Looks like a lot of fish for one person and a dust bunny."

"Rex is a hearty eater. But before you hear it on the street, I've got a dinner guest tonight."

Myrna's expression brightened. "Charlotte Enright?"

"Amazing detective work. No wonder you're in law enforcement."

Myrna ignored that. "About time, if you don't mind my saying so. First date you've had since you arrived."

"Give me a break. I've only been in town less than a week." He started down the hall toward the break room.

"I've got a terrific recipe for tartar sauce," Myrna called after him. "I'll write it down for you."

CHAPTER 3

Devin stopped in front of the entrance to Looking Glass Antiques and peered through the window. He could see Charlotte Enright moving about inside the shop. She was dressed in black jeans and a black, short-sleeved T-shirt. She had a little blue triangle-shaped scarf tied around her hair. She was unpacking a crate.

She was busy. He could come back later.

He started to move on but for some reason he could not. Sure, he had to apologize, but Nate was waiting down at the marina. They had plans to make for the hike out to Hidden Beach. He could always apologize later. Like maybe right around five thirty when Charlotte was closing up for the day. She would be in a hurry to go home and he would be able to get the whole thing over with fast.

Or he could get it done now. He thought about how the chief would handle things and groaned. The chief would take care of it now.

Reluctantly he opened the door of the shop and moved inside. The old-fashioned bell chimed overhead. The subtle vibes hit him. It was as if he'd run through an invisible waterfall. The interior of the antiques shop did not exactly get brighter but it seemed to him that it was lit by something more than just normal light and shadow. He could see strange colors but he had no names for them.

He stopped, distracted by the intriguing sensations. It was so ice-rez, this feeling. Scary, sometimes, but incredibly ice-rez. Reluctantly he withdrew into himself. The unnatural colors and lighting in the atmosphere faded back to normal. He was still vaguely aware of some of the sparkling waterfall-like sensations but they no longer distracted him. He could control this feeling, he realized. That was also very cool.

"Hi, Devin." Charlotte straightened up from the crate she had been unpacking, brushed off her hands, and walked toward him. "I'm glad you stopped by today."

She knew, he thought. He felt as if he'd been shoved off-balance. Belatedly he remembered to remove his sunglasses. He reached up and took off the shades with the smooth, deliberate motion that the chief always used. The action bought him a little time to recover.

"Why?" he asked warily.

He should have known that Charlotte had guessed the truth about last night. She was a little weird. The chief was weird, too, but in a different way, and that was okay. The chief was a man and understood stuff. Charlotte, on the other hand, was a woman. He liked her but she made him uneasy. It was as if she could see inside his head or something. That was the main reason he had not ventured into the shop when it was open during the day.

There was another reason why he hadn't come into the shop, as well. He couldn't afford to buy any of the cool antiques. He just wanted to hang around them for a while. Shopkeepers didn't like people who wandered into a store and hung out. They looked too much like shoplifters.

Charlotte smiled. "I came across something I think suits you perfectly. I just unpacked it." She turned and went back across the room.

He followed cautiously. "My grandma says that your aunt never bothered to unpack most of the stuff that she bought for this shop."

"No, Aunt Beatrix did not like dealing with customers. In fact, I think it's safe to say she never quite got the concept of customer service. Makes for a difficult business model."

"I don't get it. If she didn't like to sell her stuff, why was she in the business?"

"Good question. In my family we always said she was eccentric and let it go at that. But between you and me, I think she spent her life searching for something."

"Yeah? What?"

"I have no idea."

"Did you ever ask her?"

"I did one time, as a matter of fact. She said it was a key. I asked her what it opened. She said it wasn't created to open a door. It was made to lock something that should never have been opened in the first place."

"Do you think she ever found it?"

"No."

"That's too bad."

Charlotte stopped, hands on her hips and surveyed a pile of junk on the floor. At least, it looked like junk to him, but he knew that to her they were antiques.

"Let me see," Charlotte said. "I think I put it next to that old chocolate pot. Yes, there it is." She stooped down and scooped up a small object.

For a moment she gripped the object in her hand. At the same time she put the fingertips of her other hand on the mirrored pendant she wore. Light sparked on the pendant. He thought he felt a small flash of fresh energy in the atmosphere but it was hard to be certain.

Charlotte opened her hand and held out the object. "Here you go. This feels like you."

Alarmed, he took a step back. "I never even touched it, I swear it."

She smiled. "I know, but it's yours now, if you want it."

"What do you mean, it feels like me?"

"It just does. Here, take it. See how it feels to you."

He looked down at the object in her hand. The antique was a flat amber disc about two inches across and half an inch wide. It was engraved with a compass rose. The four points of the compass were set with small gray crystals. He was instantly fascinated.

"Wow," he breathed. He took the amber compass from her and examined it closely. It felt good in his hand, warm and comfortable, as if it had been made for him. A shiver of awareness hummed through him. "Does it still work?"

"Oh, yes. That's a genuine Damian Cavalon compass. He was one of the first tunnel explorers. Navigating the catacombs was impossible with standard aboveground compasses. They didn't function in the alien psi. He came up with the first design that could work in a hot-psi environment. There have been a lot of improvements in the technology over the years but any ghost hunter will tell you that there is nothing as reliable as an old-style Damian Cavalon compass. Most hunters still carry them as backup when they go into the Underworld."

"I don't see a dial or a needle. Maybe it broke off?"

"No, it doesn't work that way. You just rez the amber and the crystals light up. True north is always bright blue. Try it."

He focused a little energy into the disc, the amount he would have used to turn on a rez-screen or a toaster. Nothing happened. He pushed a little harder. The crystal set at north started to glow faintly. He turned slowly on his heel and watched it brighten. Excitement shot through him.

"That's north," he announced, pointing across the street toward the door of the Kane Gallery.

"Evidently," Charlotte said. She smiled.

"This is great," he exclaimed. Then reality hit him. He sighed and held out the compass to her. "But antiques are expensive. No way I can afford something like this."

"I don't see why we can't work out some arrangements. Are you interested in a short-term job?"

"Yeah, sure."

"I could use someone to help me clean up this place. Dusting, sweeping, and washing the windows. The glass in the display cabinets is so grimy the customers can't even see what's on the shelves. Would you be interested in doing that kind of work in exchange for the compass?"

Excitement crackled through him. He closed his fingers tightly around the compass. "That'd be great. No problem. When do you want me to start?"

Charlotte looked around. "How about next week? I need to finish unpacking these crates and it would be best to complete an inventory before I start organizing and arranging the items on display."

"Okay. See you." He started toward the door and then froze under the crushing weight of sudden dismay. "Wait, I almost forgot. You may not want to give me the compass."

"Why not?"

He turned around and braced himself.

"I'm the one who was inside your shop last night."

Charlotte folded her arms and looked at him with her knowing eyes. "I see."

"I didn't take anything, honest."

"I believe you."

"I just wanted to look around."

"Next time you want to look around, try coming through the front door."

"I shouldn't have done it."

"No," she said. "Why did you?"

"I dunno. I just wanted to. Anyhow, I'm sorry."

"Okay. Apology accepted. But don't do it again."

"Do you want the compass back?"

"No." Charlotte smiled. "We have a deal. See you next week."

"Okay."

He ran for the door before she could change her mind.

CHAPTER 4

"So, why haven't you ever married?" Slade asked.

Charlotte sipped some of the white wine and considered her answer while she watched Slade arrange the salmon on the outdoor grill. He dealt with the salmon and the fire the same way he seemed to do everything else: competently, coolly, with a minimum amount of fuss. Rex, perched on the porch railing, was watching the activity around the grill with rapt attention.

"You're really interested?" Charlotte said finally.

"Damn curious," Slade admitted. "Over the years, whenever I thought about you, I told myself you'd be married by now."

"Remember me telling you that my talent had a few downsides?"

He paused, the metal spatula in midair, and looked at her. "Fifteen years ago you said something about having panic attacks when you run hot for any length of time. Didn't you outgrow those?"

"Not entirely. I have much better control now. But I still get them if I get super jacked for too long."

He shook his head. "Definitely a downside. But what does it have to do with the fact that you've never married?"

"It's complicated." She swallowed some more wine. "Let's just say that, as far as professional matchmakers are concerned, I'm a difficult match."

"So you did go to an agency?"

"Oh, sure, I went with the best, at least the best one for a member of the Arcane Society."

"Arcanematch?"

"Yes."

"I take it that didn't go well?" he asked.

"I was reminded that no match is ever one hundred percent guaranteed perfect and that goes double for strong or extremely unusual talents. Turns out I fit both categories. Evidently that makes for a para-psych profile that has too many unknown or unpredictable elements."

He frowned. "You told me that your ability was useless for anything except reading aura rainbows and tuning antiques."

"That's all it is good for. I happen to have

a heck of a lot of talent for doing it." Time to change the subject, Charlotte thought. "What about you? Ever try a matchmaking agency?"

"Remember that Marriage of Convenience I mentioned?"

"Yes."

"We met through a matchmaker. The counselors said we had an eighty-two percent compatibility rating."

"Not bad for a strong talent," she said.

"But not exactly a slam dunk, either. Susan and I didn't want to take any chances. We decided to try an MC first."

"Good plan, since it turned out you two weren't a great match. What happened?"

"Things changed," he said. "I changed. Let's just say I no longer fit the profile that I had registered with the agency."

"I see." She didn't but it was obvious she wasn't going to get any more information out of him. Fair enough. This was a first date, after all. There were protocols.

For some reason she'd had a hard time making up her mind about what to wear to dinner that evening. It should have been a simple decision, given the venue — a backyard barbeque. Slade's weather-beaten cabin stood in a clearing on a tree-studded bluff overlooking a rocky beach and the dark waters of the Amber Sea. In the near distance a scattering of islands, some so small they were no more than oversized rocks, floated in the mist.

The temperature had been in the mid-eighties all day. It was just now starting to dip down into the seventies. The sun would not set for another three hours. Her wardrobe selection should have been a no-brainer. Jeans, a pullover top, and maybe a sweater to wear when she walked back to her own cottage later in the evening were the obvious choices. But she had dithered, rummaging around in her small closet far too long before choosing jeans, a dark blue pullover, and a sweater to wear on the way home.

First-date syndrome, she thought. A woman never outgrew it. She wondered if men had the same issues. If Slade had agonized over his own attire this evening, there was no evidence of it. At least he was not wearing his uniform. That boded well, she thought. He was dressed in jeans, a dark shirt with the sleeves rolled up on his forearms, and a pair of low boots. She was pretty sure that he had shaved again, too. There was no sign of a five-o'clock shadow.

"No such thing as a hundred percent in anything, I guess," Slade said. Satisfied that the salmon was off to a good start, he put the spatula aside and picked up the bottle of beer on the table. "Are you good on the wine?"

She glanced at her half-full glass. "Fine, thanks." She picked up the glass and took a small sip. "Something I've always wondered."

He looked at her. "Yeah?"

"How did things work out for you at the FBPI?"

Slade lowered himself onto one of the picnic table benches. "Good, for the most part. You could say I had a talent for the work."

"What, exactly, did you do for the Bureau? I realize you were a special agent, but what kind of bad guys did you go after?"

He was silent for a time. Then he started to talk. "Here's how I work, or how I used to work. Set me down in the middle of what appears to be the perfect crime or an old cold case and I can tell you if the perp committed the crime by paranormal means. I could usually find the evidence, too. I was so good at it that I eventually wound up working for a special department within the Bureau. It was known as the Office."

"Never heard of it."

"Which is exactly the way the Bureau

wants it. The Office exists for the exclusive purpose of profiling and taking down the worst of the worst, rogue psychics who use paranormal talent to commit crimes."

"The Ghost Hunters' Guild is rumored to have an agency that does something along the same lines."

"It does but its agents work almost exclusively down in the catacombs and the underground rain forest. The Office handles the aboveground cases. But in the past few years a solid working relationship has developed between the two. Some situations require coordination."

"Makes sense. Bad guys who commit crimes on the surface sometimes try to escape into the Underworld."

"And vice versa," Slade said. "It's not uncommon for a bad actor who violates the law underground to try to hide in a city or town where he knows the Guild can't easily track him."

She raised her brows. "Or apply its own brand of justice if it does find him."

Slade smiled his rare, fleeting smile. "I can see you're not a great admirer of the Guilds."

"They do have a certain reputation," she allowed.

"Things are changing. You should know

that. You're from Frequency. That Guild had the most notorious reputation of all. It will be different now that Adam Winters is in charge, trust me."

"You know Winters?" she asked.

"We've worked together a few times in the past. Good man."

"Well, he's certainly a local hero back in Frequency, I'll give you that. If you can believe even half of the news reports, he and Marlowe Jones apparently saved the Underworld from certain destruction. Their wedding will be the biggest social event of the season."

"One thing's for sure, by marrying into the Jones family, Adam has forever linked the Guild to Arcane."

"For better or worse," Charlotte said dryly.

"I can see the Frequency Guild has some public relations work to do, at least in your case."

"Yes, it does." She lounged back in her chair. "If you liked your work with the FBPI and this Office you mentioned, why change your career path?"

He drank some more beer and got to his feet to check the salmon. "It was time for me to move on."

Something bad had happened, she thought. But she knew she would not get the truth out of him that evening.

"You mentioned you had a project going," she said. "What is it? Or is it a secret?"

"I'm keeping quiet about it here on the island." He glanced over his shoulder. "And I'd appreciate it if you didn't say anything. I don't want the word to get out that I'm a short-timer. Bad for morale at the station."

"I understand. I won't tell anyone. What's the new career plan?"

"I'm going to set up a private security consulting business. Hire the talents I need. I've got some connections from my days with the Bureau. Figure those will help land the first clients."

"How is the plan going?"

"Slowly, but it's going." He turned back toward the grill. "The fish will be ready soon."

"I'll get the salad."

She went up the steps. Apparently sensing that dinner was fast approaching, Rex chortled excitedly at her as she went past him. She opened the screen door and moved into the small spare front room of the cabin. It was clear immediately that Slade was making no attempt to turn the place into a home. Everything was neat and orderly. That did not come as a surprise. But aside from the computer on the desk, there was almost nothing of Slade in the room. He was treating the place like the short-term rental he obviously intended it to be.

The cabin was typical of many of the small rentals on the island. The furniture was sturdy but battered. The well-worn couch and the pair of reading chairs set in front of the fireplace looked as if they had been around for several generations. The two framed pictures on the wall were faded generic landscapes of Amber Island scenes that had probably been in the house as long as the furniture. There was a bedroom and bath but the cabin also boasted a sleeping loft in the high-ceilinged front room designed to accommodate additional guests. The loft overlooked the main room and was accessed by a narrow wooden staircase.

She crossed the old braided rug and went into a vintage kitchen. Opening the elderly refrigerator, she took out the bowl that contained the cucumber, tomato, olive, and basil salad she had brought with her. She poured the dressing that she had made earlier over the salad and tossed everything together. When she was ready she picked up the bowl of salad and the loaf of zucchini bread she had brought and went back outside. The sun was sinking fast. The evening was growing cooler. By the time she left she would need the sweater, she thought.

"Devin Reed stopped in to see me today," she said. She set the salad and the bread on the picnic table. "I assume that was your doing?"

"I may have given him a push in that direction. I figured out he was the most likely suspect." Slade eased the fish onto a platter. "Devin just turned thirteen. He is obviously coming into a talent of some kind. He's attracted to the energy in the shop. But I'm sure he didn't steal anything."

"I gave him one of the antiques."

"Yeah?"

"An old Damian Cavalon compass."

"An original?"

"Yes."

Slade whistled. "Nice gift. Was he thrilled?"

"He seemed pleased. I did a little tuning work on the compass. It suits him now."

"The way that pocketknife you gave me suits me?"

She shrugged. "It's what I do. Speaking of young Devin, I've noticed that he hangs around you every chance he gets. Looks like he even managed to find a pair of sunglasses that looks exactly like yours."

"I talked to him today about what's happening to him."

"The development of his talent?"

"Right." Slade sat down on the opposite side of the table. "He doesn't have any idea of what's going on and he's afraid to talk to his grandmother for fear she'll think he's got mental health issues."

"It's a reasonable concern. He wouldn't be the first kid to get sent to a shrink after coming into a nonstandard, non-amber-related talent. What kind of ability do you think he has?"

"Not sure," Slade said. "It's still unfocused."

"He lost his mother a few months ago. That kind of trauma can delay or even totally screw up developing senses."

"He's a good kid but he's caught some bad breaks."

"I understand that there's no father in the picture."

"No," Slade said. "The kid's got his grandmother but that's it."

"Myrna isn't going to have an easy time of it. It's hard enough to raise a teenage boy alone. Trying to deal with one who is showing some serious talent will be even more complicated."

"Especially if the person doing the raising

isn't comfortable with the concept of non-standard talent, herself," Slade said.

"Who is, unless you happen to be Arcane? And even within the Society, very strong talents tend to make other sensitives nervous."

"That's the thing about power of any kind," Slade said. "It can be scary. I told Devin that what was happening to him was normal but that most people wouldn't think so. I advised him to keep quiet about his new senses until he's older and until he's figured out how to control them."

"Good advice. Meanwhile, he needs guidance. No matter how you label it, what he did last night certainly fits the definition of illegal entry."

"It won't happen again."

"A kid like Devin could go either way," Charlotte said.

"I know."

"Sounds like you speak from personal experience."

"I do."

CHAPTER 5

He walked her home shortly before eleven
o'clock, using a flashlight to illuminate the
unlit road that wound through the trees
along the bluff. The flashlight was for Charlotte's sake. In spite of the damage to his
talent, his night vision was still good,
especially when he was a little jacked, as he
was now. He had tried to keep his senses
tightly shuttered all evening but just being
around Charlotte was enough to give him a
slight buzz, enough to illuminate the world
with a faint ultralight radiance. Enough to
keep the sweet ache of semi-arousal going
deep inside him.

But Charlotte would have been walking
blind without the artificial light. Darkness
on the island was absolute once you were
away from the town's small business district
and marina. There were no streetlights. The
cottages and cabins scattered along the cliffs
and bluffs were set far apart and veiled by

thick woods. The branches of the trees that crowded close to the edges of the pavement blocked out what light came from the stars and crescent moon.

Charlotte glanced at Rex who rode on Slade's shoulder. "You two are lucky. You can both see in the dark. Must come in handy."

"Night vision has its uses." He wondered how much longer he would have the paranormal eyesight that allowed him to see in total darkness. He wouldn't need it to know if Charlotte were nearby, though, he thought. No matter how psi-blind he became, something in him would always respond to her presence.

"When did Rex attach himself to you?" Charlotte asked.

"Shortly after I got out of —" He stopped abruptly. "After I finished my last job for the Office. I was living in an apartment in Crystal City. Heard a sound out on the balcony one night. I opened the slider and there was Rex. He just sat there for a while staring at me. He looked like he was waiting for something."

"Food?"

"That's what I figured. I gave him some leftover chicken. He ate it and then he left. The next morning he was back on the balcony with a nice little rock."

"A rock?"

"A very green rock, psi green. I knew it had come from the underground rain forest."

There was no mistaking the unique, acid-green glow that was the hallmark of so much of what the long-vanished aliens had constructed. Aboveground the ancient ruins of their dead cities glowed with green energy after dark. Down below, the endless labyrinth of catacombs they had built were lit with the strange green light day and night. The vast reaches of the bioengineered jungle buried deep in the Underworld were illuminated with an artificial green sun.

No one knew what had happened to the aliens who had first colonized Harmony. But human anthropologists and researchers had concluded that something in the environment of the planet had proved poisonous to them. The psi infused into the walls and buildings of their elegant, graceful cities and into the engineering marvel that was the Underworld had clearly been intended to be the antidote.

But in the end the forces of nature on Harmony had evidently proved too much for the aliens. No one knew if they had simply died out as a species or if they had called it quits and abandoned the planet. Whatever the case, they had vanished thousands of years before the human colonists from Earth had arrived on Harmony. The experts could not establish a firm date for the era of the alien colonists because the green quartz that they had used to construct virtually everything they had built or manufactured was indestructible. It showed no signs of weathering or erosion.

"So Rex brought you a rock from the rain forest to cement your relationship," Charlotte said, amused. "What a clever, charming gift."

"He's been hanging around ever since," Slade said. "Sometimes he takes off on his own for a while, usually at night. He started doing that here on Rainshadow on the night we arrived. I've gone with him a couple of times."

She laughed. "Isn't trespassing still illegal?"

"As illegal as it was fifteen years ago when you and I went in. But things have changed."

"Like what?"

"For one thing, I'm the chief of police now. I can go anywhere I want on the island without having to worry about getting arrested for trespassing."

"Oh, right. I forgot. You carry a badge. Must come in handy."

"It does." He paused, wondering how much to tell her. "But that's not the only thing that has changed here."

She must have picked up on the seriousness he had injected into the words because she turned her head quite sharply to look at him.

"What do you mean?" she asked.

"According to Chief Halstead's notes, the fence was strengthened about five years ago after two people managed to sneak into the Preserve and died on the grounds. The Foundation's search-and-rescue team brought the bodies out. Then they sent an engineering crew to crank up the power of the fence. It's definitely much stronger now, a lot harder to get through than it was the night I took you inside. But that's not the only thing that has changed. The Preserve itself feels different, at least in parts."

"Really? How?"

"It's hard to explain. There are still a lot of pretty places, but in some sections the energy is darker and heavier."

"I recall that it was very disorienting the night you took me in," Charlotte said. "If you hadn't been with me I would have been hopelessly lost within ten or twenty feet."

"Back in those days the psi fence and the fear of getting lost was enough to keep out most folks. But now I'm pretty sure that only someone with a heck of a lot of talent and just as much determination could get through the barrier."

"You said some of the places inside feel different?"

"I spent a lot of time inside the Preserve fifteen years ago. It was an irresistible attraction to a nineteen-year-old guy who had come into a strong talent."

"I remember," she said. She smiled, thinking about it. "I felt the lure, as well."

"The two times I went in this past week I came across some features that were definitely not present fifteen years ago."

"Such as?"

"Ponds and lakes that seem to simmer with dark energy. Canyons of intense night."

"Canyons of night?" she repeated, fascinated.

"I don't know what else to call them."

"But the beautiful places are still there? That meadow that you showed me that night, for instance. It was like a fairyland. I've never forgotten it."

"It's still there," he said. "Still as pretty as ever. But it feels hotter now."

"Got any theories?"

"Not yet. But I've been doing some research online and I'm working on a theory. Ever heard of a para-nexus?"

"Sure. According to the Arcane experts it's a natural geologic hot zone of paranormal forces, a location where there is a confluence of several kinds of powerful natural energy currents. Similar to a vortex, I think. There are records of such places back on Earth and I've heard that they've found some here on Harmony down in the catacombs."

"A nexus is more powerful and more complex than a vortex because there are more forces at work. In addition to the energy of the planet's magnetic field, there are ocean currents and strong tides, as well as tectonic and geothermal forces involved in a true nexus. When they come together in certain ways in certain locations they produce a lot of ambient energy like the kind inside the Preserve."

"You think it's a nexus?"

"Yes."

"How did you do your research on the Preserve?"

"I found some old navigational charts and ships' logs and diaries from the First Century expeditions. They're housed in the online collections of the University of Old

Resonance. I also turned up a few accounts of the Amber Sea Islands left by smugglers and pirates. I haven't had a chance to read all of them yet but I can see that a theme is emerging."

"What kind of theme?"

"Some of the early navigators were convinced that Rainshadow was haunted by ghosts of the aliens."

She laughed. "Okay, that's an original notion but I think you can ignore that theory."

"The first expedition that went into the part of the island that is now the Preserve disappeared. There were two rescue attempts made but in both cases the teams were forced to turn back. The bodies of the first group were never recovered. Later a couple of expeditions were able to get a short distance inside but none of them got far and most of the territory remains unmapped."

"When did the Preserve go into private hands?"

"Good question. Shortly after the Era of Discord, a corporation called Amber Sea Trading Company claimed most of Rainshadow under the old Exploration Laws that were established to encourage private exploration and development."

"When did the legal entity called the

Rainshadow Preserve Foundation come into existence?"

"A few years after staking a claim to the island, Amber Sea Trading established the Foundation to govern the Preserve. It's been under the control of the Foundation ever since. Halstead left a phone number to call in the event that anyone else gets lost inside the Preserve. The Foundation will send out a search-and-rescue team."

"Why do you think you can go into the Preserve without getting lost?" Charlotte asked, very thoughtful now.

"Damned if I know. I have to assume it's got something to do with my talent." *Or what's left of it,* he added silently.

"There must have been at least a few similar hunter-talents on some of the early expeditions."

"Which may explain why some of the teams were able to get at least partway into the Preserve," he said. "But evidently that kind of talent wasn't sufficient to allow full exploration of the island."

"Have you encountered anything inside that stops you?"

"Not yet. The night canyons are the most serious obstacle I've come across so far. And I sure as hell wouldn't go swimming in any of the ponds or lakes now. But thus far I

haven't experienced the extreme disorientation that the survivors who have been pulled
out by the Foundation's search-and-rescue
teams have reported. I've only gone in twice
in the past week, though. I haven't had a
chance to do much looking around."

"Planning on going in again anytime
soon?"

He was amused. "You want to go in, don't
you?"

"I've never forgotten that first visit." Her
voice turned wistful. "I've even dreamed
about it from time to time over the years."

"I've had a few dreams about the Preserve,
myself," he admitted. "I'll take you back
inside."

"Okay," she said. "I'd like that."

"But not tonight."

There was a faint rustling in the undergrowth at the side of the road. Rex went
very still on Slade's shoulder. He sleeked
out and his second set of eyes, the amber
pair that he used for hunting, snapped open.
He bounded down to the pavement and
vanished into the woods.

"Ugh," Charlotte said. "Nature in the
raw."

"What do you expect? Dust bunnies are
omnivorous and they are predators."

"That may be true, but as far as I'm

concerned, there's a reason why grocery stores were invented. Makes things ever so much tidier." She glanced toward the night-shrouded woods where Rex had disappeared. "I take it he doesn't have any trouble navigating the Preserve with you?"

"As far as I can tell Rex has no problem at all inside. But dust bunnies get around in the Underworld just fine, too. They seem to be well-adapted to heavy psi environments."

He stopped. Charlotte stopped, too.

"Something wrong?" she asked.

He aimed the beam of the flashlight at the graveled lane that intersected the road. "This is your driveway."

She smiled. "Good thing you noticed. It's so dark out here, I didn't even see it. If I'd been on my own, I would have kept walking."

They followed the narrow, rutted drive through the trees and into a clearing. With the canopy of overhanging branches gone, the starry night sky sparkled and glittered in all its glory.

Charlotte looked up. "It's incredible, isn't it?"

He watched her face, fascinated. He could have watched her all night long, he thought. In spite of the control he was exerting over his senses, he went a little hotter.

"Yes," he said. "Incredible."

"This was one of the things I have always loved about the island," she said. She headed toward the front steps, fishing her key out of her purse. "Back in Frequency the city lights combined with the glow of the ruins make it impossible to see anything but the moon and the brightest stars. But here the night sky is always an amazing sight."

He followed her up the steps, wishing he could think of a way to make the night last longer.

Charlotte's cottage was set on a bluff overlooking a rocky cove and a handful of small, neighboring islands. Unlike his own spartan cabin, her place had a quaint, cozy look. Small and compact, it consisted of two floors, a gabled roof, and a wraparound porch. Baskets of flowers hung from the eaves of the wide, overhanging roof.

He studied the scene for a couple of seconds, trying to understand why Charlotte's cottage looked so different from his own. It wasn't just the flowers, he thought. There was something else about the place. Then it came to him. *It looks like a home,* he thought.

Charlotte was just about to unlock the door when the vast waves of eerie green light flooded across the heavens. The night lit up as though it had been ignited by supernatural energy. She gave a small shriek and jumped. The key clanged on the wooden porch.

"What in the world?" she gasped. "Oh, my goodness, look, an aurora. You can see them only a few times a year here on the island. Atmospheric conditions have to be just right."

"I remember seeing an aurora the summer I worked at the marina," he said. "This is the first time I've seen one since then."

She laughed. "Maybe it's a good omen, hmm?"

"It's a natural atmospheric phenomenon," he said. "Not an omen."

"Give me a break. Surely a man who can come up with a phrase like *canyons of night* can allow me a little poetic license here."

He smiled. "You're right. Maybe this is an omen."

He switched off the flashlight and guided her down the steps to get a better view of the spectacular display.

"Talk about special effects," Charlotte breathed.

"No movie studio could produce a light show like this."

The brilliant green lights crashed and

cascaded endlessly across the night sky, creating an otherworldly effect that dazzled all of the senses.

Energy heightened in the atmosphere. Slade realized that Charlotte had jacked up her talent a few degrees in order to savor the full effects of the aurora. His own senses responded, not to the rippling, glowing lights in the sky but to Charlotte's energy.

He knew then that he had miscalculated badly. He had told himself that sex with Charlotte did not have to be complicated, just a simple case of two adults who were attracted to each other acting on that attraction. But he had been wrong. Sex was going to be very complicated. In that moment, however, entranced by Charlotte's upturned face and the air of wonder and fascination that shimmered around her, he did not give a damn about the potential complications.

He put his arm around her shoulders, acutely conscious of the delicate, feminine body beneath the light sweater she wore. Her scent stirred the banked fires deep inside. He turned her toward him. She did not resist.

"Charlotte," he said. And stopped because he could not think of what to say next.

"I know, I know," she said, her voice a

little husky now. "You're not long for this island. You've got plans for the future that don't involve hanging around here. We're just two talents passing in the night, blah, blah, blah."

"I may have said blah, blah, blah, but don't think I actually said that we're just two talents passing in the night."

She put her hands on his shoulders and smiled up at him. Her eyes were luminous pools of mystery.

"How about two talents who happen to find themselves stranded together on an island," she said.

He pulled her closer. "I don't think I said that, either."

"No, I did."

"That works."

He brought his mouth down on hers and kissed her beneath the radiant green night skies. Heat and energy flashed in the atmosphere. Charlotte made a small sighing sound and melted against his chest. Slowly, he reminded himself. You don't want to screw this up by running too hot.

But the fires of passion were already flaring and getting hotter by the heartbeat. Against his better judgment he deepened the kiss. It was okay. He could handle this. He was in control. It was just a kiss.

Charlotte's mouth softened and opened under his. He felt her fingers tighten on his shoulders. A shiver swept through her. The knowledge that she was responding to him was making him reckless.

He eased his hands down her sleek back until his palms rested on the enticing curve of her hips. He cradled her snugly against his thighs. He heard Charlotte's sharp breath when she felt his erection through the fabric of his jeans.

"What's the matter?" he asked into her ear. "Didn't you realize how much I want you?"

Her fingers clenched tighter around his shoulders. "It's not that," she said tightly. "It's just . . . never mind."

She kissed his throat and then he felt her teeth on his earlobe. There was a sense of urgency about her now, as if she was suddenly desperate to leap off an unseen cliff. He almost laughed.

"It's okay," he said. "We've got all night."

"No," she said. "We don't. We need to do this now. Before I — Never mind."

"Before you what?"

"It's not important now."

"Whatever you say. Maybe we should find a bed, first?"

"There's one in my cottage."

He scooped her into his arms and carried her up the front porch steps. She managed to find the key where she'd dropped it, fumbled, got the lock opened, and then they were inside.

"The lights," she whispered. "On the wall."

"Don't need them," he said.

"Oh, yeah, right, the night-vision thing. Wow, that's handy."

"Oh, yeah."

He got her up the stairs to the second floor and down a short hall to a bedroom. There he fell with her onto the bed. He managed to sit up long enough to get her shoes and his boots off and then they were locked in sensual combat on the quilt.

She twisted into his body. He found the sweet, vulnerable skin of her throat. He was playing with fire but he was satisfied that he was still in control.

He removed her glasses and set them carefully on the nightstand. Without the crystalline armor of the lenses, she suddenly looked more innocent and vulnerable. It brought back a vivid memory of how she had looked that night fifteen years earlier. He leaned down and kissed her forehead.

"Ack." She turned her head aside, batting at his shoulders with both hands. "Don't do

that. I promised myself you wouldn't kiss
me like that."

"Like what?"

"Like you did that night. As if I were your
kid sister."

He grinned. "Trust me, I never thought of
you as a sister, not fifteen years ago, not
tonight."

"You're sure?"

"There are some things a man knows with
absolute certainty."

"Okay, then. If you're sure."

He kissed her on the mouth, letting the
heat rebuild. When she groaned and shuddered beneath him he unfastened her
sweater and peeled it off. He slid his hands
under her blue pullover. The fine bones of
her rib cage felt bird-light and bird-delicate
under his big hands. Her breasts were small,
full, firm, and ripe, the nipples like berries
between his fingers. He squeezed gently and
Charlotte seemed to levitate off the bed.

"Ah," she gasped. "Yes."

She got his shirt open, got her hands
inside. When he felt her palms on his bare
skin another wave of heat rolled through
him.

He raised his head to look down at her.
Charlotte's eyes burned with passion. He
knew that his own eyes were equally hot.

The scent of her body acted like a drug on his senses, threatening to suppress what remained of his control.

He'd thought he could handle this, but things were getting out of control fast.

He could not resist moving one palm down to the crotch of her pants. He could feel her heat even through the fabric. He cupped her and pressed hard.

"Yes." She clutched at him.

There was more than urgency in her hoarse voice now, he thought. There was an element of desperation. He did not understand it but the desire to sink into her was so strong now that he did not want to take the time to ask questions.

It wasn't until he started to undo the fastenings of her jeans that he realized that his fingers were trembling and his mind was clouded with need. Shock slammed through him. The atmosphere in the small, shadowed room was too hot, way too hot.

His senses flared higher and suddenly he was far out on the spectrum, heading into the red zone, staring into the dark storm of psychic oblivion that awaited him.

He had to crank it down a few notches, he told himself. He could do that. Grimly he reached for and found his control. He was still rock hard, still ready to explode, but he was able to partially close down his senses. The dark storm receded.

He went back to work undressing Charlotte but he discovered she had gone very still beneath him. Her fingers wrapped around his wrists. She stared at him with wide, unfocused eyes.

"No," she said. "No, that's enough. Please."

A flicker of raw panic shot through him. Had he hurt her?

"Are you all right?" he said.

"Yes, I'm okay. I'm sorry. It's just that things are moving too fast here. I mean, we haven't seen each other for fifteen years and now here we are in bed together."

"I got the feeling a few minutes ago that you didn't think that was a problem."

"I'm really sorry. This is my fault. I know that."

She sounded miserable. He leaned over her, resting on his elbows so that he could frame her face with his hands. "I'm not trying to assign blame here. I just want to know what's going on. You went cold on me like a de-rezzed light. Something I did?"

"No, of course not. It's me. My problem. I'm sorry."

"Stop apologizing and tell me what the hell went wrong with the two-talents-

118

stranded-together-on-an-island concept?"

"I thought that logic would work," she admitted sadly. "I should have known better. I made a mistake. You're not an easy man to read."

"Care to explain?"

"Think about it, Slade," she said earnestly. "This is a small community and you are the chief of police. That makes you a very high-profile person in town. For the next six months or however long you're here, we'll be running into each other at the post office, the grocery store, the coffee shop, the bookstore. You know how it is."

"No. Explain."

"It would be extremely awkward for both of us if we sleep together tonight and then in the morning one of us concludes that it was all a mistake," she said.

"You suddenly decided that one of us would regret it tomorrow?"

She cleared her throat. "I'm not one hundred percent certain, but yes, I think there is a strong likelihood of that."

"And you went with the worst-case scenario?"

She sighed. "Better to be safe than sorry. I think."

"Which one of us did you decide was going to regret having sex tonight?"

"Does it matter?" She sounded anxious.

"It matters."

She drew a deep breath. "Okay, then. You. You're the one who would have regretted it. I think. Like I said, it's a little unclear."

For an instant he was too shocked to speak. After a couple of seconds he pulled himself together, pushed away from her, and sat up on the edge of the bed. He looked down at her.

"How the hell do you know that?" he asked.

She levered herself up on her elbows. "You're sure you want to go into this?"

"Yes, damn it," he said through his teeth. "Not like the mood hasn't already been ruined."

She took a deep breath. "Okay. I guess I owe you an explanation."

"Yes."

"A few minutes ago when you were running hot?"

"What about it?" he said. "You were pretty damn hot yourself, as I recall."

"I saw your aura rainbow," she said quietly, apologetically. "Sex always produces a lot of psi, you see, and I was jacked myself and —"

"I don't want a lecture on para-physics. What did you see in my rainbow that made you freeze up on me?"

"It was obvious that you felt deeply con-flicted about what was happening. You wanted the sex, all right, but I got the distinct impression that there was something about our encounter that you were dread-ing. I assumed that it was the thought of having to face me in the morning. Or maybe you were worried that I'd get too emotion-ally involved and you didn't want to hurt me. I don't know. Sorry."

"Stop saying that."

She sat up and slipped off the opposite side of the bed. "I don't know what else to say." She found her panties and hastily stepped into them. "If it's any consolation, I run into this problem a lot."

"You do?"

She pulled her crumpled top over her head and snatched her glasses off the night-stand. She plunked the glasses on her nose. "It's probably the reason Arcanematch was never able to match me successfully."

"No kidding."

"Every time they sent me out on what was supposed to be a serious date I ended up viewing the man's rainbow. Once I saw it, I just knew things weren't going to work out. Things always fizzled after that."

He pulled on his boots, got to his feet,

and faced her across the bed. "What is it with the rainbow reading?"

She struggled into her jeans. "Look, you've been very fair about this. I knew going in tonight that whatever we had together wasn't going to be long-term. You made that perfectly clear. I was okay with that. Going with the flow. Rezzing with the frequency, as they say. But then I saw your rainbow and realized that you were anticipating a full-scale disaster."

He shoved his fingers through his hair. "You misread the situation. Or my rainbow."

"I could live with the commitment-free scenario but I don't like the idea of you regretting things afterward." She drew herself up. "A woman has her pride."

He tried hard to follow her logic. It wasn't easy. After a few seconds he abandoned the attempt.

He circled the bed, closing in on her. She retreated quickly until she came up hard against the wall. He stopped inches away and planted his palms on either side of her head.

"You are not nearly as good at reading rainbows as you think you are," he said.

Her mouth fell open. "But I am. I'm the best. Just ask anyone at the Arcane lab where I was tested."

"Your talent may be as good as it gets but I am here to tell you that it is not infallible, not by a long shot."

"What do you mean?"

"I may have some concerns about my personal future but I can guarantee you that I would not have regretted sleeping with you tonight. Not in a million years. Not ever. Regardless of the outcome."

"But I saw the tension in your rainbow," she said. "I could tell that you were deeply conflicted about the consequences of a physical relationship with me."

"You sound like a para-shrink. Personally, I have had enough of para-shrinks."

She winced. "Men hate it when I start talking like this."

"No shit."

"The history of my social life is filled with disastrous first dates. Well, sometimes I make it to two or three. Once in a while I get all the way to five."

"If you start talking like this on every date, I can see where there might have been a few problems," he said.

"In fairness to myself, I have to say that I've tried keeping my mouth shut in hopes that I'm wrong."

"Must have been hard for you."

"I gave all my Arcanematch dates at least

three chances," she assured him.

"How very broad-minded of you."

"The point is, I gave the professional matchmakers a chance. But in the end it always turned out that my rainbow-reading intuition was accurate the first time. More accurate than their para-psych profiles. If I tried to override my intuition I invariably had a panic attack."

"Are you having a panic attack now?"

"No." She frowned, as though somewhat confused. "Probably because we stopped in time."

"Your intuition told you that I was the one who would have regrets so you pulled the plug before you found out whether or not that would actually happen. And before you found out if you would have a panic attack."

"Like I said, a woman has her pride. Besides, I thought it would be easier, socially, for both of us that way. We have the next six months to get through together here on this island."

"You make it sound like we're doing time in a prison cell together. Do you really think it's going to be easier to deal with me at the post office and the grocery store now after what just happened between us?"

She exhaled slowly. "I didn't handle this

very well, did I?"

"Let's just say that I feel like banging my head against this wall." He pushed himself away from her. "I think I'd better go back to my place now."

"Okay, but one question before you leave," she said quickly.

"Now this I'm pretty sure I will regret. What?"

"Were you by any chance conflicted about having sex with me tonight because you're on the rebound from that Marriage of Convenience that you told me about?"

"No. That was easy." He turned to go. "I'm leaving now before this conversation deteriorates any further."

"Maybe it's a physical problem that worries you?" she said very earnestly. "Have you seen a doctor?"

"Forget hitting my head against the nearest wall." He kept walking. "I think I'll go back to my place and pour myself a real big glass of Hot Ruins Whiskey."

There was a lengthy pause behind him.

"Good night, Slade. I'm sorry I screwed this up."

The sad wistfulness in her voice stopped him in the doorway. He turned around and walked deliberately back toward her.

"Did you forget something?" she asked.

He clamped both hands around her shoulders and hauled her close.

"Promise me something," he said.

"What?"

"Promise me that you will not say another word until I am back out there on the road and too far away to hear you."

"Okay."

He took one hand off her shoulder and put it across her lips. "Hush. Not a single word."

She nodded once but said nothing. Her eyes were wide and deep and full of an expression of bewilderment that he found very gratifying.

"For the record," he said, "there is no physical problem involved."

She blinked but she did not try to speak.

He took his finger off her mouth and tightened his grip on her shoulders. He kicked up his senses a few notches, not trying to focus, not going into the danger zone, but hot enough so that Charlotte would be aware of the energy. He kissed her before she could think twice about speaking.

He did not kiss her the way he had earlier. He did not ask for a response. He was not trying to seduce her now. His only goal was to leave an indelible impression.

She did not go up in flames when his

mouth came down on hers. She froze, shocked or stunned or maybe simply dumbfounded. He held the kiss for a short time, letting her feel the heat.

He raised his head. "There will be a second date."

She blinked several times. "What?"

He touched her full lips with his forefinger. "No talking, remember?"

She looked at him with a dazed expression. "Huh?"

"Forget it. There's really no point in trying to make you stop talking, is there?"

"Probably not."

"Just remember." He brushed his mouth against hers once more. "There's a second date coming up."

He walked out of the bedroom before she could think of anything else to say.

He went out onto the porch and into the night. The green waves of the aurora still flooded across the sky. He realized his senses were still a little heightened. He walked down the driveway to the road and started back toward his cabin.

Rex materialized out of the woods, chortling a greeting.

"Sounds like your night went a lot better than mine," Slade said. "But there will be a second date. She owes me that much."

CHAPTER 6

The phone rang just as Charlotte reached into her voluminous shoulder bag to find the key to the back door of Looking Glass. She took out the phone instead and glanced at the screen.

"Hi, Mom," she said. "Before you ask, yes, I'm fine. Things are going swell."

"What did you have for dinner last night?" Marilyn Enright demanded.

"Grilled salmon, a lovely salad of vegetables fresh from my neighbor's garden, and some homemade zucchini bread."

"You've never cooked anything on a grill in your life."

"That's because whenever a grill was involved Dad and Cort always took over. Something about it being the manly way to cook, remember?"

"It's the fire thing," Marilyn said absently. "Men can't resist an open flame. So, if you didn't cook the salmon, yourself, what did you do? Eat out?"

"No, it was a home-cooked meal."

"Someone cooked it for you?"

"The salmon was grilled by my host. But I made the salad. Doesn't that count?"

"Yes, of course it counts." Marilyn's voice softened. "Sounds like you're making friends there on the island."

"Getting to know people, yes, indeed."

Marilyn pounced. "What's his name, dear?"

"Mom, we've talked about this. You promised me that you would respect my privacy, remember? We both agreed that at my age a woman no longer has to give her mother an account of her personal life."

"I know, dear, but I'm a mother. I can't help but worry. Let's face it, your personal life tends to be somewhat volatile where men are involved. That situation with Jeremy Gaines a few months ago became quite worrisome. Your father was starting to think that Gaines might be stalking you."

"Jeremy wasn't a stalker. He was just very tenacious."

"Regardless, we're all very glad that he's out of the picture. But your father and I don't like the idea of you being so far away."

"I didn't move to a desert island, Mom. I'm only a couple of hours from Frequency by ferry, for crying out loud. Forty-five minutes by float plane."

"Technically, maybe. But an island is an island. It feels like you're a long way from us."

"Mom, I've got to go. I'm at the shop and it's after eight."

"I thought you didn't open the shop until nine," Marilyn said.

"True, but I'm trying to conduct an inventory this week. It's easier to do that before I open up. Once the morning ferry arrives I'll be dealing with customers."

"All right, I'll let you go. But first tell me how your date went last night."

"How do you think it went? It was a disaster, as usual. Got to go. Bye."

"Wait, who is he?" Marilyn demanded.

"The chief of police here in Shadow Bay."

"Is he registered?"

"With Arcanematch? No, not any longer. Evidently things didn't work out when he went the matchmaking route. I thought it gave us something in common but I think I was wrong about that."

"What's his name?"

"Slade Attridge. He used to work for the Federal Bureau of Psi Investigation. Talk to you later, Mom."

She cut the connection, dropped the

phone back into her purse, and started to undo the lock. It took her a second to realize that the door was already unlocked.

"Devin, I swear, if you've been prowling through my shop again, I'm going to report you to your grandmother this time. Forget the local cops."

She opened the door and moved into the cluttered back room. A trickle of unease fluttered through her. She knew the sensation all too well. Her intuition was kicking in. But this ominous crackle of awareness was much different from the one she had experienced yesterday when she'd discovered the unlocked door.

It dawned on her that the back room was even more disorganized than usual. The lids of several packing crates had been pried off. The contents were strewn everywhere. The drawers of an antique rolltop desk stood open. The top of a fine First Generation steamer trunk had been raised. The bubble wrap had been ripped off several small antique glass items.

Yesterday she had sensed that someone had been inside the shop but the knowledge had not filled her with sharp, clawing dread. She had been annoyed but she had not been scared. This morning she was scared. She was also angry.

She started to back out of the shop. She was going to feel like an idiot calling Myrna at the station again this morning to report another intruder. This time it would be a thousand times worse because she would have to deal with Slade after their dreadful date. She had not yet decided how she wanted to handle that situation. She had been awake most of the night thinking about it. No solution had presented itself.

She saw the shoe sticking out from between two stacks of shipping crates just as she stepped back and reached for her phone. A man's shoe.

Adrenaline shot through her. Her senses flashed high in fight-or-flight mode. She struggled to lower her talent. The last thing she wanted to do was go back inside but she had no choice. She had to make certain the man was truly dead, not bleeding to death or suffering a seizure.

She made her way around a stack of wooden crates. The unnerving sensation grew stronger as she got closer to the body. When she saw the face of the man sprawled on the floor she froze.

There was no need to check for a pulse. Although there was no blood and no signs of obvious violence, the aura of death was palpable. Besides, fear and adrenaline had kicked her senses into high gear. She could see very clearly that there was no hint of a rainbow around Jeremy. The lack of a reflection meant that there was no aura energy.

Jeremy Gaines had seriously complicated her life while he was alive. She had a feeling that he was going to make things even more difficult now that he was dead.

She started to shiver. *Damn.* She hadn't had a panic attack in months. She went into the deep-breathing exercise immediately, hoping to regain control before things got worse.

It was all she could do to take out her phone. It required a couple of attempts to call the emergency number. But she managed to keep it together while she reported the situation to Myrna.

"The chief is on his way," Myrna said, sounding uncharacteristically authoritative and thoroughly professional. "Do not go back inside your shop until he gets there. Understand?"

"Got it," Charlotte said.

"Are you okay?" Myrna asked. "You sound a little breathless."

"I'm fine. Thanks."

Charlotte hung up the phone and sank down onto the back step. She forced herself to breathe the way she had been taught, fighting the panic attack with every ounce of her willpower. She hated using the pills.

Breathe.

CHAPTER 7

Slade crouched beside the body, pulled on the plastic gloves that Myrna had magically produced from the back of a cupboard beneath the copying machine, and cautiously opened his senses. The haze of violent death shivered in the atmosphere. He didn't have to go any hotter to know murder when he saw it.

"Who was he and what was he doing here in your shop?" he said to Charlotte.

"His name was Jeremy Gaines," Charlotte said. She stood some distance away from the body, arms tightly folded beneath her breasts. "He was a former client of mine. I haven't seen him since I left Frequency. I have no idea what he was doing here. I didn't even know that he was on the island."

Slade pulled a ticket receipt out of one of the dead man's pockets. "Looks like he arrived on the last ferry yesterday evening."

"I had closed up and gone home by then."

"Later you walked over to my place."

"Yes." She fell silent.

He knew that she was remembering that he had left her at her door around eleven thirty. She had no alibi for the remainder of the night. He studied her for a moment.

"You look pale," he said. "Are you okay?"

Her mouth tightened resolutely. "I'm fine. Had a bit of a panic attack when I found the body but I'm okay now."

"You're sure?"

"I'm sure." She raised her chin. "Don't worry, I have pills if I need them."

She did not want to talk about the panic attack, he realized. Fair enough, he didn't like talking about his senses-related problem, either.

"Was Gaines a talent?" he asked.

"Yes," Charlotte said. "He is also a member of the Arcane Society, for what it's worth."

"Like you."

"Back in Frequency I catered primarily to collectors who are Arcane."

"How long was he a client?"

"Not long." She stopped.

"Might as well tell me the rest," Slade said. "I'm going to find out eventually."

She grimaced. "Jeremy was a client. He was very knowledgeable about antiques and antiquities. And he had money. I found a couple of nice Post–Era of Discord items for him. Then he asked me to locate a certain piece of late Nineteenth-Century Old World glassware for him. A snow globe."

"Go on."

"Old World antiquities are not my area of expertise. That is a far more rarified market. Most of the good pieces are in museums. But it was an interesting challenge so I agreed to see what I could do. Eventually I traced rumors of an Old World snow globe to the private collection of a woman named Evelyn Lambert. Mrs. Lambert was amazed that I had been able to track it down to her collection. But she declined to sell. I told Jeremy that she was not interested."

"What happened?"

"Jeremy got angry when I informed him that the collector who owned the snow globe did not want to sell. In fact, he was furious."

"Did you give him Mrs. Lambert's name?"

"Certainly not." Charlotte was indignant. "I always respect and protect the privacy of my clients. A lot of collectors are very secretive. Mrs. Lambert was one of those."

"What happened after that?"

"Mrs. Lambert was so impressed with my expertise she wanted to talk to me about her plans to give her collection to one of the Arcane museums. I told her who to call to make the arrangements. We got to be friends. She was in her eighties and she lived alone. Her house was filled with the most incredible collection of glass antiques. She knew everything there was to know about glass, not just Colonial antiques but Old World antiquities, as well. I had tea with her almost every Thursday afternoon for two months until she died. I learned a great deal from her."

"When did she die?"

"Several months ago. She left most of her glass to the Arcane Museum in Frequency but she was kind enough to leave a few very nice pieces to me."

"What happened to Jeremy Gaines?"

Charlotte's jaw tightened. Her eyes narrowed a little at the corners. "This is where it gets messy."

"Talk to me."

"I thought Jeremy had disappeared for good. I didn't see him for months after he flew into that rage in my shop. But he showed up one afternoon shortly before I moved here to the island. He turned on the charm. Jeremy had a lot of that. My mother said it was probably an aspect of his talent."

"Any idea what kind of talent he was?"

"I never asked. I didn't want to get too personal. But I assume he had a strong psychic sensitivity for old paranormal objects since he was such an avid collector."

"Ever see his collection?"

She made a face. "You know, you sound just like a cop."

He looked at her.

She cleared her throat. "Right. The answer is no. He never offered to show it to me. I never asked to view it."

"What did he want when he reappeared in your life?"

"He said he'd been thinking about me and he wanted to get to know me in a personal way. He said we had so much in common. He apologized for losing his temper the last time I had seen him and he asked me out on a date."

"What did you do?"

"I declined. I had seen his aura rainbow the day he lost his temper. I didn't like what I saw." She shuddered. "Not that I needed to view his rainbow after that display of rage. That would have been enough to put off any sensible woman."

"Anger-management issues?"

"Definitely. But in addition there was something else that I didn't like. I've seen it before a few times. The ultralight in Jeremy's rainbow was very similar to the bands of colors I've seen in the rainbows of the few true sociopaths I've had the misfortune to meet from time to time."

The hair lifted on the nape of his neck. "You can see that kind of thing in a rainbow?"

"Yes, but only when someone is really jacked up. Unfortunately, I can't detect the bad stuff in someone who is just walking down the street. Rainbows are linked to auras. They're generated by strong emotions or strong talents. Or both. That's why I didn't . . ."

She stopped abruptly but she did not need to finish the sentence, he thought. They both knew what she had been about to say. She hadn't perceived the true colors of his aura rainbow last night until things had gotten hot and heavy between them.

"I think I'm starting to understand why you didn't have a lot of luck with your Arcanematch dates," he said neutrally.

She exhaled slowly. "Sometimes it's better not to know too much about a person."

"You may have a point there."

On the other hand, her talent was evidently what had kept her single all these years, he thought. It had kept her free until he could get back to her. But now he was the one who was facing a psychic prison sentence that would not allow him to be with her for long.

"Did you ever see Gaines again?" he asked.

"Yes. He seemed to become obsessed with trying to convince me to give him another chance. There were phone calls. He sent flowers. He discovered my address and showed up on my doorstep one evening with a bottle of champagne. He stopped by my shop the next day, apologized again and asked me out to coffee."

"Stalker?"

She hesitated. "Well, my family worried that he was becoming one but I honestly don't think that was the case."

"Sure sounds like a stalker scenario."

"Maybe." But she was clearly not convinced. "In any event, after a week or ten days he gave up and went away. I truly believe that he just wanted me to take him back as a client. Jeremy being Jeremy, he assumed charm would do the trick."

"Why was he so determined to become your client again? There must be a lot of good antiques dealers around."

Charlotte's brows rose. "Not a lot who have the feel for para-antiques that I possess. I told you, I'm very, very good at what

I do. I have a certain reputation in the field. Jeremy knew that. It's why he sought me out in the first place. He was a very serious collector. He wanted only the best."

"And you're the best?"

"I'm certainly one of the best. But that means that I can afford to be choosy when it comes to my clients."

Slade contemplated Gaines's expensive black turtleneck sweater, black trousers, and black running shoes. "Looks like he came dressed for a night of breaking-and-entering and dropped dead on the job."

"Jeremy had no need to steal anything. He could have afforded to buy whatever he wanted."

"But you refused to do business with him."

"True, but there were ways around that. Gaines could have used another dealer as an intermediary. I probably wouldn't have found out. Dealers work together all the time without revealing the names of their clients."

"It wasn't my area of expertise when I worked for the Office, but I've heard that the world of collectors who specialize in the paranormal is a very gray market that often slides all the way into the black market."

"Collectors do tend to be reclusive, eccentric, and secretive," she admitted. "Dealers who don't respect that don't last long in the business."

Slade studied the body. "Gaines died here, inside your shop, sometime during the night. If he wasn't stalking you, he must have been after something that he thought you had but which you wouldn't sell to him if he came through the front door."

"I honestly can't imagine what he would have wanted that badly from my collection. He went for the more exotic objects."

"But if he did want something from your collection, why didn't he use another dealer to get it for him?"

"Exactly. It makes no sense." She looked at the body. "This doesn't look good for me, does it? I mean, what are the odds that one of my ex-clients who just happens to be wearing a lot of black breaks into my shop and drops dead from a heart attack?"

"Not good but fortunately for you, that's exactly what it looks like, a heart attack or stroke. Got a feeling that's what the medical examiner over in Thursday Harbor will call it."

"But you don't buy it, do you?"

"No," he said. He got to his feet. "This was death by paranormal means."

She looked shocked. "Are you telling me

that someone actually used *talent* to murder Jeremy?"

"Talent or a device that generates lethal paranormal energy."

Shock turned to bewilderment in her eyes. "What kind of weapon can generate that kind of radiation?"

"Certain crystals can be alchemically altered to become weapons-grade. But there are also some very high-level talents who can kill with their own natural power."

She shuddered. "I've heard a few horror stories over the years. Everyone in Arcane has. But I thought the ability to kill with psychic energy was just another Arcane legend."

"It's extremely rare. Takes a hell of a lot of power and only certain kinds of talent can be focused in a lethal way. Since it invariably looks like the victim died from natural causes, the murder usually goes undetected."

"You sound like an expert on the subject."

"Detecting murder by paranormal means is what I do, Charlotte, remember? Or, rather, what I did when I worked for the Office."

"Right. Sorry. I'm getting a little frazzled here. I can't help but point out that if Jeremy was murdered, I'm the obvious suspect. He and I had a history and I don't have an alibi for half of last night."

"True, but what you do have is a talent for reading rainbows. Not exactly the kind of ability that your average rogue psychic uses to commit murder."

She brightened. "And I certainly don't possess any of those crystal guns you mentioned."

He opened his senses a little higher and studied the darkly radiant pools of energy on the floor. "Someone does."

"You're sure?"

"Down in the tunnels it's possible for a very powerful ghost hunter to commit murder from a distance by generating certain types of ghost light. But aboveground the killers who are strong enough to kill with their natural energy almost always have to have physical contact with the victim. Whoever killed Gaines did it from a distance of several feet."

"You can tell that, as well?"

"Yes," he said.

"What happens now?"

"Standard procedure. I'll notify the authorities in Thursday Harbor and try to get in touch with Gaines's family."

"Are you going to tell them that you think Jeremy was murdered by paranormal means?"

"No. Like I said, the ME will call it death by natural causes."

"Hang on. I admit, I was not a fan of Jeremy Gaines. Still, it doesn't seem right to just ignore his murder. There's a killer running around. For all we know he might still be on the island."

"I didn't say I wasn't going to investigate. I just said that it's unlikely that I'll find any usable evidence. It doesn't mean I won't find the killer."

"But if you can't arrest him, what will you do if you identify a suspect?"

"It depends."

"It *depends?*" She unfolded her arms and waved her hands. "What kind of cop talk is that? There are rules about this sort of thing. At least there are supposed to be rules."

"When it comes to crimes committed by paranormal means, the rules are a little vague."

She gave him a speculative look. "In other words, if you decide that I murdered Jeremy, a lawyer wouldn't do me much good."

"If it's any consolation, I don't think you killed him," he said.

She stared at him, her mouth slightly open. It took her a second to get it closed.

"Good," she said finally. "Great. I mean, that is a huge relief."

"But if you did kill him, you probably had a real good reason."

"Thanks. That's supposed to reassure me?"

"It's the best I can do at the moment."

"And to think that I was worried about the two of us feeling a bit awkward the morning after."

CHAPTER 8

Fletcher Kane opened his senses and studied the painting on the table. The image on the canvas was similar to the others that lined the walls of the gallery, a vision of a fantastical, otherworldly forest landscape lit by an eerie phosphorescence. The picture should have looked like an enchanted fairyland but the strange canyon just barely visible through a stand of trees gave it a hellish quality. The canyon was filled with a disturbing darkness that was slowly seeping out into a glowing forest world, threatening to consume the luminous scene.

Like the others, the painting would sell quickly enough, Fletcher thought. A daytripper off the ferry or a visitor staying at a local bed-and-breakfast would respond to the intensity of the picture and snap it up. But it was doubtful that whoever bought it would see the deeper reality that he perceived. The painting seethed with ominous energy.

"The dreams are getting worse, aren't they?" he said quietly. "I heard you get out of bed and take the meds again last night."

Jasper Gilbert exhaled and walked to the window. He watched the small crowd of tourists prowl the boutiques and galleries on Waterfront Street.

"These aren't the old dreams, Fletch," he said. "These are different. Something bad is happening out there in the Preserve."

"Take it easy. I don't doubt your visions."

Jasper snorted. "Even if the Guild shrinks think I'm a crazy thanks to that last trip into the Underworld?"

"You're not crazy, and what the Guild doctors didn't understand is that you've always had weird dreams." Fletcher tapped the edge of the painting with his finger. "But it's clear your dreams about the Preserve are getting darker and more intense."

Jasper clasped his big hands behind his back and looked across the way at the entrance of Looking Glass. "Two people connected to the antique shop are dead. First Beatrix and now that stranger they say was stalking Charlotte Enright. What are the odds?"

"Beatrix was an elderly woman. She died of a heart attack."

"Gaines was only about forty years of age."

"It happens, Jasper."

"Two deaths within the past six months and both linked to Looking Glass. And now the shop has a new owner."

"I understand," Fletcher said.

He and Jasper had been bonded both professionally and personally for a long time. They had met back when they had both been young Guild men. Like most of those who worked the Underworld, they had retired in their forties. Guarding the corporate and academic expeditions that explored the tunnels was hard, risky work. Burning ghosts in the catacombs took a lot out of a man, and Guild retirement benefits were very good.

They had married and moved to Rain-shadow to pursue their dreams. Jasper had always longed to concentrate on his art. Fletcher had been surprised to discover that he had a knack for business. They made a good team in the art world just as they had in the Underworld. Years ago they had discovered that their ghost-hunter talents had given them the ability to penetrate partway into the Preserve where Jasper had taken inspiration from the eerie landscape inside the fence.

But things had started to change five years ago, Fletcher thought. Two strangers had managed to go deep into the Preserve. This time there were no survivors. The search-and-rescue team sent out by the Foundation had brought out the bodies.

Immediately afterward the mysterious people who ran the Foundation had intensified the force field that functioned as an invisible fence. Jasper and Fletcher could barely make it through now, and when they did they were no longer able to navigate the terrain. They dared not go more than a short distance inside, but that was far enough to tell them that something dark was stirring deep in the forbidden territory.

It wasn't just the atmosphere inside the Preserve that had changed, Fletcher thought. Jasper's dreams had begun to change, too.

Fletcher walked through the gallery to join Jasper at the window. Together they watched Slade Attridge leave Looking Glass and walk down Waterfront Street toward the police station.

"When do we tell him that we think there's something dangerous going on inside the Preserve?" Jasper asked.

"When we know for sure that he's the

right man for the job. When we can be certain that he'll stay on in Rainshadow."

CHAPTER 9

"They took the body away on a police boat out of Thursday Harbor," Charlotte said. "The chief says I can open the shop anytime I want but somehow I don't feel in the mood to conduct business as usual."

"I don't blame you." Rachel Blake came out from behind the counter, two steaming mugs of tea in her hands. She set both mugs down on the small round table. "Finding a dead body first thing in the morning is not a great way to start the day. Are you okay?"

"Yes." Charlotte picked up the mug of tea. "Well, I am now. I had a panic attack when I found the body but, hey, I think I deserved it under the circumstances."

"Absolutely. A dead body is enough to give anyone a panic attack." Rachel paused, the mug halfway to her lips. Her dark eyes shadowed with concern. "You're still having problems with panic attacks?"

"They aren't nearly as frequent as they

were when I was coming into my talent, thank heavens. But if I get too anxious or badly shaken, my talent automatically flares from zero to sixty. If that happens, it can set off an attack. I'll concentrate on starting the inventory this afternoon. That will take my mind off what happened this morning."

They were in the small coffee shop at the back of Shadow Bay Books. Like Charlotte, Rachel had spent many summers on Rainshadow. They were the same age and, in addition to sharing the normal trials and tribulations of the teenage years, they had shared the bond that came with the development of talents that neither of them had wanted or understood.

Rachel's great-aunt and the aunt's lifelong partner had owned the bookshop in those days. But a year ago the couple had retired unexpectedly and offered the business to Rachel. They had instructed her to do whatever she wanted with the shop and then they had moved to the sunnier climes of a desert retirement community.

Rachel had confided to Charlotte that at first she had been stunned because she had no idea the pair had the financial wherewithal to finance a high-end retirement community in the desert. *I always thought they were just squeaking by on the income*

154

from the bookstore and a few investments they made over the years. Who knew the investments were in a couple of small start-ups that got bought out for a fortune?

Rachel had matured into an attractive young woman. There was a lively energy about her that was infectious. But Charlotte sensed shadows and mysteries in her friend's amber brown eyes that had not been present all those years ago.

The summer friendship between the two women had gone into a long period of hibernation after they went off to college and started their separate adult lives. But when they had both found themselves back on Rainshadow it was as if they had never been apart. There was still a lot of history to catch up on but the old bond between them had snapped back into existence immediately. It was as if they had never been apart.

"So this Jeremy Gaines was a client of yours?" Rachel asked.

"Ex-client." Charlotte sipped some tea. "Can't imagine why he came here or why he was in my shop last night."

"Got any ideas?"

Charlotte smiled wryly. "You sound like the chief. The answer is no idea whatsoever."

"How did your association with Gaines end?"

"Badly. And from the way you phrased the question, I think you've been reading too much suspense and mystery fiction."

"Not like there's much else to do here on Rainshadow," Rachel said.

"Which brings up the obvious question — why did we both come back?"

"Don't know about you," Rachel said, "but I needed a change and I've always had this fantasy of operating a bookstore. You didn't answer my question."

"I more or less fired Jeremy as a client. He got pissed. Made a pest of himself for a while."

"Stalker?"

"My family was starting to think so," Charlotte admitted.

"And then he shows up here inside your shop. You know what? I'll bet he *was* stalking you. Probably came here last night to do something very nasty inside Looking Glass. That's the sort of thing stalkers start out with."

"I suppose it's a possibility," Charlotte said.

"Lucky he dropped dead of a heart attack when he did. Guys like that, they just keep going and the violence tends to escalate.

The only way to stop them is to kill them."

A chill shivered through Charlotte. "You speak from experience, don't you?"

"Yes," Rachel said. "I do."

CHAPTER 10

"Word around town is that the guy who dropped dead in Charlotte's shop was stalking her," Myrna said. "Probably came here to vandalize her store or leave a dead rat on the premises in order to frighten her. Good thing he dropped dead when he did."

Slade stopped at the desk and scooped up a stack of printouts. "It was convenient."

Myrna started to say something else but she got distracted by Rex, who came bouncing down the hall from the direction of the break room.

"Oh, good," Myrna said. "Looks like he finished the rest of today's loaf of Thelma's zucchini bread."

"You gave him some more?" Slade asked.

"It's either that or I start dumping the bread off the cliff at Lighthouse Point. No human being could possibly eat as much zucchini bread as Thelma is making this year. She had a bumper crop of zucchini, enough to go into commercial production."

Rex vaulted up onto Myrna's desk and chortled a greeting. He clutched a black beaded object.

"What on earth does he have in his grubby little paws?" Myrna asked. "He'd better not be bringing a dead bird in here. Hmm. Looks like an old evening purse, one of those tiny little bags ladies use to hold a lipstick and a compact."

Slade looked at the beaded purse.

"Damn," he said. "Rex must have snuck into Charlotte's shop while we were getting Gaines's body ready to transport."

"Uh-oh," Myrna said. "If it came from Looking Glass, it's probably not just some old evening bag. It's probably a valuable antique."

"Probably," Slade said.

Rex put the purse on the desk. He selected a few shiny paperclips from Myrna's stash and put them into the bag. When he was satisfied, he grabbed the purse and jumped back down to the floor. Then he dashed off in the direction of Slade's office.

"Something tells me the purse may have lost some of its value," Myrna said.

"I'll put it down as an office expense," Slade said.

"Speaking of Charlotte, how's she doing?

Must have been quite a shock for her, walking in on a dead body like that."

"She said something about conducting an inventory, so I think she's recovering."

"Not to change the subject, but how was your date last night?"

"We both survived it," Slade said.

The door of the station opened. Kirk Willis, Slade's one and only officer, entered. He used both hands to remove his sunglasses in a practiced, deliberate gesture.

Myrna smiled but said nothing.

"Heard the dead guy was a stalker," Kirk said.

Kirk was in his early twenties, a tall, still-gangly young man who didn't look a day over nineteen. He had been with the department for less than a year when Slade had arrived to take over as head of the department. Kirk had made no secret that he was not enthralled with his job. He had entered the police academy only after he had been forced to accept that his dream of working as a ghost hunter down in the catacombs was not going to happen. Kirk could pull a little ghost light but not enough to make him a Guild man.

Police work was a fallback profession as far as Kirk was concerned. Winding up in a small department in a town that was nothing more than a dot on the map on an island that wasn't even on a lot of maps had been a soul-crushing experience for him.

Kirk's attitude had improved briefly after they had taken down the drug runners who had ducked into the harbor earlier that week, but Slade didn't expect the newfound professional pride to last long. He empathized with the younger man. After all, he was planning to get the hell off the island, himself, as soon as possible. But being a short-timer was no excuse for an unprofessional attitude. He was going to have to have a chat with Kirk. There was a job to be done, and as long as Kirk was getting a paycheck from the town of Shadow Bay he was going to do that job right.

"The stalker theory makes sense," Myrna said. "I heard that Gaines was a former client of Charlotte's back in Frequency. Evidently he tried to date her and she declined."

"Explains what he was doing on the island," Kirk said. "Right, Chief?"

"It does," Slade said. "And for the moment, that is the official theory of the death."

Kirk and Myrna stared at him, eyes widening.

"Official theory?" Kirk repeated cautiously. "Are you saying it might not be the correct theory?"

"We are going to conduct an investigation to rule out homicide," Slade said. "But this will be a very low-profile project. Neither one of you will say a word about it outside this office. Not to anyone. Is that understood?"

"You got it, Chief." Kirk's dark eyes brightened with enthusiasm. "You really think someone murdered Gaines?"

"Yes, and before you ask, it wasn't Charlotte."

Myrna cleared her throat. "And we know this, how?"

Slade raised his brows. "I used to work for the FBPI, remember? I've done a lot of crime-scene investigation. The psychic evidence at the scene of Gaines's murder tells me that Charlotte was not the killer."

Myrna nodded. "You're the expert on paranormal forensics. But you're sure this is murder, not a heart attack?"

"I'm positive," Slade said.

"Poison, maybe?" Kirk offered. "They say some poisons don't show up in autopsies."

"That's true," Slade said. "But there's another possibility. A severe shock from a power source can stop the heart. We'll know more when we have the three basics."

"Means, motive, and opportunity," Kirk said. He was practically vibrating with enthusiasm now.

"Right." Slade looked at him. "You're good with a computer. I want you to do a background check on Gaines. There's reason to believe that he was involved in black-market antiquities. He may have made some enemies."

"I'll start on it right away."

Slade looked at Myrna. "Any luck locating Gaines's relatives?"

"No, oddly enough. It's as if he doesn't have any family."

"More likely he was living under a fake ID. Look deeper."

"Will do," Myrna said. Excitement lit up her face. She straightened her shoulders and swiveled her chair to face her computer.

"Remember," Slade said. "No one in this office talks to anyone about the investigation. Clear?"

"Clear," Kirk said.

"Clear," Myrna said. "Nothing like this has happened around here since those two hikers got lost in the Preserve five years ago."

The door opened. Devin charged into the office. In his excitement, he forgot to remove his sunglasses.

"What's a stalker, Grandma?" he demanded.

They all looked at Myrna.

"A stalker is a very bad person," Myrna said. She glanced at Slade. "Right, Chief?"

"Right," Slade said. "Very bad."

Devin frowned. "Do you think the dead guy came here to hurt Miss Enright?"

"It's a possibility," Slade said.

"In that case, I'm glad he croaked," Devin said fiercely. He whirled and ran back toward the door. "I gotta go tell Nate."

The door closed behind him.

Myrna sighed. "Some things seem so much simpler when you're that age."

"Yes," Slade said. "They do. I'll be in my office if you find anything."

He went down the hall. Rex was napping on his back on top of the row of file cabinets that lined the wall. All six paws were in the air. The stolen purse was nearby.

"I hope you're enjoying the hell out of that purse because you're the one who's going to have to deal with Charlotte when she discovers you ripped it off," Slade warned. "Don't expect me to pay for it."

Rex's blue eyes snapped open. He rolled to his hind legs, picked up the purse, and hopped down onto Slade's desk.

Slade reached for the crystal-studded bag.

"Let me see that thing."

Rex chortled and graciously released the antique purse. When Slade took it he got a little jolt of energy. It was like inhaling a woman's tantalizing perfume. Pleasant and ever-so-slightly exhilarating.

"You're getting a rush out of the energy infused in this thing, aren't you?" he said to Rex. "Must be a psychic version of dust bunny catnip."

Rex chortled happily. He retrieved the purse and scampered up onto the wide windowsill. He started to bat the cord that controlled the slatted shades.

"Don't worry, I'm not going to try to take it away from you," Slade said. "That purse is your problem. I've got enough of my own."

He lowered himself into the ancient chair behind the big, battered desk. Both pieces of furniture looked as if they had served several generations of his predecessors. He was pretty sure that the desk, along with the vintage wooden chairs, slatted window blinds, and file cabinets filled with yellowed paperwork, qualified as antiques. Like the town, the police station looked as if it had been caught in a time warp.

The desk chair groaned when he turned to face the computer. He had thought about picking up a can of oil down at Herb's Marine Supply but decided it wasn't worth the trouble. He wouldn't be hanging around long enough to bother with repairs and maintenance issues.

The one piece of equipment in the office that qualified as state-of-the-art was the computer. It was not department issue. It was his personal computer. He fired it up and settled in to do some serious research on Jeremy Gaines. Kirk could handle the routine background check. He would be able to access police department and business records but he did not have access to the FBPI files. If Gaines had been involved in the dangerous world of the para-weapons business, the information was more likely to be buried in the Office files.

Half an hour later he sat back and thought about what he had discovered. He contemplated possibilities for a while and then he picked up the phone and made a call.

When he finished the phone call, he got up and started for the door.

Rex grabbed the purse and leaped down to the floor to follow. Slade picked him up and plopped him on his shoulder.

"If I were you, I'd hide the purse," he said.

Rex ignored him.

CHAPTER 11

"Yes, Dad, I'm fine, really." Charlotte stood behind the sales counter, holding the phone to her ear with one hand while she studied the screen of her computer. "It doesn't look like I'm going to be arrested for murder, at any rate."

"Arrested." Daniel Enright was both stunned and outraged. "Are you telling me that there was ever the slightest possibility of your being charged with that bastard's murder? You said the authorities called it a heart attack."

"Right, right, a heart attack," Charlotte said soothingly. "I was just trying to reassure you."

"Using the words *arrested* and *murder* in the same sentence is not a good way to reassure me."

"I didn't mean to alarm you, really. Everything is under control."

"I was right about Gaines, wasn't I?" Daniel said grimly. "He was stalking you."

"Maybe."

"What do you mean, maybe? Why else would he have followed you to Rainshadow?"

"I'm not sure, Dad, but it's possible he came here to steal something from my shop."

"And dropped dead at the scene?" Daniel did not try to hide his skepticism.

"I know, it doesn't sound very likely, does it? But that's how it looks."

A dark shadow blocked the light that had been streaming through the glass door pane. Charlotte looked out toward the street and saw Slade. Rex was on his shoulder. Slade tried the door. When it did not open he looked at her through the window.

Phone clamped to her ear, she moved out from behind the counter and crossed the room to unlock the door.

"There's really nothing to worry about, Dad," she said. "The local chief of police happens to be a talent who used to work for the FBPI. He knows what he's doing."

"Since when does a former FBPI agent take over a small-town police department?"

"He's making a career change. Hang on a second. He's here now. His name is Slade Attridge." She opened the door.

Slade walked into the shop. Rex made excited noises. He waved the beaded purse at Charlotte.

"So that's where it went," Charlotte said. "I had a feeling it had been stolen."

"What's going on?" Daniel demanded on the other end of the phone. "What was stolen?"

"Nothing, never mind," Charlotte said. She pointed to the phone and mouthed the words *my dad* to Slade.

"Let me talk to him," Slade said. He plucked the phone from her fingers before she could object. "This is Slade Attridge. Yes, Mr. Enright, I'm the chief of police here on Rainshadow. Right. Yes. I understand, sir. No, she's not a suspect. Yes, believe it or not, I do know what I'm doing. I'll give you the name and number of my former boss. You can call him to get some background on me if you've got questions. Got a pen?"

There was a pause. Charlotte heard her father's muffled voice. She raised her eyes to the ceiling, exasperated. Of course her father had questions. Daniel Enright was a strategy-talent. He hadn't become the CEO of a successful corporation by taking others on faith. He always looked below the surface.

A few seconds later Slade spoke into the phone again. "His name is Special Agent Thomas West. He works out of the Resonance City office." Slade rattled off a phone number. "Tell whoever answers the phone that I gave you that number. Yes, sir, I'll keep an eye on Charlotte."

Charlotte made a face. "This is so irritating."

Slade met her eyes while he continued talking to her father. "Yes, sir, I am aware that there was some history between Charlotte and the victim."

Charlotte winced.

"Yes, I agree. Gaines's death was more than a little suspicious under the circumstances. If it was murder it was by paranormal means and there's a special department within the FBPI that investigates those kinds of crimes. As it happens, that's the department I worked for when I was with the Bureau. Yes, sir, I have investigated this kind of thing before." Slade paused, listening. "Charlotte told you I was making a career change?"

Charlotte started to smile. Slade raised his brows but his tone remained respectful.

"Yes, sir, I'm planning to open a private security consulting firm," Slade said. "I'll be catering to Arcane-connected corporations like Enright, Inc., as a matter of fact. Yes, sir, I'm aware that there are very few security consultants who understand the problem of securing data and records against corporate espionage agents who possess paranormal powers. It's a niche market but, I think, a potentially lucrative one."

There was another pause.

"Yes, sir. Getting back to Jeremy Gaines, I did some research on him this morning. Looks like he probably had more than a few enemies. I have reason to believe that he was in the business of peddling stolen antiquities."

Charlotte blinked. "Jeremy was in the black market?"

"Yes, sir, I'll keep you informed," Slade said into the phone. "Now you'll have to excuse me. I've got work to do here."

He ended the connection and handed the phone back to Charlotte. "Your father is calling my contact at the Bureau as we speak to make sure that I'm actually qualified to keep an eye on you."

"Sorry about that," she said ruefully. "My family has always been a little overprotective of me. You know how it is when you're the youngest and the only girl."

"No," Slade said evenly. "I don't know

how it is to be the youngest and the only girl."

She flushed. "Sorry. I guess you don't. You'll just have to take my word for it. It's not just that I'm the only girl in the family, it's the panic attack thing and the fact that it's linked to my talent. Everyone has the impression that I'm delicate. Never mind, tell me what you discovered about Jeremy. Was he really dealing stolen goods?"

"Looks like it. I did some rough research using the Bureau's files. I haven't had time to check out the details but from what I could determine Gaines moved in murky circles. I don't think he was actually a collector, just a broker."

"That explains why he never offered to show me his private collection. He probably didn't have one."

"It gets more interesting. He wasn't just dealing stolen antiquities. There are strong indications that he specialized in the really dangerous stuff."

She frowned. "What do you mean by dangerous?"

"Weapons-grade para-antiques and antiquities. Objects that are powerful enough to kill."

"Oh, man. I know there's a market for that kind of thing but I've never gone anywhere near it. I told you, he came to me looking for an Old World snow globe, a pretty toy, not some kind of para-weapon."

"And you did locate the snow globe."

"Yes. But as I said, I never gave him Mrs. Lambert's name."

"Doesn't mean he wasn't able to find out her identity. If I'm right about Gaines, he was a pro. He survived for quite a while in a very dangerous business. All he had to do was follow you around or bug your phone calls or download data from your computer in order to discover Lambert's identity."

She chilled. "Do you really think I led him to her? I have always tried to maintain good security for my clients."

"If Gaines was working the para-weapons market, he would have had the skills and the talent to break through any security system you bought off the shelf."

Charlotte felt utterly stricken. "If he managed to find Mrs. Lambert through me, then maybe her death wasn't from natural causes. Maybe he killed her. Maybe I'm responsible."

"Take it easy." Slade frowned. "You're starting to hyperventilate. Breathe."

"Right." She forced herself to go into the breathing ritual. "Damn, I hate this."

"You're not responsible for Mrs. Lambert's death. I checked that angle out, too. She died in the hospital of natural causes. She was there for several days. Her family was at her bedside."

"You're sure?"

"I'm sure."

"Where does that leave us?"

"You said Lambert gave the bulk of her collection to one of the Arcane Society museums before she died?"

"Yes, the Frequency City branch. The museum got everything except for the few pieces that she bequeathed to me in her will."

"Where are those objects?"

"Here." Charlotte waved a hand toward the crowded back room. "In some of those crates that Jeremy pried open. But there was an inventory with the bequest and I can assure you that there was no Old World snow globe listed. Believe me, anything that valuable would have gone to the museum."

"I checked," Slade said. "The museum staff is still unpacking and cataloging the glassware they received from Lambert but they've got a detailed inventory. Someone is going through it now to see if there is an Old World snow globe on the list. I should have an answer tomorrow."

She was impressed. "You did all of that

research today?"

"It helps to have Bureau connections."

"Sounds like it."

Slade surveyed the shop. "Gaines thought there was something here that was of value to him, presumably that snow globe. He broke in to search for it. Someone else followed him here to kill him. Whoever it was must have been after the globe, too. The question is, did the killer find it?"

"If he did, it would have been by pure chance. The objects that Mrs. Lambert left me were packed in with a lot of other glassware from my shop." She paused. "Hmm."

"What?"

"All of the glassware I deal in is psi-infused."

"Para-antiques are your specialty," Slade said. "What about it?"

"I'm sure you're aware that glass is tricky in general because it doesn't conform to the standard laws of para-physics."

"Something about it having the properties of both a solid and a liquid."

"Right. And glass infused with paranormal energy is downright unpredictable. What's more, a lot of psi-glass packed together in a crate would produce a tremendous amount of interference. Even a talent with a strong affinity for glass, like a glass-light reader, for instance, wouldn't be able to identify the radiation given off by a particular item if it was surrounded by a lot of other hot objects." Charlotte looked around at the crowded shop. "And the problem would increase exponentially if there was a lot of other energy in the vicinity."

"Which would definitely be the case in here," Slade concluded.

"So, it's just barely possible that the killer found what he was looking for that night but the odds are against it."

"Which means that he may come back to take another look," Slade said.

Charlotte pursed her lips, thinking. "Seems like it would be a lot easier to just pop into the shop posing as a collector of old snow globes."

"Good point," Slade said. "Let me know if that happens."

"Don't worry, you'll be the first to know. I have to say, it has occurred to me that there's an upside to this situation."

"That would be?"

"You indicated that you were bored with your job here on Rainshadow. Now, at least, you have something to keep you occupied."

The edge of his mouth kicked up a little at one corner. "I'll try to remember to think

176

positive. I've advised Willis and Myrna that we've got a murder case on our hands but I've ordered them not to talk about it to anyone. Meanwhile, we're going to let the stalker-who-dropped-dead-from-a-heart-attack scenario stand as the official explanation of this situation."

"Why?"

"Because, with luck, the killer will conclude that there is no active investigation and that you are not a threat to him."

She took a sharp little breath. "Do you really think that whoever killed Gaines might come after me?"

"I think you'll be safe as long as you and the local police appear to be satisfied that Gaines was a stalker."

"*You* are the local police."

Slade gave her his hunter's smile.

"Yes," he said. "I am."

"So, what are you going to do?"

"What I just promised your father I would do. Keep an eye on you."

CHAPTER 12

The following morning Slade opened the door of the Kane Gallery and moved inside. Rex rode on his shoulder.

Fletcher Kane, the proprietor of the gallery, stood at a table with Jasper Gilbert, the artist whose work hung in the Kane Gallery. They were examining a canvas on the table. The men looked up when Slade entered.

"Good afternoon, Chief," Fletcher said in his urbane, cultured tones. "Hope you aren't too put off by recent events here in Shadow Bay. I can guarantee you that dead bodies don't routinely turn up in our fair town."

"That's what people keep telling me," Slade said. "Thought I'd bring you up to date, Mr. Mayor."

His senses were closed down but the paintings on the walls of the gallery still succeeded in stirring the hair on his nape. The images were fiercely luminous scenes of the island. What set them apart from the works of other local painters was the surreal, otherworldly quality. The greens were psi green, the kind of green that was found only in the ruins and the Underworld. The reds and yellows were so hot it was a wonder that they did not set fire to the canvas. Whether by intention or artistic intuition, Gilbert succeeded in capturing the nexus energy of the island, Slade thought.

Fletcher Kane was currently serving as Shadow Bay's part-time mayor. He looked very much the way one expected the owner of a modestly successful gallery to look. With his lean frame, silver hair, and patrician features he exuded a refined elegance. Amber and gold rings gleamed on his long, tapered fingers. You had to look hard to see the dangerous edge beneath the surface.

Jasper Gilbert, on the other hand, possessed just the right degree of scruffy eccentricity that one expected from an artist. He was big and bearded. His sweatshirt and baggy pants were stained with ancient and new paint splatters.

Both men were in their early seventies. According to the background research Slade had gathered on them, they had lived on the island for nearly three decades.

Jasper eyed Rex. "Does the rule against bribing an officer of the law extend to said officer's dust bunny?"

"No," Slade said. "As far as I can see Rex doesn't pay a lot of attention to the rules."

"Well, in that case, I believe I've got some leftover zucchini bread in the back room."

"Rex will be thrilled," Slade said.

"I'll go get it."

He disappeared into the back room.

Fletcher Kane studied Rex. "What's he got in his paw? Looks like an old evening bag."

"Rex purloined it from Looking Glass."

"Purloined? Would that be professional cop jargon for 'ripped off'?"

"It would," Slade said. "Charlotte tells me the damn purse is worth a few hundred bucks."

"Don't even think about trying to slip that into departmental expenses," Fletcher warned. "As mayor, I assure you I would spot it immediately."

"I'll try to hide it under office supplies."

"Forget it," Fletcher said. "How goes the investigation?"

"The investigation is ongoing, as we in the police business like to say," Slade said. "But for now it looks like a guy who was stalking Charlotte dropped dead in her back room."

"Convenient," Fletcher observed.

"Yes," Slade said. "Very."

Fletcher looked knowing. "You're not buying it are you?"

"Not for a minute," Slade said. "My department is aware that we are conducting a murder investigation and so is Charlotte. I'm keeping you in the loop because you're the mayor. I realize that means that Jasper is also in the loop."

"A goodly number of people."

"Yes."

"You know what they say — if two or more people know a secret it is no longer a secret."

"I'm going to have to take that chance for now."

Jasper emerged from the back room with a large slice of zucchini bread on a plate. He set the plate on the counter. Rex watched each move with close attention.

"Help yourself, Wonder Bunny," Jasper said.

Rex chortled with glee and hopped down onto the counter. He put his purse aside and attacked the zucchini bread with gusto.

"That zucchini bread looks vaguely familiar," Slade said. "I'm going to go out on a limb here and guess that it was made by Thelma Duncan."

"Good guess," Jasper said. "It's not that it isn't great zucchini bread. It's more a case of, who really likes zucchini bread?"

"Rex, evidently," Fletcher said.

They all watched Rex polish off the bread.

"It's amazing," Slade said. "He's been eating zucchini bread every day since we hit the island last week and he never gets tired of it."

"Lucky Rex," Fletcher said. "We had our fill about forty-eight hours into zucchini season. Don't tell Thelma but we started composting the stuff."

Jasper lounged against the counter. "So what really happened in the back room of Looking Glass, Chief?"

"Death by paranormal means," Slade said.

Fletcher and Jasper exchanged an unreadable look.

Fletcher turned back to Slade. "That's not good. Ghost-hunter work? Some hunters can pull a lot of ghost light aboveground."

"No, I've seen people who were killed with ghost fire. This is different."

"Got any theories?" Jasper asked.

Slade gave them what he had. Both men absorbed the information in a thoughtful silence.

"Black-market antiquities," Jasper said. "Interesting. I always figured there was nothing but junk in Looking Glass."

"Gaines may have been after some relic that was shipped from Charlotte's Frequency City shop," Slade said. "She handled some high-end objects. I stopped here today to ask a favor."

"Certainly," Fletcher said. "What can we do for you?"

"Willis and Myrna are good but they've had zero experience in the illegal antiquities trade. Can't say I've had a lot, myself. It wasn't my specialty when I was an agent. But I figure you two probably know as much if not more about the business than most people do. It would be helpful if you could give me some background."

Jasper looked intrigued. "You think we're experts because we're in the art world?"

"That and the fact that you are both Guild men. A lot of smuggling goes on in the Underworld. The Guilds handle protection for every corporation and research lab working the ruins underground. That means you know smuggling and you know antiquities."

Fletcher and Jasper looked at each other again, once more exchanging a silent message. Then they turned back to Slade.

"Out of sheer curiosity, how the hell did

you figure out that we were both Guild men?" Fletcher asked.

"I've worked with some ghost hunters," Slade said. "There's a look."

Jasper elevated one bushy brow. "FBPI intuition?"

"Well, that and the fact that I ran you both through the Bureau's files."

Fletcher grimaced. "Should have seen that coming."

"Guess it's what we get for asking Adam Winters to recommend a candidate for the police chief position here on Rainshadow," Jasper said.

CHAPTER 13

There was something very powerful inside the wooden crate. An icy-hot frisson feathered Charlotte's senses. She had unpacked about half of the objects. She studied the jumble of bubble-wrapped antiques that remained inside. It was impossible to tell which one of them was giving off the currents of strong energy.

The doorbell chimed just as she selected one of the bulky packages. A subtle sense of awareness shifted through her. She did not need to look toward the door to know that Slade was there. She watched him walk into the front room. His lean frame and broad shoulders were silhouetted against the daylight filtering through the windows. Rex was with him. The dust bunny chortled a greeting.

She put down the bulky, plastic-shrouded object she had just taken from the box and walked into the sales room. She stopped a short distance away.

"Good morning," she said. She looked at Rex. "Glad to see that Rex is enjoying his clutch."

"He carries it everywhere," Slade said.

"Are you, perhaps, a tad concerned about what it does to your image to be seen with a sidekick who carries a beaded clutch bag?"

"No," Slade said.

She smiled. "Of course not."

"I stopped in to tell you that I just talked to the ME over in Thursday Harbor. They're calling Gaines's death a heart attack. There are no signs of foul play and they have no one pushing them to do an autopsy."

"As you predicted," she said. "But you're still certain that Jeremy was murdered?"

"No question."

"What happens now?"

"I'm looking deeper into Gaines's background but it's going to take time. He was a pro. He knew how to cover his tracks."

"What exactly are you looking for?"

"Clients, other dealers he may have worked with. His competition. When a guy like Gaines gets killed, it's almost always business-related. I thought I'd take another look at the scene of the crime."

She waved a hand toward the back room. "Help yourself."

"Thanks."

"I've moved some stuff around," she warned.

"Doesn't matter. The kind of evidence I'm looking for will still be there."

"Psi residue?"

"Right." He walked into the back room and crouched down in the area where Jeremy's body had been found. Charlotte started to follow him and then stopped. There was no sign of Rex.

"Where's your dust bunny?" she said.

"Not my bunny." Slade crouched down and studied the floorboards.

Charlotte did a quick search of the premises. She found Rex perched on a Second Century tall clock. He had the clutch purse open beside him. When he saw her he chortled innocently and blinked his baby blues.

Satisfied that Rex was not bent on the destruction of her shop, she went to stand in the doorway of the back room. Energy shivered in the atmosphere. She knew that Slade was running a little hot, not fully cranked but definitely rezzed. She folded her arms and propped one shoulder against the doorjamb.

As she watched, he ran his fingertips across the floor. After a moment he got to his feet and walked slowly toward the rear door. He hunkered down a second time.

"What do you see?" she asked, fascinated.

"Same thing I saw the first time. I told myself that I was wrong but now I'm not so sure."

"Not sure about what?"

"Cause of death." He got to his feet.

"But you said it was by paranormal means."

"No question about that. But as I told you, the ability to commit murder with psi energy is extremely rare. Any talent who could kill from this distance aboveground would have to be unusually powerful or possess an enhancing device. Maybe both."

"Right. So?"

Slade looked down at the floor just inside the door, a cold, thoughtful expression hardening his features. "I can see the residue of the energy that was laid down by the killer when the murder was committed. It's strong." He walked slowly back to where Gaines's body had been found. "But it is not, in and of itself, a lethal type of talent."

"Meaning?"

"Meaning that the killer must have used a device of some kind to commit the murder. The thing is, para-weapons leave traces just like mag-rez pistols leave shell casings. This stuff doesn't look like anything I've ever seen before. Definitely not crystal-based energy."

"Alien technology, maybe?"

"No, alien technology leaves its own unique tracks. No question but that this was human psi generated through a para-weapon. But whatever it was, it was not a crystal gun."

"It was bad enough knowing that Jeremy was involved in the black market, but to think that he might have been dealing para-weapons is appalling. How could he do such a thing?"

Slade looked amused. "Do I really need to answer that?"

She sighed. "No. He was a sociopath so I guess it's no surprise that he had no qualms about the kind of antiques and antiquities he traded. Any luck tracking down his associates?"

"Some. Kane and Gilbert gave me the names of some heavy players in the black market. I came up with a few more from the Bureau's files. But it takes time to check alibis. I've got Willis working on it now."

"What happens next?"

"As I told Kane and Gilbert, the investigation is ongoing."

She took a deep breath and braced herself.

"Given that status, would you like to have dinner at my place tonight?"

He did not answer immediately, just studied her with a speculative expression.

She flushed, took off her glasses and concentrated on removing a tiny smudge with the hem of her T-shirt. "Sorry. I had the impression that you might be willing to risk a second date. If I got that part wrong, it's okay. I understand, really."

"You didn't get it wrong," he said, his voice perfectly neutral. "What do you want me to bring?"

Her spirits lifted. "Maybe you'd better bring the beer. I don't have any and I wouldn't know what brand to buy for you."

"Fine. I'll bring the beer. What time?"

She eyed him closely. "You're really not worried about another date?"

"What additional damage could you possibly do to my ego this time around that you didn't do the first time?"

She cleared her throat. "That's one way to look at it. Why don't you come over around six thirty? That will give me time to close the shop and pick up a few things at the grocery store."

"That works. See you tonight."

He walked past her into the front room.

Charlotte plunked the glasses back on her

nose, got unstuck from the floor, and hurried after him.

"Wait," she called.

He stopped, one big hand wrapped around the doorknob. "What?"

"Thanks," she said. She stopped. "I appreciate the second chance. I'll try not to screw things up this time around."

"Sounds like a plan."

"We'll keep everything casual," she promised. "Just a couple of friends getting together for dinner."

"As opposed to the two-talents-stranded-on-an-island scenario?"

"Right."

"Is that the way you want it?"

"It's probably best for now," she said. Wistful regret shadowed her eyes.

"Why am I getting the feeling that you're the one who's nervous?"

"I am nervous," she admitted. "I told you, when it comes to dating I've got a lousy track record."

"Maybe you should stop trying to analyze your dates' rainbows."

"It's a hard habit to break," she said.

"Maybe you need more practice."

"That's a possibility."

"See you at six thirty."

She relaxed slightly. "Great."

"I'll bring the zucchini bread."

"Don't bother. Thelma Duncan left two more loaves on my doorstep this morning."

"Rex will be excited."

A small, distinct clang reverberated from the corner of the shop.

"*Rex!*" Charlotte yelped. She glared at Slade. "Your dust bunny is destroying my business."

"Not my dust bunny," Slade said.

Charlotte whirled around, searching for signs of mass destruction. She saw movement near the back wall and rushed through the tightly packed space. She finally saw Rex. He was perched on top of a dusty glass cabinet that contained an array of small amber and crystal objects. He had the clutch bag open and was in the process of leaning over the edge and reaching into the cabinet for one of the items on the top shelf.

"*No,*" Charlotte said sternly. "You will not touch that. It's a Marilyn Stone lady's compact and it is worth at least eight hundred bucks."

"Forget the compact, Rex," Slade said.

Rex abandoned the compact and chortled at Charlotte. He cocked his head to the side in what he no doubt thought was a cute, appealing manner.

Charlotte patted him somewhere in the

vicinity of the top of his head. "I know what you're up to," she said. "You are trying to pretend that you are a sweet, cuddly little pet, but you are not fooling me. Not for a minute."

"Let's go, Rex," Slade said from the door.

Rex bustled down from the glass cabinet with his clutch and flitted across the floor. Slade scooped him up and tucked him under one arm.

"Tonight," Slade said to Charlotte.

There was a dark promise in the words. Charlotte stilled.

"What about tonight?" she managed to ask.

"I'll take you into the Preserve after dark."

Excitement flashed through her. She smiled. "Great, something to look forward to. Besides the zucchini bread, I mean. It's been fifteen years since I last broke the law and did some trespassing."

"I don't want to spoil the moment but I have to tell you that, technically speaking, you won't be breaking any laws if you go into the Preserve with me this time."

"To say I'm disappointed would be an understatement. Why won't I be doing anything illegal with you tonight?"

"As the duly constituted representative of the forces of law and order in these parts,

I'm expected to deal with any illegal activities therein."

"But there isn't much in the way of illegal activity due to the fence."

"Doesn't mean I'm not obligated to go in and patrol the place once in a while."

She laughed. "So I'll be doing a sort of civilian ride-along tonight?"

"Except we'll be on foot."

He opened the door and went outside onto the street with Rex. She leaned on the counter for a moment, watching Slade until he was out of sight. Little thrills of anticipation splashed across her senses. *You're getting a second chance, woman. Whatever you do, don't screw up this time. You can do this.*

She straightened and went into the back room to finish unpacking the crate. Now that Slade was no longer around to distract her senses, she became aware once again of the dark energy leaking out of one of the bubble-shrouded antiques inside the shipping container.

She jacked up her talent a couple of notches and reached for the bundled object that she had been about to take out when Slade had interrupted her.

The instant she touched it, she knew that whatever was inside was the object emitting the strong energy. The object was surprisingly heavy for its size.

Carefully she started to unwrap the antique. As she got closer she could make out the dome shape. A chill of awareness and excitement shot through her. The antique was very similar to a snow globe in shape.

But when she peeled away the fine layer of bubble wrap, disappointment settled on her like a wet blanket. She was holding a paperweight, not a snow globe. The antique was made of glass but it was opaque, not clear. She shook it gently. Nothing happened. There was no scene inside, no sparkling snow.

The paperweight was quite old. She kicked up her senses again. *Really old,* she thought. It was almost certainly an Old World object. In addition there was a large amount of energy in it. The combination made it almost priceless to certain collectors and museums. The paperweight might be a dull-looking object but it held the potential to be the biggest sale of her career.

She put it on a table and picked up the itemized list that had accompanied the bequest. She had already examined it but she wanted to be certain.

As she had remembered, there was no gray glass paperweight with an Old World provenance on the list. *Don't get your hopes up,* she thought. A mistake had no doubt been made when the museum staff had packed up Evelyn Lambert's vast collection. It was easy enough to see how a simple, rather unattractive paperweight had been overlooked and put into the wrong box.

There was only one way to be sure that she had a right to the paperweight. She would contact the Lambert family lawyer to explain the situation. Meanwhile, the first priority was to find a secure place to stash the object. She remembered the old antique safe that her aunt had installed years earlier in the floor. It would be perfect.

She picked up the paperweight. Her senses were still a little jacked. She did not notice that the object was starting to lose its opaque quality until she was just about to set it on the shelf inside the old safe.

The first hints of a small scene appeared inside the glass dome. She had seen similar images in old photos in the Arcane Society Museum. The tiny, exquisitely detailed Old World cityscape was complete, with a stately clock tower and imposing buildings. It was familiar to anyone who had grown up within Arcane.

London, England. Late Nineteenth Century, Old World Date. The era was known

to historians and antiquities experts as the
Victorian Age.

CHAPTER 14

Slade contemplated the antique object for a long time. She watched him from the other side of the table, aware that he was running a little hot. So was she. It seemed to her that their jacked-up auras, combined with the radiation from the nondescript artifact that sat between them made the atmosphere inside the shop feel thick and ominous, like the energy of an oncoming storm.

After a while Slade looked up and fixed her with his cop eyes.

"You're telling me that this might be the artifact that Gaines wanted you to find for him? The one he broke in here to steal?"

"I think so," Charlotte said. "I know it doesn't look like much but that's not unusual when it comes to paranormal objects. Watch what happens when I generate a little energy."

She put her fingers on the dome and heightened her senses. The glass cleared, slowly revealing the miniature landscape.

"Doesn't look like any city I've ever seen," Slade said. "Are you sure that's the Old World town where Jones & Jones was founded?"

"I verified it on the computer. That clock tower was a chiming clock. The bell was nicknamed Big Ben."

"Big Ben who?"

"Darned if I know who Ben was. But I'm positive that's the city that was home to Arcane and J&J in what was known as the Victorian Era."

"Who was Victoria?"

"An ancient queen, I think. She ruled during the period when J&J was founded."

"You're sure the snow globe is authentic and not a replica?"

"Trust me, it's the real thing."

"There's no snow," Slade said.

"Well, this globe is hundreds of years old. It's hardly surprising that it no longer produces fake snow. But there is a lot of energy embedded in that thing. I've never come across anything like it."

"Must be worth a fortune."

"Oh, yes." She smiled. "I sent an email to the lawyer who handled Mrs. Lambert's estate. My main concern is that this is all a mistake. I wouldn't be surprised if this object was supposed to go into the museum collection. I can't risk putting it on the market until I know for sure that it's mine to sell."

"I can sense that it's giving off some energy," Slade said. "But I don't recognize it."

She understood what he meant. Power was power, and most sensitives could pick up on the vibes when there was a lot of it around. But by definition a talent could only recognize — and work — the ultralight currents that emanated from the distinct narrow bands on the paranormal spectrum to which he or she was personally sensitive.

"If we're right about Gaines, he dealt in para-weapons," Slade said. "Do you think this globe might be weapons-grade?"

"No," she said, on firm ground now. "It's certainly powerful but it doesn't feel like any para-weapon I've ever handled."

Slade smiled faintly. "How many have you touched?"

"Very few. One doesn't come across them very often in my end of the business. But I have come in contact with some and I can tell you that this energy feels different. I'm sure it's as strong as any weapons-grade artifact but I don't think it was designed to kill. At least, not all by itself."

"What does it do?"

"This is going to sound strange but it feels a bit like a generator or an engine."

Slade picked up the globe and held it to the light. "Maybe it was meant to power or fuel a weapon."

"That's possible. But even though it isn't a para-weapon I can assure you that Jeremy would have wanted to get his hands on it simply because of its enormous value."

"Priceless?"

It was her turn to be amused. "I learned long ago that there is no such thing as priceless, not in my business. No matter how rare or valuable an object is, there is always a price and always some collector willing to pay it."

"And maybe one or two who would be willing to kill for it?"

"Oh, yes."

Slade raised his brows. "You know, until I met you I had no idea that the antique trade was such a rough business."

"It has its moments."

He set the globe back down on the table. "And this particular almost-priceless object might be yours."

"I'm trying not to get my hopes up. Logic tells me it was supposed to go to the museum."

"Looks like I now have my motive for murder."

"Absolutely."

Slade put his fingertips on the globe. Energy crackled briefly in the atmosphere. "I told you that I don't recognize the psi emanating from this thing, but I do recognize some of the residue *on* it."

"What do you mean?"

He took his hand off the globe and looked at her.

"More than one person has died while clutching this globe," he said.

"Are you sure?"

"I'm sure. There are several layers of violent energy. But the most recent one is at least forty years old."

"The globe was probably tucked away in Mrs. Lambert's personal vault for the past forty years," Charlotte said. "It's too late now to ask her how she acquired it. She seemed like such a nice old lady. Maybe I don't really want to know how it came into her possession."

"You did say that sometimes it's best not to know too much about someone. She never mentioned that she intended to leave the globe to you?"

"No." Charlotte sighed. "Which is why I suspect that it will soon be going to the

Arcane museum. But who knows? I might get lucky. Maybe the lawyer will tell me that Mrs. Lambert wanted me to have it."

"Meanwhile it needs to be held in safe-keeping."

"It just so happens that years ago my aunt installed a fabulous old Greenleaf amber-lock safe in this shop. There is certainly more sophisticated technology on the market now but no one has ever crafted better locks."

"I've come across a few Greenleaf safes in my time. They're solid. Sounds like a good place to store the globe."

CHAPTER 15

"If I never eat another slice of zucchini bread again in my entire life, I don't think I'll mind," Charlotte said.

"I believe Rex now considers it a staple of his diet." Slade switched on the small flashlight he had taken out of the pack slung over his shoulder. "He's going to be crushed when the season is over."

"I'm sure he'll move on. He's a dust bunny. He lives in the moment."

"Zucchini issues aside, dinner was good tonight. I liked the way you fixed the tomatoes."

"Thanks. But I gotta tell you, I'm even running out of things to do with tomatoes. Luckily Mrs. Duncan says her broccoli, kale, and peas are coming in nicely so we should have some changes in the menu soon."

"I've never been a broccoli fan and I wouldn't know what to do with kale,"

Slade said.

"You wash it, dry it, cut it up, toss it with olive oil and salt, and then you roast it in the oven until it gets all crispy."

"Yeah?" Slade sounded skeptical.

"Tastes just like potato chips."

"I'll take your word for it," Slade said politely.

"You'll see. I'll fix some for you as soon as Mrs. Duncan brings me a batch."

"Deal."

There had been a little light left in the sky when they had set out from her cottage in Slade's SUV. But darkness was coming on fast as they walked into the trees at the end of Merton Road. Rex, clutch purse in paw, was bobbing about at their feet, dashing hither and yon to investigate interesting rocks and clumps of vegetation. Occasionally he disappeared altogether into the undergrowth only to reappear a short time later with some small treasure — a rock or a flower — to show them.

The night seemed filled with promise. Charlotte was intensely aware of a sparkling sense of anticipation, as if an important door was about to open and everything in her life was going to change. She hadn't felt anything like this since the night she had gone into the Preserve with Slade fifteen years ago. No, she reminded herself, she had experienced it on one other occasion. That was the morning last week when she stood with the others and watched Slade walk off the ferry to take the chief's job.

It only went to show how poor her intuition was, she thought, because when you got right down to it, nothing had changed after those other two encounters.

Nevertheless, she felt thrilled tonight. There was no other word for it.

"I'm really excited about this, you know," she confided.

Slade smiled his faint smile. "Yeah, I can see that."

"I don't get out much."

"Nobody does around here, as far as I can tell. Probably because there's no place to go."

"I'm not talking about traveling or entertainment. I meant that I've had a hard time doing the really interesting things."

"Such as?"

"I told you that my family expected me to end up selling antiques. They were right. But fifteen years ago my secret dream was to become a para-archaeologist and work in one of the Arcane museums."

"I remember. I take it that didn't work out for you."

"I got my degree and I applied to the Arcane museums in each of the four city-states and all of the regular public and private museums as well. But every single one of them turned me down."

"Did they give you a reason?"

"Just the usual *sorry, we don't need your particular talents at this time* crap. But I did some investigating on my own and found out the truth. My rainbow-reading ability isn't considered useful in the field. I've got a good feel for identifying para-artifacts and antiques, but that's hardly unique. There are people with a lot more specific talent for that kind of thing."

"What about that tuning trick you do?" Slade asked.

"That's just it. Everyone considers it a neat trick, a novelty. But I can't even use it to tune standard resonating amber for focusing purposes. It doesn't work that way. The fact is, my little trick has no academic-related uses."

"Just good for selling art and antiques?"

"Yes. I can't complain. It's worked out very well for me from a financial point of view. And I really do enjoy the work. My family was very relieved when I made the decision to go into the business."

"Why?"

"They were afraid that working with some of the seriously powerful antiquities in museum collections would cause me to have more panic attacks." She paused. "Me being so damn delicate and all."

There was a long silence before Slade finally spoke.

"You're not the only one who got slapped with that label," he said. "I did, too."

"What?" Startled, she glanced at him. "Are you serious? There's nothing delicate about you."

"Cut me some slack here." He managed to sound hurt. "I may be a cop but that doesn't mean I don't have feelings."

She laughed. "You know what I mean. You were an FBPI agent and you worked for that special Office and now you're a police chief investigating a murder by paranormal means. Somehow I just can't see anyone labeling you as delicate."

"You'd be surprised."

The silence that fell between them was longer this time. Charlotte sensed that Slade regretted having gone down this particular conversational path. She pulled up the collar of her jacket and waited to see if he would tell her the rest of the story.

The night was cool but not cold. She was dressed for the trip into the forbidden zone in jeans, a sweater, and a jacket. She listened to the sounds of the gathering night. Small creatures chirped in the grass. A light breeze sighed through the branches and boughs and rustled leaves. Birds called in the trees.

Slade did not speak.

In the end she couldn't stand not knowing.

"Okay, okay, who called you delicate?" she asked.

At first she thought he was not going to answer the question. But he must have concluded that, since he had brought up the subject and since she had answered his questions, he owed her some sort of response.

"A team of doctors and para-shrinks at a clinic," he said.

"Oh, *geez*." She stopped, stunned, and stared at him, trying to read his profile in the low light. "Talk about a career-killer for someone in your line. I don't believe it. You have got to be kidding."

"No." Slade halted. He did not turn to face her. Instead he gazed steadily ahead at the trees that marked the boundary of the Preserve. "Although to be fair, I don't think *delicate* was the exact word that was used in the file. The terms were *unstable* and *deteriorating* and a few others in the same vein.

But the result was the same. Everyone concluded that I was no longer fit for the kind of work that I do. That I did. The official story is that I'm taking time off until my senses heal."

"But?"

"But the para-shrinks and the doctors don't think there's a chance in hell that I'll ever regain the full use of my talent. In fact, things are expected to get worse."

"What happened?"

"Long story," Slade said.

She knew from his tone that he was not in the mood to tell her the rest. Not yet.

"Right," she said. "But I have to tell you, you are not psychically delicate."

"Yeah? And just how would you know that?"

"Beats me. It's part of what I do. I've seen your rainbow when you're partially jacked. Everything looked clear, strong, and stable. If your senses were deteriorating, that fact would be reflected in the primary ultralight colors that I saw."

"I thought you said I looked conflicted."

"I did sense that, but the rainbow itself was strong."

"I'm sure the para-shrinks would be interested to know that an antiques dealer has declared me not delicate."

The icy edge on the words was enough to silence her.

"Not much farther now." Slade started walking again. He aimed the narrow beam of the flashlight at the ground in front of her. "You'll feel the fence soon."

Time to shut up about his aura rainbow, she thought. He had a right to his secrets.

The first shiver of dark, ominous energy whispered across her senses. *Like a warning shot over the bow,* she thought. They were moving through the trees now. The woods seemed to close in more tightly around them and the atmosphere darkened.

"You're right," she said. "The fence energy feels different tonight. It's much stronger."

"It gets worse."

"Why do I suddenly know how Little Amber Riding Hood felt when she started out to Grandmother's house?" she said. "Or maybe I'm thinking of Hansel and Gretel."

"There was a reason why forests have always been considered dangerous places in fairy tales," Slade said. "And this particular forest has never been explored. Add in the nexus factor and whatever the hell that fence is supposed to be protecting, and you're dealing with a lot of unknowns here."

The flickers of energy intensified, jangling her nerves. It was like brushing against a lot

211

of small, live wires. She flinched and gritted her teeth against a near-painful jolt.

"Lot of hot psi, too," she gasped.

"For the next few yards we'll be walking through a heavy psi-storm. My advice is to run a little hot until we're through the force field. That seems to ward off the worst of the effects, at least for me. Speak up if you want to turn back."

"I will not be turning back," she said briskly.

"Didn't think so."

"But it is definitely hotter than it was fifteen years ago."

"Yes."

Cautiously she elevated her senses. The downside was that she could now perceive the psychic electricity that flashed and crackled in the atmosphere. She understood why the Preserve had a reputation for being haunted. Anyone who got this far through the barrier could be excused for believing that there were howling, wailing apparitions everywhere. The sensations were disturbing and oppressive and flat-out scary.

The upside of walking with her senses slightly heightened was that Slade was right. Running a little jacked dampened some of the terrible sense of dread that threatened to overwhelm her.

Slade took her hand and squeezed it tightly. The psi-fire faded even more with the physical contact. She realized that he was using some of his energy field to shield her.

"Better?" he asked.

"Yes, thanks."

The psychic noise caused by the screaming phantoms was more tolerable now.

"Not much farther." Slade gripped her hand more firmly. "There's Rex."

She looked down and saw Rex trotting calmly through the energy field, evening clutch gripped in one paw. All four eyes were open and he was half-sleeked but there was no indication that he was experiencing any discomfort.

"The force field is probably tuned only to human psi frequencies," Charlotte observed. "Then again, what else could they be tuned to? No one has ever figured out how to measure animal psi."

They moved out of the trees and into a small meadow. The disturbing energy field winked out with disconcerting suddenness. The psychic scream inside her head fell silent. She breathed a sigh of relief. At least the experience hadn't triggered a panic attack, she thought.

"We're in," Slade said. He stopped and let

go of her hand.

She gazed at the incredible scene around her with a sense of awe and wonder. "This is absolutely amazing. You're right. It's so much stronger and more spectacular than it was fifteen years ago. It's still an enchanted fairyland but it's a much brighter version of the original. I've never seen anything like it in my life."

"There are some places in the Underworld that rival this but none that I know of aboveground," Slade said.

"You know what?" she said softly. "This reminds me of some of Jasper Gilbert's paintings."

"I had the same thought."

"Think he's been in here?"

"He and Kane are both retired ghost hunters, strong ones, I think. That means they have a talent for working amber and alien psi. It's possible that is enough to get them through the fence."

The moonlit meadow and the small pond looked as if they had been painted with a brush dipped in silver light. The soft radiance that illuminated the landscape was clearly paranormal in nature. The ultralight given off by the grass and other foliage was not the only discernible energy. Charlotte realized she felt warmer now. It was as if someone had switched on the heat.

"The bio-phosphorescent effect isn't so obvious during the day," Slade said. "The visible radiation from the sun tends to overwhelm it. But at night the paranormal energy really pops if you've got enough talent to see at least partway into the ultralight end of the spectrum."

"I can't believe the Arcane researchers haven't set up a lab here," she said.

"As far as I can tell, Arcane doesn't even know this place exists," Slade said. "Neither do any of the other big labs. The Rainshadow Foundation has done a very good job of keeping the Preserve secret. The question is, why?"

"I wonder what those who can't see far into the paranormal spectrum perceive when they look at scenes like this inside the Preserve."

"According to the few reports that exist from the old days, those with limited psychic senses who managed to get in and back out thought they were seeing ghosts. Phantoms and spirits. Flickering shadows at the edge of their vision."

"What about those canyons of night that you mentioned?"

"I haven't found any descriptions of them in the old records and, as I told you, I didn't come across any fifteen years ago, either. I'm sure they're new. Want to see one?"

"Yes."

"There's one not far from here."

They set off across the meadow. Charlotte kept her senses heightened, entranced and fascinated by iridescent wildflowers and grass that flashed with eerie silver luminescence. Banks of radiant ferns surrounded a pond that gleamed obsidian dark.

It wasn't just the plant life that radiated bio-psi. Charlotte heard a small lizard skittering away into the foliage and caught a glimpse of a jeweled tail. Winged insects flitted and danced on the night air like so many sparkling fairy-sized flashlights.

They circled around the pond. Charlotte saw that the surface was darkly, ominously luminous.

"What in the world?" she whispered.

"I have no idea," Slade said. "What's more, I don't think it would be a good idea to put on a dive suit to find out why the pond seems to be glowing."

She shuddered. "I agree."

When they reached the trees Slade took Charlotte's hand again.

"The entrance to the canyon is just inside the tree line," he said. "You probably won't be able to see a thing. Don't worry, I can. I won't let you get lost."

They moved into the trees. The darkness closed in abruptly. Between one step and the next all of the enchanting fairy lights of the meadow winked out, plunging Charlotte into the deepest, densest night she had ever known. The first whispers of panic flickered through her. Instinctively she went into deep-breathing mode. Slade's hand tightened on hers. She sensed his silent inquiry.

"I'm okay," she said.

Cautiously she pushed her talent a little higher. Two apparitions moved in the absolute darkness. She realized she was looking at Slade and Rex. A fierce rainbow formed around one of the shadows. Slade, she thought. She would know him even in the darkest place in the universe.

"I understand what you mean by canyons of endless night," she said.

"Can you see anything at all?" he asked.

"I can definitely sense the energy here. It's dark and it's scary. I can see your rainbow quite clearly. But you and Rex are just shadows within shadows."

"I think that's more than most people, even those with talent, could see. There's a lot of energy in the vicinity but most of the currents are coming from the farthest end of the spectrum, the dark ultralight end."

"What do you perceive?" she asked.

"Infinite night. Like something out of a nightmare."

"What do you suppose is generating the heavy ultralight?"

"I don't know."

"You're worried?"

"Power in large quantities is always a concern, and whatever is going on here involves a lot of energy. The changes inside the Preserve raise questions."

She smiled. "And you like answers."

"Yes."

"You said yourself that the Preserve has always been a dangerous place."

"True." He guided her back out of the dense night to the edge of the glowing meadow. "But I think it's becoming more so. The Foundation was right to strengthen the fence but I don't think it's going to be enough."

"Doesn't seem to be working too well. We got in."

"If we got in, other strong talents can make it, too. But I doubt if most of them will have the ability to navigate it. GPS and compasses don't work."

"What about the locator devices that ghost hunters use in the Underworld?"

"I tried one. It doesn't work, either. They're designed to handle environments that generate a lot of alien psi. This is different. It's nexus energy. And something else. I think."

"You aren't sure?"

"I'm certain that the nexus forces are involved but they may simply be enhancing whatever is really going on here," he said.

"You're not having any problem staying oriented."

"I told you, something about my version of hunter-talent allows me to navigate the Preserve."

"Well, I'm thoroughly lost at the moment," she said. "If you weren't with me I could probably make it across the meadow, but once inside the trees I'd be completely disoriented again. I don't even want to think about what it would be like to blunder into one of those night canyons. A person could wander in circles forever."

He led her back out of the trees into the twinkling fairyland meadow. She looked around, searching for a small scruffy shadow carrying a clutch. She didn't see one.

"Where's Rex?" she asked.

"Probably got bored and decided to go hunting. I told you he disappears a lot at night. It was the same way back in Resonance City. There he used to go down into the Underworld to meet his buddies."

"Perhaps there are other dust bunnies here in the Preserve. Maybe he's hoping to meet a girlfriend." She thought about the clutch purse. "Or a boyfriend."

"There's enough uncharted territory here in the Preserve to conceal a whole herd of dust bunnies."

Charlotte stopped to drink in the luminous landscape. "This place really is extraordinary. Make my night, lie to me and tell me that you never brought any other girl here fifteen years ago."

"No."

She sighed. "I should have known better than to ask a former FBPI agent to lie."

"No, I never brought anyone else here," he said very steadily. "Just you."

She turned quickly. "Really?"

"Only you."

She looked into his heated eyes.

"Tiger, tiger, burning bright," she quoted in a whisper.

"What's a tiger?" Slade asked.

"Old World beast of prey. Something like a specter-cat, I think. The line is from an ancient poem."

"I remind you of a beast of prey?"

"No," she said. She touched the side of

his sternly etched face. "But I have always known that you were born to guard and protect. I am quite sure that you could be as fierce and relentless as a tiger or a specter-cat if it proved necessary to defend those who are weaker than you."

He reached up and caught her wrist. Very deliberately he turned his head and kissed her palm. A great longing rose deep inside her, a longing that she knew had been there all along, unacknowledged, for the past fifteen years.

Slade looked at her with all the fierceness she knew was locked inside him.

"I don't know what you saw in my aura rainbow that made you think I would regret making love to you," he said. "But whatever it was you were wrong."

"Was I?"

"I want you, and I don't give a damn what it costs me."

"There shouldn't be a price to be paid," she said.

"There is always a price. I want you to understand that I am willing to pay it."

He let the pack slide off his shoulder and then he drew her close, wrapped his arms around her, and kissed her with all the dark fire that she had seen blazing in his aura rainbow. Instinctively she started to touch

221

the pendant at her throat but she stopped just before her fingers brushed the silver mirror. Perhaps it was the energy in the atmosphere around them. Or maybe it was simply that she did not want to screw up again and miss the experience she had been yearning for all these years. Whatever the explanation, she knew that this time she would try very hard not to view his rainbow.

He said he was willing to pay the price. She would take him at his word. Because she knew now that there would be a price for her as well, and she, too, was willing to pay it.

Her hand fell away from the pendant. She gripped his shoulders, savoring the sleek power she could feel there, and returned the kiss with a passion she hardly recognized as her own.

The kiss was desperate and all consuming; a kiss unlike anything she had ever experienced. She was suddenly shivering but not because of a panic attack; rather from the force of raw physical desire. Everything about Slade was hard, demanding, implacable, and relentless.

He wrenched his mouth away from hers and imprisoned her head gently between his two powerful hands.

"This is about you and me tonight," he

said. "Nothing else matters."

"Nothing else," she agreed.

He used his grip to bring her hard against him and kissed her again. She wound her arms around his neck and clung to him to keep from drowning in the sparkling, effervescent whirlpool. But she fell deeper and deeper into the churning energy. Slade groaned and crushed her lower body against his own.

He did not try to hide his hunger for her. He was hot and aroused and he obviously wanted her to know it. Liquid heat and a tight, urgent tension built deep inside her. He got her jacket open. She found the buckle of his leather belt. And then his hands were gliding up her body beneath her top. When he got her bra unfastened he closed his palms over her nipples. She was so sensitive now that she gave a small, startled cry.

He kissed her throat. "Are you all right?"

"Yes, yes." She fumbled with the zipper of his trousers. "I'm not *that* delicate."

"Ah." He sucked in a sharp breath and pulled back. "I'll get the zipper."

Appalled, she went very still. "Did I hurt you?"

His laugh was half groan. "No. But timing is everything."

She freed herself from her boots while he unzipped his trousers and got out of his own boots.

He reached into the pack and pulled out a plastic pouch. He tore open the bag and removed a thin emergency blanket. When he spread it out on the ground the tarp proved to be surprisingly large.

He drew her onto the blanket and then he went down on his knees in front of her. He pulled her down with him. She pushed her hands inside his shirt and let the heat of his body warm her. She was about to unfasten her jeans when he stopped her.

"Let me," he said, his voice low and dark.

He eased the zipper down and worked the jeans over her hips. When he could not get them any farther he pushed her gently onto her back and peeled the denim all the way off. Her panties went with the jeans.

For a moment he knelt beside her, studying her with burning eyes as though he had never seen anything quite like her before, as if he did not want to forget a single detail. With his strong shoulders silhouetted against the night sky, his features starkly etched in psi-light, he could have walked straight out of her most intense fantasies.

He put one hand on her thigh and moved his warm palm upward until he cupped the full, damp place between her legs. Her body reacted instantly to the intimate touch. She lifted her hips, straining against him. He stroked her slowly until she was as tightly coiled as a spring, until she was trembling with the force of the urgent need inside her.

She seized his wrist and pulled him down alongside her. He rolled onto his back, taking her with him. She tumbled across his granite-hard body. His rigid erection pressed against her bare thigh.

He arranged her so that she straddled him and then he worked her with his hand until she was almost screaming with need.

He gripped her hips and pushed himself slowly inside her. As badly as she wanted him, her body resisted at first. He was too big. She hesitated, not knowing if it was going to work.

He felt her go still and he stilled, too. She did not need to view his rainbow to know that he was fighting for his control. The heat of his body and the sweat on his chest told her very clearly. She also sensed that he would not lose the battle. Slade was always in control.

"Okay?" he got out hoarsely.

"Yes," she whispered.

Tentatively she allowed him to go deeper. Her body slowly opened to accept him but the steady invasion caused the tension inside her to heighten to a level that was almost unbearable.

"Yes," she said. She tightened around him. *"Yes."*

He locked his hands around her hips and started to move, driving in and out of her in a powerful, relentless rhythm.

In the end, she could not resist temptation. She had to know the truth. She touched her pendant with her fingertips and opened her senses to the fullest extent.

Slade's dark rainbow blazed in the night. She knew then that he was not holding anything back this time. He had told her the truth. He wanted her and he did not give a damn about the consequences, whatever they were.

But her intuition told her that he still expected to pay a heavy price.

There was no time to second-guess what was happening and she had promised herself she would not ruin things by trying to analyze him. She took her fingers off the pendant.

"Slade."

In the next moment the tension inside her was released in wave after wave of deep, satisfying currents. She was flung into the heart of the glorious storm.

Slade's fingers tightened around her thighs. He thrust one last time. With a hoarse, husky growl, he came in a surging, pounding climax.

The silver meadow blazed around them.

CHAPTER 16

He felt Charlotte stir beside him. He opened his eyes and his senses to the night and watched her sit up on the blanket. She reached for her panties and jeans. Her hair had come free. In the otherworldly glow of the meadow she looked magical, mysterious, and incredibly sexy. He could have looked at her for the rest of the night, the rest of his life.

Something twisted deep inside him. How much longer would he be able to see her like this, with all of his senses? Whatever happened, he would never forget this night. He wondered if she would remember him in the years ahead.

He pushed the dark thoughts aside. He had made his decision and he was content. He would not destroy what was left of the night with questions that had no answer.

He levered himself up on one elbow. "Hey there, gorgeous."

She paused in the act of wriggling into the jeans and looked at him over her shoulder. Her eyes were still gently luminous.

"Hey there, yourself, handsome," she said.

Her voice had a sexy, throaty quality that stirred the embers all over again. He tried to come up with something clever in the way of postcoital conversation but nothing occurred to him. He did not want to chat. He wanted to drag her back down onto the blanket and make love to her again and again before he lost his talent forever.

But for all its heat-retention and waterproof capabilities, the sheet of high-tech plastic did nothing to soften the ground underneath it.

He watched her shimmy partway into her jeans. Then she got to her knees in order to pull the pants up over her hips.

"It's getting late," she said. She stood and adjusted her top and the jacket. "We both have to go to work in the morning."

He sat up reluctantly. The plastic crinkled under him.

Charlotte watched him close his jeans.

"I'd like to hear the story," she said.

"What story?" He leaned down to pick up the blanket. It dawned on him that he felt incredibly relaxed, better than he had in months. Maybe better than he ever had in his entire life.

"Earlier you said that some doctors at a clinic had slapped you with the 'delicate' label. I asked you why. You said it was a long story. We have a long walk out of here. I thought it would be a good time to tell me the tale."

"Damn. Should have seen this coming." Talking about his problems was the last thing he wanted to do.

Charlotte stiffened. "Don't ask." Her voice had gone very cool.

He concentrated on folding the blanket into a small square. "Don't ask what?"

"Why women always want to chat after sex. Speaking personally, I don't. Not usually. In my experience it invariably leads to a bad outcome. But, then, all my dates end badly."

"At least you're consistent."

"True. But I think I need to know why you wound up here on Rainshadow."

He thought about it while he crammed the blanket back into the pouch.

"What the hell," he said finally. "It's not like it's not in both my Bureau file and the Arcane clinic files."

"My goodness," she said. "What on earth happened?"

He was saved from an immediate answer

by a familiar chortle. Rex fluttered across the glowing meadow. When he reached them he bounded up to Slade's shoulder. He was still holding the small purse.

"Well, well, well, where have you been, Big Guy?" Charlotte said. She reached up to pat Rex. "I'll bet you went hunting, didn't you? I don't even want to think about what you dined on this evening."

Slade knew he was probably anthropomorphizing, but judging by Rex's jaunty attitude, he had a hunch the dust bunny had gotten lucky. Probably hadn't had to have a complicated, mood-shattering postcoital chat afterward, either.

He slung one strap of the small pack over his shoulder. "Let's go."

They tromped across the sparkling meadow, past the obsidian pond and into the trees. Slade gathered his thoughts, searching for an entry point into a nightmare he relived every night.

"It happened on my last assignment," he said finally. "It was supposed to be a straightforward investigate-and-take-down-if-necessary job. A researcher from a low-profile government lab died in a diving accident on an island in the Harmonic Sea. Seemed routine, but any time a government lab employee goes missing or dies unexpectedly, the Bureau looks into the situation."

"So you went to check out the accidental death and concluded that it was murder?"

"No, I concluded that there had been no death at all," he said. "Well, there was a dead guy and he had been murdered while diving but he was not the missing researcher. He had, however, been killed by paranormal means in an attempt to make it look like a heart attack. The missing lab tech's ID was on the body."

"So you investigated further," Charlotte said.

"That's the job. Turned out the lab tech was very much alive and working for a drug lord named Masterson, who had a walled compound, more like a fortress, on one of the other nearby islands."

"What on earth would a drug thug want with a government researcher?"

"You may be surprised to learn that the drug trade is highly competitive," Slade said.

"Gee. Who would have thought so?"

"For obvious reasons a successful drug lord needs to stay one step ahead of the competition. It just so happened that the lab tech's expertise was in pharmaceuticals. Masterson wanted him to produce a new designer drug for the gray market."

"A club drug," she said. "One that's not

quite illegal because the chemical composition has been tweaked just enough to keep it off the list of banned pharmaceuticals."

"Law enforcement is always one step behind the chemists in the drug trade."

"So this drug lord abducted the researcher with the goal of forcing him to make a new drug?" she asked.

"As far as I could tell, there was no strongarm work involved," he said. "Masterson used a more traditional business approach. He paid the lab tech a hell of a lot of money up front and offered to cut him in for a share of future profits."

"You interrupted the plan, I assume?"

"I went into the fortress one night with the intention of searching the lab. I was about to crack a mag-steel vault when things got complicated."

"How?" she asked.

"What I didn't know until then was that Masterson had rounded up a few end-of-the-line alcoholics and junkies to use as subjects in the drug experiments. The poor bastards were locked up in a lower level of the basement. I went down to get them out."

"Of course you did," she said, sounding very certain. "It's what you do. What happened?"

"I got the prisoners out of the basement

but when I went back in to open the safe, Masterson, the lab tech, and a couple of Masterson's enforcers were waiting for me. I took down Masterson first. Evidently they had not expected me to be able to do that."

"Because of his talent?"

"He was some kind of hunter. I never did discover the exact nature of his ability."

"So, how did you manage to take him out?"

"The old-fashioned way. Mag-rez pistol."

"Oh. Right. That would work."

"It does if you're faster than the other guy. The enforcers fled. With their boss dead there was no reason for them to stick around. But they laid down a lot of covering fire on the way out. One or more of the shots struck a gas canister in the corner of the room. There was an explosion. It killed the renegade lab tech instantly because he was standing so close to the canister. Next thing I knew the whole lab was going up in flames and a lot of dark smoke."

"How did you survive the explosion?" she asked.

"I was in the basement stairwell, using it for cover. The stone walls shielded me from the worst effects of the explosion but not from the gas that was in the canister. There was no way I could avoid inhaling some of it when I made a run for the door."

"What kind of gas was it? Some sort of illicit drug?"

"No one knows what it was," he said. His hand tightened around the flashlight. "A team went into the ruins of the lab later but they didn't find anything aside from traces of a few chemicals known to have some psycho-pharmaceutical properties. The assumption is that the gas was a new experimental drug."

"What effect did it have on you?"

"It didn't do any damage to my lungs but it acted like acid on my senses."

Charlotte came to an abrupt halt. "You were psi-blinded?"

He stopped because he didn't have much choice. "Temporarily. Couldn't use any of my talent for a couple of weeks."

"How awful. But your senses recovered, thank heavens."

"Only partially," he said. "The experts tell me they probably won't come all the way back."

"I don't understand. You used your talent to determine that Jeremy Gaines was murdered by paranormal means and you can navigate here inside the Preserve."

"For now I'm at a Level Seven on the Jones Scale."

"That's very strong. Well above average, certainly."

"I used to be a Nine," he said.

"I see."

She was silent for a moment, taking in the full meaning of what he had just said. She understood, he thought. The loss of two full points on the scale was dramatic. Now she would feel sorry for him. That was the last thing he wanted.

"Are you sure that the new measurement is accurate?" she asked finally.

Might as well tell her the rest, he thought. She would continue to feel sorry for him but she would also realize that she had to put some emotional distance between them. The sex had been great but he knew that in spite of her decision to enter a no-strings-attached relationship, deep down she wanted something a lot more intimate and enduring. That meant a lover who was psychically compatible. He could not promise her that kind of bond. He might as well get to the bottom line and get it over with before any real damage was done. *Correction,* he thought, *make that before any more damage was done to either of them.*

"According to the para-psych doctors at the clinic there's an eighty-five percent chance that I won't remain a Seven for much longer," he said. He started walking again. He kept his tone calm and clinical. "They warned me that my aura is unstable in the regions that are linked to the psychic senses. I was told that in all likelihood my condition will continue to deteriorate."

She hurried to fall into step beside him. "What does that mean?"

"It means that I have to find a new line of work, among other things," he said. "Which, as I mentioned, is what I'm trying to do here on Rainshadow."

"Please don't try to brush me off, Slade. I want to know what's happening to you."

"Why?"

"Why?" She spread her hands wide in a gesture of frustration. "Because of what we just did back there in that meadow, for heaven's sake. We're lovers now."

Okay, this was where things were going to get dicey, he thought. He realized he wanted the lovemaking to mean something to her, something important. But he also knew that it would be infinitely better for both of them if she stuck with the resonate-with-the-moment approach.

"Look," he said, "the truth is, no one knows what's going to happen to my talent. The experts don't know if I'll stabilize at some point or if I'll lose my para-senses altogether. I was told to plan for the worst-case scenario. Any other questions?"

"No." She touched the pendant at her throat and then she shook her head firmly. "But I think the experts misread your aura. Or maybe they couldn't see far enough along the spectrum. Or maybe they just did not understand what they were viewing. That happens a lot when it comes to analyzing high-end talents, you know."

"So now you're a trained aura-reader?"

"No," she said. "But I know what I see in your rainbow. I've told you that rainbows are a reflection of the primary ultralight colors in a person's aura."

"Are you saying that you can see something in my aura that none of the experts saw? Thanks, but no thanks. I can't afford to waste time with that power-of-positive-thinking crap."

"That's the spirit," she shot back. "Think negative. That way you're never disappointed."

The sharpness of her tone caught him by surprise. She was usually so cheerful, so sunny and warmhearted. Like a dust bunny, he thought. But dust bunnies had teeth. He thought about that night fifteen years ago when Charlotte had tried to fight off a bigger, stronger attacker with only a flashlight.

Underneath all that sweetness and light, Charlotte was a fighter.

"I'm just trying to be realistic," he growled, feeling defensive now.

"What happens when you push your talent to the upper limits?"

"I was told not to risk it."

"Why?"

"The theory is that the more I use my talent, the harder I push it, the faster it will deteriorate," he said.

"I don't understand. Everyone knows that if a strong talent runs in the red zone for a prolonged period, he or she can certainly exhaust his or her senses temporarily. But it takes only a couple of hours to recover completely."

"The folks at the clinic warned me that I probably wouldn't recover from a serious burn," he said quietly.

"But knowing you, you have experimented a bit, right?"

She knew him too well, he thought. How had that happened? He had never let anyone get close. But somehow she was right next to him, physically and psychically. She had somehow slipped through the invisible barricades he had spent a lifetime building and shoring up.

"I had to see for myself," he admitted.

"And?"

"Let's just say that I learned my lesson. I saw my future and there's nothing good waiting there. All I can do is try to buy as much time as possible."

"What, exactly, did you experience when you rezzed your talent to the max after the explosion?"

They were inside the trees again. The silver meadow disappeared behind them. The thick darkness dropped like a shroud. He jacked his talent up just enough to guide her through the trees and summoned the scenes of his recent nightmares.

"A storm of energy," he said. "It was like looking at an advancing hurricane or a tornado."

She touched the mirror pendant. "That's not what I saw reflected in your rainbow earlier tonight when you took me into the night canyon."

"I was only partially jacked then."

"It was enough for me to see your true colors. I saw them the other night when you kissed me and I saw them again tonight when you made love to me."

He studied the tiny mirrored pendant at her throat. Moonlight glinted on it. He was uncomfortable with the knowledge that Charlotte seemed to be able to dig out his secrets. But he knew a few things about her, too. One of the things he knew was that she would not lie to him.

"What, exactly, did you see?" he asked.

"A lot of powerful ultralight. I can't put a name to all of the various primary colors because I've never seen them before, but I can tell that they come from the far end of the spectrum and that the frequencies of the radiation are rock steady. There was no sign of instability."

"What does that mean for me?"

"Well, for one thing, it means that you've got some serious talent you don't seem to be aware of," she said.

"Whatever is out there in that storm that I can see when I go hot is not my old talent. I don't recognize it, Charlotte. The energy looks chaotic to me. That is never a good sign when you're talking about human psi. You know that as well as I do. Chaos on the spectrum is one of the surefire indicators that a person is either going psi-blind or mad."

"It's not chaos. I told you the bands of light in the rainbow are strong and stable."

"Then why don't I recognize the energy?"

"I don't know," she admitted. "You're going to have to find out for yourself."

"How the hell do I do that?"

"The same way you did when you first came into your talent back in your teens," she said patiently. "The way I did it. The way Devin will eventually figure out his developing psychic nature. You work with it and you experiment until you understand how to focus and control it."

He went cold. "Damn it to hell. Are you telling me that I'm coming into a new talent?"

She smiled. "Relax, you're not becoming a Cerberus. You won't go rogue."

Cerberus was Arcane slang for those who developed more than one kind of talent. Such individuals were so rare as to be the stuff of dark myth and legend. True multi-talents generally died in their teens or early twenties. The problem, according to the Society's experts, was that the human mind could not handle the high levels of stimulation and acute sensory perception that accompanied multiple talents. Cerberus talents invariably went insane and self-destructed. Most of the handful of recorded cases took their own lives early but a few had survived long enough to become murderous para-psychopaths.

When it came to dealing with Cerberus talents, Arcane policy was simple and straightforward. *Get rid of them.* The corollary to that policy was *by whatever means necessary.* He happened to know from his time working for the Office that the FBPI and the Guilds had similar policies.

"You're sure?" he said.

"Oh, yes."

"Because I have to tell you that having Arcane, the Office, and the Guilds coming after me is all I'd need to make my life full, rich, and complete."

"Well, you did indicate that you were a trifle bored with being chief of police here on Rainshadow."

"I'm not joking," he said. "How can you be certain that I'm not developing a second talent? No offense, but you sell antiques for a living. You're not a para-shrink or even an aura-reader."

"I know." Charlotte's voice went flat. She folded her arms around herself and started walking again, very quickly. "You're right. You probably shouldn't be taking advice from a low-rent talent like a rainbow-reader."

He moved then, taking two long strides to catch up with her. He wrapped his fingers around her arm. "I didn't mean that I don't trust you."

"I know. It's my talent you don't trust. Believe me, I understand."

Coolly, she tried to pull free of his grasp. He wanted to hold on to her but he knew she would fight him. He let her go and clenched his hand around the barrel of the flashlight.

"I'm sorry," he said. "But I've spent the past three months dealing with the fallout of whatever that gas did to me. I was told that my talent and my life would never be the same."

"Well, for what it's worth, I think the experts who told you that were right. I doubt if your talent or your life will ever return to whatever was normal for you before you were hit with the gas."

He frowned, hardly daring to allow himself even the slimmest ray of hope. "You really don't think I'm going to go psi-blind?"

"No." She hesitated. "But I think there is definitely the possibility of another, equally bad outcome."

"What could be worse?"

"Living with a lot of powerful energy that you don't know how to focus or control. That kind of situation truly will drive you mad."

He took a deep breath. "You think that I should push my talent. Start working with the dark energy that I see at the end of my spectrum."

"There's an ancient Arcane saying that applies here. *Learn to control your talent or it will control you.*"

Chapter 17

"I don't believe it." Devin came to a halt in the trees and looked down the steep granite cliff at the rocky beach below. A small boat powered by an outboard engine had been drawn ashore. "Some jerks found Hidden Beach."

Nate stopped beside him. "I don't recognize the boat. They didn't rent it from Dad."

Nate Murphy had just turned thirteen. He was Devin's best friend on the island. Nate had grown up on Rainshadow and knew all the hidden coves and secret inlets along the forbidding shoreline. Devin envied his knowledge of boats and all things connected to the water. Nate had worked around his dad's marina his whole life and was really good when it came to that kind of stuff. He even had his own kayak and he was teaching Devin how to handle one.

Devin wanted very badly to tell Nate about his developing psychic senses but he was pretty sure the chief was right. Nate would probably think he was weird.

"How did they find this place?" Devin asked. "You said boaters hardly ever come to this side of the island because of the rip currents and the tides. You said there wasn't any place to come ashore."

"Except Hidden Beach," Nate pointed out. "They probably found it by accident." He lowered his day pack to the ground and sat down on it. "So much for hunting for Captain Sebastian's treasure today."

"Maybe those guys will leave soon." Devin looked around. "Wonder where they are?"

"Probably trying to see how far they can get inside the Preserve. Every so often someone tries it on a dare or just to see what will happen. They'll find out soon that they can't get through the fence."

"If they're trespassing, Chief Attridge can arrest them."

"He won't do that," Nate said with cool certainty.

"Why not? The chief used to work for the FBPI. Those guys are tough. They arrest serial killers and drug lords and really dangerous dudes."

"I'm not saying he couldn't arrest 'em, just that he won't. Why bother? Everyone knows that the fence stops most folks from getting more than a couple of feet inside the Preserve. People who do manage to get inside don't come out alive. Why put folks in jail for trying to get themselves killed?"

"Yeah, I guess."

"What do you want to do? Find another place to look for treasure or wait and see if those guys with the boat leave soon?"

Devin hesitated. The logical decision was to move on up the shoreline. There were plenty of other interesting locations to explore on the perimeter of the Preserve. But Hidden Beach was the one that intrigued him the most. He wanted another look at the cavern.

"We've been planning this trip for days," he said. "Those guys will probably leave soon. Let's wait and see what happens."

"Okay."

They took a couple of energy bars out of their packs and hunkered down to wait.

"Do you really think we'll find Captain Sebastian's treasure inside the cave?" Nate asked after a while.

"Maybe." Devin wasn't sure how much more to say so he decided to keep quiet.

The entrance to the cave down below on the beach was almost invisible, a narrow crevasse in the rocks that widened unexpectedly once you got inside. Devin had sensed something intriguing inside the cavern the last time they had explored it, something that needed to be found, but he had no idea what it was. Some part of him was certain that the secrets hidden inside the cavern were valuable. He could not explain how he knew that to Nate, though, without explaining his new senses.

"I wonder if the guys who came here in that boat found the cave and went inside to look for the treasure," Nate said. "Maybe that's where they are now."

"I hope not. That cave is ours."

They munched the energy bars and drank the bottled water. Time passed. Devin was about to suggest that they dig out another round of energy bars when he heard the low rumble of voices. The sound did not come from the nearby woods where the Preserve fence began. It emanated from the hidden entrance to the treasure cave down on the beach.

"I don't believe it," he said softly. "They *did* find it."

"Yeah," Nate said. "But they're leaving now. We've still got plenty of time to look for the treasure."

Down below two men squeezed out of the slit in the rock face and emerged into the open. A jolt of fear flashed through Devin when he saw the mag-rez pistols on their hips. Beside him, Nate froze, too.

"Oh, shit," Nate whispered. "They must be smugglers or drug runners."

Real-life pirates, Devin thought. He felt a terrible prickling sensation on the back of his neck.

"Come on, we'd better get out of here," he said.

"If we move they might see us," Nate said.

"Okay, okay."

Devin stilled. Beside him, Nate seemed hardly to breathe.

As if sensing that they were being observed, one of the men glanced up. His eyes locked with Devin's. He reached for his gun.

"Company," he snarled to his companion.

The other man looked up. "Couple of kids."

"Doesn't matter. They've seen us."

Both men bounded up the trail that would take them to the top of the cliff. They moved very fast, faster than Devin had seen anyone move in his entire life.

He jumped to his feet. "We've got to get out of here."

Nate watched the men coming up the cliff trail. It was as if he were paralyzed with fear.

"Come *on.*" Devin reached down and grabbed his friend's arm. *"Run."*

Nate scrambled to his feet. "We'll never make it. They've got guns."

"They can't follow us into the Preserve."

"We can't get inside, either."

"I think maybe I can get us in," Devin said.

He did not know where the knowledge came from. Some voice inside his head was screaming at him that the Preserve was their only hope. He ran for the trees, hauling Nate with him.

"What about the fence?" Nate gasped.

"I think I can get you through it. Just don't let go of my hand, okay?"

"Are you sure?"

"It's not like we have any choice."

He sensed the first jarring sparks that told him they were entering the strange energy field that marked the outer boundary of the invisible fence. Beside him Nate sucked in a sharp, startled breath.

"You okay?" Devin asked.

"Yeah. I think so. I've never been this far inside. It hurts."

Devin risked a glance back over his shoulder.

The men were at the top of the cliff now.

"They're heading into the Preserve," one of the smugglers shouted. "We can't let them get away."

Devin heard gunshots but neither he nor Nate went down so he figured the shooters had missed. He ran as fast as he could. Nate pounded along beside him. The freaky energy was pulsing all around them now. It was like running through a lightning storm, Devin thought. Jolt after jolt shot through him but he pushed his new senses as hard as he could and the pain of the shocks seemed to diminish. Nate gripped his hand harder.

"I can't see them anymore," one of the gunmen shouted. "I can feel the fence. This is as far as we can go."

Both men slammed to a halt.

"Forget 'em," the second man said. "The Preserve will take care of them for us."

CHAPTER 18

"How did your date with Charlotte go last night?" Myrna asked from the doorway of the office.

Slade did not look up from the list of names on the computer screen. "If one more person asks me that question, I may have to fire everyone in the department."

Rex was on the desk. He had his beaded clutch open and was busy selecting paperclips to go inside. He paused long enough to chortle a greeting to Myrna. She went to the desk and patted him a couple of times. Then she studied Slade.

"Fire everyone, hmm?" she said. "All two of us?"

"Yes."

"Did things go that badly or that well?"

He pretended that he had not heard the question. "Where's Willis? Did he finish checking out the alibis of Gaines's known associates?"

Kirk Willis materialized in the doorway. "Just finished the last one, Chief." He walked into the office and put a file folder down in front of Slade. "None of the people on your list seems to have been anywhere near the island in the past year, let alone on the night Gaines died. What's our next move?"

Slade turned away from the screen and opened the folder. "There's a rule that applies to situations like this. It comes from an Old World investigator, Sherlock somebody. Something to the effect that once you have excluded the probable, whatever remains, however improbable, is the answer."

Myrna frowned. "What the heck does that mean?"

"It means," Slade said, "that there's a high probability that our killer is still here on the island."

Kirk and Myrna stared at him, disbelief in their eyes.

"You really think so?" Kirk asked, dubious but intrigued.

"Yes," Slade said.

"I can't believe that any of the locals is a killer," Myrna said slowly. "This is such a small town. Everyone knows everyone else."

"You're forgetting the B&Bs that are scattered around the island and the folks attending those Reflection Retreats out at the lake lodge," Slade reminded her. "We can get the names and addresses of the guests from the innkeepers."

"What, exactly, are we looking for?" Myrna asked. "We already know most of them probably don't have solid alibis. Any one of them could have snuck out of a B&B or the lodge and met up with Gaines at Looking Glass."

"But most of them probably aren't serious collectors of the kind of antiques that Charlotte handles," Slade said.

Kirk brightened. "You want me to see if I can find out if any of them are collectors?"

"I want to know about any connections at all that any of them might have to the antique or antiquities trade."

"I can do that," Kirk said.

"I know you can," Slade said. "But do it quietly. I don't want the killer to get the idea that we think we have a murder on our hands or that we're looking for him on the island. He'll be gone on the next ferry and we might lose him altogether."

"What makes you think he didn't leave the day after the murder?" Myrna asked.

"I don't think he got what he wanted," Slade said. "He stuck around because as far as he knows there is no murder investigation going on. He feels safe. We want him to continue to feel that way."

"I'm on it," Willis said. He straightened away from the doorjamb, preparing to head out.

"One more thing," Slade said. "Good work on these alibis. I know that some of the people on that list were very low profile. I'm impressed that you were able to confirm their whereabouts on the night of the murder."

Kirk reddened a little. "Yeah, well, I've always liked working on a computer."

"Good skill to have on this job. Get back to me as soon as you've got some information on the island guests."

"Yes, sir."

Kirk turned and went briskly down the hall. A moment later the front door closed behind him.

Myrna gave Slade a knowing smile. "Young Officer Willis has certainly developed a lot more enthusiasm for the law enforcement profession since you arrived on the island. I think he's starting to feel like a real cop."

"It's his first murder investigation," Slade said. "The experience tends to have that effect."

"Actually, I think it may be the first

murder investigation we've had on the island since Letty Porter decided she'd had enough of her husband getting drunk and beating up on her. She got him drunk one last time, drove him to Death Wish Point, and pushed him off. They never did find the body. That was almost twenty years ago."

"What happened to Letty Porter?"

"She's still here. Has a cabin out on Higgins Road. She's in her seventies now. Chief Halstead was new on the job at the time. He was never able to prove murder. Not that he tried real hard. As far as everyone around here was concerned, George Porter had it coming. He was one mean drunk."

Slade leaned back in his chair and drummed his fingers on the desktop. "She killed once."

"Forget it," Myrna said. "Take my word for it, Letty Porter has absolutely no interest in antiques. And knowing Letty, even if she had wanted to kill Gaines for some reason, she would have used the nearest blunt object."

"All the same, see if you can find out where she was on the night Gaines died."

"Okay." Myrna glanced at her watch. "It's not quite four o'clock. I can take a run out to her place right now."

"Do that."

Myrna started to step back from the doorway. She hesitated. "You know, I'm starting to get a little worried about Devin and Nate."

"Wasn't this the day of the big treasure hunt?"

"Yes, but they left early this morning," Myrna said. "I expected them back by lunchtime. They've only got a few energy bars and some bottled water with them. They're thirteen-year-old boys. They should be starving by now."

"Maybe they're living off the land."

"Trust me, a few summer berries wouldn't do it for boys that age. I called Nate's mom a short time ago. Laurinda said she had expected them back earlier, too, but she wasn't worried."

"You are?"

"Devin's a city kid. He doesn't know his way around the island."

"Nate does."

"I know." Myrna nibbled on her lower lip. "I'm being overly protective, aren't I?"

"He's a growing boy. He needs to spread his wings. This island is a lot safer place to do that than the big city."

"I know that, too."

"But you're still worried."

"It's just that I've had this weird feeling since this morning." Myrna sighed. "There are some dangerous places on the island. Steep cliffs. Rip currents in the coves and inlets. What if one of the boys fell?"

"The other would have come back to town to get help," Slade said.

"What if they tried to get through the fence and got lost inside the Preserve?"

"When was the last time an island kid got through the fence?"

Myrna sighed. "It's never happened as far as I know."

"The fence works, Myrna," Slade said.

At least it did when it came to keeping out those with no measurable levels of talent, he thought. Devin, with his newly stirring senses, might have been tempted to try to get inside but Nate would not have made it. If Devin had managed to get lost in the Preserve, Nate would have raced back to town to report the problem.

"There are other things that can happen to a couple of kids alone," Myrna said.

"It's okay to worry," he said.

"Gee, thanks for that, boss. I feel so much better now."

"Sorry," Slade said. "That wasn't very reassuring, was it? Look, Devin said that he and Nate were going to Hidden Beach to do their treasure hunting. They would have taken Merton Road. You could drive out there and see how they're getting on for yourself."

"Are you kidding? I can't check up on Devin. He would be absolutely mortified if I did that to him in front of Nate."

"True. I'll tell you what, I'll drive out there and take a look."

Myrna looked inordinately grateful. "Thanks, Chief. I really appreciate this."

Slade looked at Rex. "Let's go, buddy."

Sensing a new adventure, Rex chortled, grabbed his clutch, and bounded up onto Slade's shoulder.

Slade looked at Myrna. "It has been suggested that hanging out with a dust bunny who carries a purse might have a negative impact on my image as a hard-core crime fighter."

"Don't be ridiculous," Myrna said. "It's a very nice clutch."

CHAPTER 19

Nate grabbed Devin's arm. "Did you hear that?"

"Ouch." Devin winced. "Yeah, let go, man. That hurts."

They were sitting side by side, their backs against a massive granite rock. Nearby a waterfall splashed into a pool. It was late afternoon but night fell fast and early inside the Preserve. The last of the sun had vanished a few minutes ago and a deep twilight was descending.

The plunge through the weird energy fence had been bad for both of them, although Devin suspected that it had frightened Nate more than it had him. Nevertheless, they were now facing the prospect of spending the night inside the Preserve and he was not looking forward to it any more than Nate was.

At least there had been no sign of the two smugglers. The really bad part, Devin thought, was that they did not have a flashlight. They hadn't had anything to eat for hours. He thought wistfully about the packs they had left on top of the cliff above Hidden Beach.

"There's that creepy noise again," Nate whispered. "Maybe it's those two guys."

Devin stared hard at the dense darkness between the trees. Nate was not imagining things, he decided. Something had moved in the shadows. He could have sworn that for a couple of seconds he saw a pair of glowing eyes but it was hard to be certain because whenever he concentrated with all of his energy it seemed to him that there were a lot of small, strange things glowing in the dark around them. He'd realized very quickly that Nate could not see all the scary glow-in-the-dark stuff so he had decided not to mention it. Nate was already freaked out enough as it was. One of them had to stay calm.

"No," he said. "It's not the smugglers. If they had found us they would have shot us by now. You heard them back there at the cove. They said they couldn't follow us into the Preserve."

"They think that whatever is in here will get us. Don't know about you but that doesn't make me feel any better. Who knows

262

what's in this place?"

"You've lived on Rainshadow all your life. If there were dangerous wild animals in here you would have heard about them by now."

"I'm not talking about wild animals. I'm talking about other stuff. Lots of people have gone missing in the Preserve over the years. What if they didn't just die? What if they're still around?"

"There's no such thing as ghosts."

"How do you know that?"

It was, Devin thought, a legitimate question. How did he know there was no such thing as ghosts? He decided he did not want to pursue that line of logic.

"At least it's not too cold in here," he said. "If we have to spend the night we won't get that hypo thing."

"Hypothermia," Nate said automatically.

"Yeah. That."

Devin took out the old compass that Charlotte Enright had given him. He held it tightly in his hand. He had already discovered that it didn't work inside the Preserve. When he'd tried to use it earlier he saw that all four points of the compass were glowing equally brightly. There was no way to tell which way was true north. But it felt good to hold it in his hand. Comforting.

"I'm thirsty," Nate said after a while. "I'm

going to get some water."

"Me, too." Devin got to his feet.

They moved across the grass to the grotto pool and looked down at the frothy water.

"Huh," Nate said. "Something weird about that water."

"Like what?"

But he could sense it, too, Devin thought, probably better than Nate could. There was something strange about the water in the pool.

"You can't see the bottom," Nate said. He looked down into the pool as if he was fascinated by it.

"The rocks at the bottom are dark so the water looks dark. That's why you can't see anything," Devin said.

"Oh, man, there's something down there," Nate whispered.

"A fish, maybe," Devin said uneasily.

"Whatever it is, it's big. Don't know about you but I'm not thirsty enough to put my hand into that water."

"It's just a fish." Devin started to lean forward to scoop up some of the water.

Something dark swirled in the depths of the water. He realized he suddenly felt an overpowering urge to plunge into the pool. The darkness down below summoned him with a force that was slowly becoming irresistible. His heart started to pound. He leaned a little farther forward.

"Are you crazy, man?" Nate shouted.

He grabbed Devin's arm and yanked him back from the edge.

Devin felt as if he had just awakened from a nightmare. He gasped for air and took several deep breaths trying to calm his racing pulse.

"Thanks," he managed.

"Come on, we need to get away from this place," Nate whispered.

"If we start running around in the Preserve no one will ever find us."

"No one's ever gonna find us, anyway," Nate said. He did not take his eyes off the dark surface of the pool.

"Wrong," Devin said. "The chief will find us."

CHAPTER 20

Slade brought the SUV to a halt at the end of Merton Road and sat quietly for a moment, hands resting on the wheel. The first frisson of unease shifted across his senses.

"This is not good," he said to Rex. "We should have passed the boys on their bicycles somewhere along the way."

Rex was perched on the back of the passenger seat where he had a good view out the windows. Sensing Slade's concern, he muttered.

"We'd better go take a look." Slade opened the door. "If Devin did decide to try to get Nate and himself into the Preserve and it turns out they got lost, I'm going to be pissed."

Clutch in paw, Rex sidestepped along the back of the seats and hopped onto Slade's arm. From there he scrambled up onto Slade's shoulder.

They made their way through the trees

along the top of the cliffs. To the left sheer rock walls plunged into the cold, churning waters of the Amber Sea. Slade knew that the rock face went down several hundred more feet below the surface. Rainshadow was a natural fortress, he thought. It wasn't the first time that realization had crossed his mind. If you wanted to conceal some serious secrets, this was a good place to do it.

Fifteen minutes later he stood on top of the low cliff above Hidden Beach. There was no sign of Nate and Devin. He tried to shake off the chill factor but his senses were growing colder and more acute. His hunter intuition was telling him the truth, whether he wanted to acknowledge it or not.

He went down the rough trail to the rocky beach. Small pebbles and debris skittered from under his boots.

The beach was clean. *Too clean,* he thought. You'd never know a couple of teenage boys had spent time here looking for the lost treasure of a legendary pirate and smuggler who had worked the Amber Sea Islands fifty years earlier.

"The boys have been taught to pack out all of their trash but there should be some traces left behind," he said to Rex. "We're talking about a couple of teens. They can't even keep their rooms this clean."

He jacked up his senses a couple of notches. The action was automatic. He did not expect to find anything, he did not *want* to find anything, because the only psi he could detect was the burning radiation that indicated violence. With his talent he could pick up only the bad news. But somewhere along the line he had slipped into hunting mode. There was no turning back.

The flaring acid light he dreaded viewing was splashed like blood all over the rocks on the beach.

"Shit," he said very softly to Rex.

Rex mumbled ominously, tumbled down to the ground, and began exploring.

The energy was fairly fresh, Slade decided, only a few hours old. It had not been laid down by either Nate or Devin. He knew both boys. Neither of them could have generated such a cold, violent fever. What he was looking at had been left by adults. Two of them, if he was analyzing it correctly. The ultralight in the prints told him that they both possessed some talent. The chill on his senses went glacial.

Rex was at the far end of the tiny beach, investigating the rocks. He appeared very intent on whatever it was he had discovered. *A crab,* Slade thought, *or maybe some other small creature trying to hunt or hide at the water's edge.*

There was no time to waste but for some reason he felt compelled to find out what had captured Rex's attention. He crossed the beach and studied the rocks.

"What do you see?" he asked softly.

Rex pawed at one rock as though he wanted to play with it. But there was nothing playful in his demeanor. He, too, was in serious hunting mode.

Slade crouched. "Let's see what you've got."

He picked up the rock, prepared for a multilegged shore denizen to scuttle away. But it was not a crab that gleamed in the light. It was a spent shell casing. Someone had recently fired a gun here in the cove. Or from the top of the cliff.

He glanced up, thinking about how casings scattered. The violently luminous light was splashed all the way up the trail. He ran the scenario in his mind. The shooters had been surprised while they were on the beach. They had rushed up the trail in a killing frame of mind. It didn't take any psychic talent to figure out that the boys had been spotted by a couple of thugs who did not want any witnesses.

The sons of bitches went after a couple of

unarmed kids, Slade thought.

The hunting fever was upon him now. He took the notebook out of his shirt pocket, ripped out a sheet of paper, and used it to pick up the casing. He folded the paper around the casing and tucked it back into his shirt. While talent could be used to track down criminals, very little evidence of a straight paranormal nature was allowed in court. Judges and juries still liked hard evidence.

He got to his feet and looked at Rex. "How the hell did you know the shell casing was important?"

Rex fixed him with a disturbingly intense look and growled darkly.

"Let's go," Slade said.

He started up the trail. Rex scrambled after him.

At the top of the cliff Slade stopped, trying to think like a couple of teenage boys who had inadvertently surprised a pair of men with guns. If they had been scared, which was the only reasonable response, they would have run. If they had fled, they would have dropped their packs. So where were the packs?

The most likely answer, the one he did not want to acknowledge, was that the gunmen had killed the boys and dumped the bodies and the packs into the deep, cold waters of the Amber Sea. But he would not go there yet, not until he had ruled out all other possibilities. The boys might have had time to escape.

He forced himself to look for the black ultralight that indicated spilled blood. Relief roared through him when he did not see any on the ground. He fought back the emotional response because it would interfere with the hunt. Still, it was useful information, a solid fact. He could use a few more facts of that nature.

"No blood," he said quietly to Rex. "They were shooting at the boys but they didn't hit either of them. At least not here."

That left a lot of equally awful possibilities. The gunmen could have chased the boys into the trees, grabbed them, and murdered them elsewhere.

But there was one other possible scenario. The outer edge of the energy fence that marked the Preserve was not far from here. Both boys were aware of it.

He looked at Rex, who was now staring intently into the trees where the fence began. Slade got the impression that he was waiting. *Waiting for me to start the hunt?* Rex was acting as if they were a team.

Cautiously he eased his talent up another

notch. The first whispers of the dark storm-light energy at the far end of the spectrum flickered across his senses. He could not risk going any hotter, he decided. If Charlotte was wrong, he might trigger total and complete psi-blindness right here and now. He needed what was left of his senses to find the boys.

But Devin and Nate had been in a flat-out panic when they ran. They had left tracks that were vivid enough to be seen with his senses only partially elevated. One set of tracks glowed hotter and more vividly than the other.

"Smart boys," Slade said softly. "You made a run for the Preserve."

Devin's newly emerging intuition might have told him that he could get through the barrier. He might even have realized that he could drag Nate with him. It would not have been a pleasant experience but a couple of scared kids could overlook a lot of disturbing energy when they were running for their lives. Adrenaline would have fueled their flight. It was a potent drug and it left seething tracks.

Slade started toward the fence line.

The shooters' prints stopped short of the invisible energy barrier. Relief surged through Slade. The gunmen had not pur-

sued the boys into the Preserve. That made
sense. They clearly possessed some talent,
but not a lot, probably not enough to make
them want to risk going into the Preserve.

Slade loped after Rex, who was trotting
eagerly ahead. Rex's mood had changed.
He chortled enthusiastically, evidently
enjoying himself. It was obvious that he was
following the boys' prints. He knew both
Devin and Nate. Maybe he thought this was
some sort of psychic game of hide-and-seek.

With his talent slightly elevated, Slade had
no trouble following the trail into the denser
stand of trees. The oppressive energy of the
fence was strong now, but he had entered
the Preserve often enough to be able to
push through it. Devin and Nate had managed to get through it, too. Their psi-prints
were still visible and still leading deeper into
the Preserve.

There was one last blast of nightmarish
energy from the fence and then Slade was
through the force-field barrier. He stopped
long enough to orient himself and adjust
his talent to a lower level. When he looked
down he could still see the glowing trail.

"Once inside they probably wouldn't have
gone far," Slade said.

But Rex wasn't listening. He bounded
ahead with his purse.

Slade followed the prints through a jumble of boulders and another stand of trees. Rex vanished into the woods, chortling cheerfully. A short time later Slade heard Devin's voice.

"Look, it's Rex. What are you doing here, Rex? How did you find us? Where's the chief?"

"Right here," Slade said. He walked out of the woods into a small clearing.

He took in the scene in a single glance. Devin was perched on a rock, patting Rex. Nate was nearby. His face lit up when he saw Slade.

"Chief Attridge," he said. "You found us."

"Told you he'd get us out of here," Devin announced proudly.

He gave Rex one last pat and jumped to his feet. He dashed toward Slade. So did Nate.

There was a disconcerting moment when it looked like both boys were going to throw their arms around Slade. He breathed a sigh of relief when the teens stumbled to an awkward halt a short distance away.

"Nice work," he said to cover up the embarrassing moment. "You saved yourselves and you stayed put until someone got here. Your families are going to be proud of you. So am I."

Devin and Nate grinned.

"Two guys shot at us," Nate said.

"We think they were drug smugglers," Devin added.

"Devin got us through the fence," Nate said. "I didn't think he could but he did it. That was one weird trip, let me tell you. I thought my head would explode or something."

"I know," Slade said.

Devin's triumphant expression faded. "I know we aren't supposed to go into the Preserve, Chief."

"You did what you had to do to save Nate and yourself. It was the right thing."

Devin flushed but he grinned again.

"Did you catch those two guys who chased us in here?" he asked.

"No," Slade said. "They're long gone and the site has been pretty thoroughly cleaned. I couldn't find your packs or your bicycles."

"Those two assholes probably dumped them into the water," Nate muttered. "My bike was brand-new. Dad said if I let anything happen to it he wouldn't replace it."

"I'll have a talk with your dad," Slade said. "Got a hunch he'll be reasonable, given the circumstances. Let's get out of here. You can give me the whole story on the way home."

"They wore caps," Devin said.

"And they had guns," Nate added.

"I know," Slade said. He looked down at the ground around Devin's feet. The boys' footsteps were still glowing hot. "Devin, are you carrying amber or anything with crystals embedded in it?"

"Just my compass. But it doesn't work in here."

"Let me see it."

"Sure."

Devin fished the compass out of his pocket. Slade took it from him. All four crystals were glowing brightly.

"Huh," he said.

"I told you, it doesn't work in here," Devin said. "It's been lit up like that since we went through the fence."

"It's not functioning as a compass," Slade said. "But I think it is working as some kind of tracking device. It might explain why your prints were so clear."

"What does that mean?" Devin asked.

"I don't know, but it's interesting." He gave the compass back to Devin. "We'll worry about it later. We need to get you guys back home."

Nate looked uneasy again. "Does this mean we have to go back through the fence?"

"I'm afraid so," Slade said. "But this time it will be easier for two reasons."

"What reasons?" Nate asked, still wary.

"Reason number one is that all three of us are going to go through it together. Brace yourselves, we're going to hold hands."

Devin snorted. "Yeah, that's how we did it the first time, huh, Nate?"

Nate rolled his eyes. "Why does that make a difference?"

"Hard to explain," Slade said. "But it does."

"What's the second reason it will be easier?" Devin asked.

Slade smiled. "It's always easier to get through something like this when you know what's waiting for you on the other side. In this case, it will be dinner."

CHAPTER 21

"You know, if you really want to get out of this job and off Rainshadow, you're going to have to stop playing hero," Charlotte said. She used hot pads to set the pan of hot, fragrant lasagna on the table. "Now that Myrna and Officer Willis as well as everyone else in town know that you can go into the Preserve to rescue lost kids, the locals are going to pull out all the stops to keep you from resigning in a few months."

"I wasn't the hero today." Slade studied the lasagna with a sense of great anticipation. It occurred to him that he was hungry, especially for Charlotte's home cooking. "The kids saved themselves. All I did was go into the Preserve to retrieve them."

"Well, in case you hadn't noticed, being able to go into the Preserve is considered an impressive feat in these parts. The ability to track a couple of people inside the grounds is held to be downright amazing.

This is the first time anyone around here can recall that a rescue was carried out without having to call the Preserve authorities. And the first time in years when the folks who needed rescuing were found alive."

"Probably the first time the local chief of police has had some psychic talent," Slade allowed.

"Or at least your particular type of talent," Charlotte said. "Clearly not every kind of ability works equally well inside the Preserve. I've got a fair amount of talent but I'm quite sure I could not have found my way back out, let alone track a couple of kids."

She cut two large portions of lasagna and set them on plates. She set one of the plates on top of the refrigerator for Rex. He favored heights, she noticed. He chortled exuberantly and bounded up on top of the appliance. He set his clutch aside and settled down to dine with his customary enthusiasm.

She put the second plate of lasagna in front of Slade. She cut a smaller slice for herself and sat down at the kitchen table.

Inviting Slade to dinner tonight had been an impulse, Charlotte thought. She had not intended to do so because she had concluded that he needed some space. He was, after all, dealing with a lot of heavy stuff these days. She knew that he had not yet allowed himself to believe that he might recover his senses. He was not a man to be pushed or manipulated. He had to come to his own decisions. Hence her give-the-man-some-space strategy.

But when he had stopped by her shop shortly after returning to town with the boys, she had changed her mind. The shadows in his eyes and the hard, grim cast of his face had told her that, unlike everyone else in Shadow Bay, he was not in a celebratory mood.

"I take it this isn't over?" she had asked.

"No, it's not," he'd said.

There had been no time to talk because Nate's parents had arrived on the sidewalk out front, eager to thank him for bringing their son home safe and sound. But she'd gotten the distinct impression that Slade wanted to talk and he definitely needed to unwind. So she'd tossed aside her carefully orchestrated strategy and asked him to dinner. She wanted to hear every single detail of the big rescue, anyway.

Slade's response had been so casual that she had known immediately that he had been planning to show up on her doorstep with or without the invitation.

"Right, see you sometime after six," he'd said.

He had walked outside, Rex on his shoulder, to meet with Vern and Laurinda Murphy.

Charlotte had rested her elbows on the counter and watched through the window for a while, debating whether or not to get seriously ticked by Slade's attitude. He was acting as if nothing had changed in their relationship because of last night.

In the end, she had decided to take a tolerant approach. After all, he'd had a hard day. And besides, to be fair, he had no way of knowing that she had made some crucial decisions regarding the future course of their relationship. She was no longer rezzing with the frequency. You couldn't blame a man for assuming that nothing had changed when you hadn't explained said changes to him, she told herself.

It wasn't until Slade parted with the Murphys and walked off toward the station that she chanced to look across the street at the front window of the Kane Gallery. She saw the familiar figures behind the glass and realized that she was not the only one who had been watching Slade talk to the Murphys. Fletcher Kane and Jasper Gilbert had

281

been watching, too.

Now, several hours later, she still wasn't sure why the memory of Kane and Gilbert observing Slade through the window of the shop was still drifting, ghostlike, at the back of her mind. There had been nothing odd about it, she thought. Everyone in town had been talking about Slade and how he had tracked the boys into the Preserve and pulled them out.

"Something interesting about that old compass you gave Devin," Slade said.

"What is that?"

"All four crystals in the compass rose were lit up when I found him. On the way in, I noticed that his footsteps glowed a lot hotter than Nate's. At the time I assumed that was because Devin has some talent. But now I'm not so sure."

"You think the compass generated some energy?"

"Maybe. You said you tuned it for him?"

"Right."

"Those old compasses were made of amber and crystals. That's always a powerful combination. I've got a feeling that when you tuned it to Devin's rainbow frequencies you did something that helped him amplify his own natural energy, at least while he was cranked up. Maybe that's how he was able to get Nate through the fence. Something else. Dev's prints were so hot that I believe any strong hunter could have followed them."

"You're saying that the old compass worked as a tracking device?"

"Yes."

"What does that mean?" she asked.

"I'm not sure, but if it works as a tracking device, it may be possible to transform it into a directional indicator like the ones ghost hunters use down in the Underworld. That, in turn, might make it possible for anyone with some talent to navigate inside the Preserve."

"Maybe it only works with certain kinds of talent. Devin's, for instance. But we don't yet know what kind of ability he possesses."

"No." Slade went back to his lasagna.

"So what really happened today and why do I think that you didn't tell everyone the whole story?" she said.

Slade did not even blink at the question. It was as if he had been expecting it. He picked up his fork and cut off a large chunk of lasagna.

"The two gunmen who chased Devin and Nate into the Preserve may have been smugglers but if so, they were not standard issue," he said.

She paused, her own fork hovering an inch above the lasagna on her plate. "What do you mean?"

"They were both talents of some kind. I could see it in their tracks. Devin says they moved very fast so I'm guessing they were hunters. But they didn't want to risk going into the Preserve, not even to chase down a couple of witnesses, so I have a hunch they were only midlevel sensitives. Either that or their brand of the hunter-talent doesn't allow them to navigate inside the fence."

"A couple of hunter-talents turned smugglers wouldn't be the biggest surprise in the world. When you think about it, hunters are ideally suited to one of two career paths: a life of crime or a life of crime-fighting."

"True." Slade ate some more lasagna. "But I've got a feeling about those two."

"What are you thinking?"

"That a murder by paranormal means, combined with a hot artifact of unknown power and a couple of talents packing guns showing up in a small cove at the edge of the Preserve adds up to far too many coincidences."

"Do you believe that the smugglers had something to do with Jeremy's murder?"

"The thought crossed my mind."

"Are they the ones who killed him?"

"Maybe. Seems logical because he was also dealing in an illicit business. But Gaines was killed by paranormal means. The pair at Hidden Beach had a preference for guns."

"So there may be another person involved?"

"Maybe."

"A lot of maybes here."

"There always are when the case starts coming together." Slade looked at the pan of lasagna. "I wouldn't mind another slice."

She smiled and picked up the spatula. "How are Nate and Devin doing?"

"They're both describing the experience as weird and freaky and they're still a little shaken. But now that it's over they are well on their way to becoming rock stars among their peers here on the island."

"That status should help Devin make new friends when school starts."

"Oh, yeah. What is surprising is that they came through it all with coherent memories. According to the old records, that is highly unusual."

"You can go in and out of the Preserve without suffering any sense of disorientation. And you got me in and out. I recall every moment inside —" She broke off, aware that she was turning scarlet.

For the first time since he had returned to

town, sexy amusement gleamed in Slade's eyes.

"You recall every detail?" he said politely. "So do I."

She beetled her brows. "You know what I meant. Obviously some people of talent can come and go through the fence without any problem."

"Which explains why Devin is okay. I assume he was able to somehow shield Nate. But I'm not convinced that the fence or the energy inside the Preserve accounts for all the reports of disorientation and memory loss among the handful of people who have been rescued over the years."

"You have another theory?"

"During the past fifty years the few people who have been rescued from the Preserve were all extracted by teams sent in by the Rainshadow Foundation or its predecessor, Amber Sea Trading."

"The members of the rescue teams are probably sensitives who can track the way you do."

"Sure," Slade said. "But that doesn't explain the survivors' memory issues. What if the rescue teams go in not only with a hunter-talent of some kind but also with a para-hypnotist or maybe a dream-talent who could ensure that the folks who were

286

rescued don't have any clear memories of their time in the Preserve?"

She stilled. "That would be highly illegal. Why would the Foundation go to such lengths and take such a risk?"

Slade shrugged and forked up another bite of lasagna. "The obvious reason. To protect the secrets of the Preserve."

An icy shiver swept across her senses. "What secrets?"

Slade looked at her. "I don't know yet."

A chortle from the front room made Charlotte glance up at the refrigerator. Rex was not in sight.

"What's he up to?" she asked uneasily.

"I think he just wants out."

She leaped to her feet and rushed into the other room. Rex was waiting in front of the door. She opened it for him. Rex chortled a cheery farewell and dashed off across the porch, clutch gripped tightly in one paw. He disappeared into the night.

Charlotte closed the door and walked back into the kitchen. "Rex is not a normal dust bunny."

"Who knows what's normal for a dust bunny?"

"Good point," she admitted.

Slade met her eyes. "I'm not normal, either. I need to know what the hell is happening to my talent. I've decided to run some experiments tonight."

"You can run them here, with me."

"No," he said. "Not a good idea. I don't know what to expect."

"There are only two plausible outcomes," she said, keeping her voice as calm and reasonable as possible. "One is that the experts are right and you'll take a heavy psi-burn from which you will not recover. The other is that I'm right, in which case, you'll get a handle on whatever is going on with your para-senses. Either way there's no reason to go through this alone."

"That's how I work, Charlotte. Alone."

"Maybe that was the way you worked in the past but things are different here on Rainshadow," she said.

"Yeah?" He smiled but there was no amusement in his eyes. "What's different?"

"I'm here. Face it, Chief, you're not alone tonight."

He seemed to struggle with that concept for a moment, then he shook his head. "No."

"Give me one good reason why I should let you do this on your own. Aside from your natural hardheaded stubbornness, that is."

"You said there are two plausible out-comes but what if you're wrong? What if there's a third?"

"Such as?"

"What if it turns out I can access the stormlight at the far end of my talent but I'm not able to control it?"

She touched the pendant at her throat. "Whatever is waiting for you, I'm absolutely sure that you can control it. But if I'm wrong, I'll know it before you do. I'll stop you."

She was not absolutely certain she would be able to do that but she had no intention of letting him know that she had a few tiny doubts. In any event, the possibility that he might not be able to control his talent was the least of her concerns. He was going to run his experiment tonight with or without her and she could not let him face his worst nightmare — permanent psi-blindness — alone.

He got to his feet and went to stand at the window. He looked out into the night for a long time and then he turned back to her.

"Okay," he said. "We'll do this together."

CHAPTER 22

Slade sat on the sofa. He waited while Charlotte walked through the small house, turning off the lights. With a few notable exceptions, psychic energy could be worked night or day. But according to most of the Arcane experts, it was easier to focus the strong stuff in darkness. The visible energy from the sun and artificial illumination did not necessarily dampen talent but it could interfere with control. At the very least, it was a distraction.

He did not need any additional distractions, Slade thought. What he needed was absolute control.

Charlotte put out the last light, the lamp on the end table. The living room was plunged into a darkness lit only by the low-burning fire. She sat down in an old, padded reading chair and tucked one black denim-clad leg under her.

"Start whenever you're ready," she said.

"I'll keep an eye on your rainbow. If I get any bad vibes, you'll be the first to know."

He looked at her. She was a dark shadow silhouetted against the night that filled the window behind her. He kicked up his talent a little so that he could see her more clearly. Her eyes gleamed a little with psi. He could feel the whispers in the atmosphere that told him she was slightly jacked. It was good to have her here, he thought. He was not sure it was wise on his part but he could not deny that it felt right.

"Thanks," he said, without thinking.

"No problem," she said.

She understood what he was thanking her for, he thought. There was no need to explain. There didn't seem to be anything else to add so he sat forward, legs braced a couple of feet apart, and rested his forearms on his thighs. He pulled his senses into a strong, clear focus.

Charlotte removed her pendant from around her neck and held the mirror in the palm of her hand.

He took his talent up slowly but steadily, watching for the thunderstorm of ultralight that was always waiting for him out on the paranormal plane. He slipped past the comfort zone and eased his way farther out onto the spectrum. The first, faint shadows of power pulsed in the distance.

"I can sense the storm," he said quietly. "Not that far off."

"You're in full control," Charlotte said. "How do you feel?"

He thought about the question, assessing his senses. "Good. But I'm picking up the currents of the heavy energy out there. This is about as far as I've tried to go since I got burned by the gas."

"The reflected bands of primary ultralight in your rainbow are still steady and strong. There are no indications of rogue waves or instability."

"I hear you but from my perspective it's like looking into a thunderstorm or a hurricane. I know that there has to be some natural pattern but I can't detect it from the outside."

"You always talk about it in terms of a storm front," she said.

"That the nearest analogy I can find."

"Maybe it's not an analogy. Maybe what you perceive is a true psychic thunderstorm or a paranormal hurricane."

He focused on the roiling, seething darkness. "Maybe. So?"

"Energy is energy. That's one of the oldest laws of para-physics. More to the point here, para-energy works on some of the same principles as normal energy."

"What are you getting at?"

"It occurs to me that if your talent is capable of generating a storm of ultralight it seems logical that the forces involved will be organized in the same way that a normal storm is, around a core. Think *eye of the storm.*"

"You're saying that I can control this damn hurricane if I find the calm place at the center?"

"I don't know," Charlotte said. "We're both winging it here."

He saw that the mirrored pendant was glowing with a silvery light in her hand.

"You said everything looks stable," he said.

"Yes."

"Looks like the only way to find out what's going on is to go into the storm."

"I think you're right," Charlotte said quietly.

There was no point hanging around out here in limbo, Slade thought. He would treat this like any other job. Go in, do what needed to be done, and get out. If he was lucky.

"One thing before I do this," he said.

"Yes?"

"If the center of the storm turns out to be chaos I might not survive it."

"You'll survive," she said fiercely.

"Physically, maybe, but we both know that's not what I'm talking about. I might not be the same. If that's how this ends up I want you to know that you are not responsible in any way. I made this decision."

"For heaven's sake, Slade, this is no time to go melodramatic on me."

"You're going to feel guilty if this doesn't work."

"No, really, I won't," she said urgently.

"Yes, you will. I don't want that. And I sure as hell do not want you thinking that you have to continue to sleep with me just because you encouraged me to take the risk of a bad burn."

"Stop talking like that. Stop it right now."

"I was going to do this, remember?" he said. "If I get burned, I get burned. If the para-psychs and the medics were right, it was going to happen sooner or later, anyway."

"What part of *think positive* don't you understand?" she said tightly. "Forget about me and concentrate on that storm you're going to control."

"Right," he said.

He went hot, all the way into the zone, just like the old days. Adrenaline and the other potent bio-chemicals associated with raising his senses to the max spilled into his bloodstream in a fierce, thrilling wave.

But a heartbeat later he knew that it wasn't like the old days. He was suddenly flying into the dark winds of the storm and it was like nothing he had ever experienced.

The hurricane of psi buffeted all of his senses, including his excellent vision and hearing. Lightning flashed and sparked. The currents roared around him, cutting off all other sensation.

An instant later, the world went black and he was drifting through a great emptiness. It was as if he had stepped into the farthest reaches of a starless universe.

This was it, the center of the storm, and there was nothing here. He had survived the howling tornado but he was now officially psi-blind. Not only had his para-senses gone dark but so had all of his normal senses. He could not see, hear, touch, smell, or taste. Charlotte had vanished, leaving him alone in the endless storm.

But he could still sense the churning energy around him. That made no sense.

Charlotte's words came back to him, blazing like lightning in the void. *You're not alone tonight.*

He had to find a way to control the stormlight energy. He concentrated with all of his focusing ability, pulling energy he had never before been able to channel.

His senses reemerged with dazzling speed. He could see again, not only on the normal plane but far out on the paranormal spectrum as well. Exhilaration ripped through him. The only sensation that had equaled this was making love to Charlotte. He knew that for the rest of his life the two experiences would be forever linked in his mind.

You're not alone tonight.

"Oh, yeah," he said. "This works."

Charlotte smiled. "I am getting that impression, yes."

The mirrored pendant in her hand flashed with silvery light.

He opened all of his senses to the wild energy that was now his to control. He called down bolts of lightning and channeled currents of ultralight that he had never known existed. The living room was ablaze with paranormal fire.

"Better tone it down a little," Charlotte said.

"Don't worry, I'm in control."

"Yes, but you're playing with psi-fire." Charlotte's voice was edged with wariness now. "Got a hunch my insurance won't cover that sort of damage."

"It's incredible." He could hardly concentrate enough to respond. A man could get drunk on power like this. Maybe he was already drunk.

"Slade, pay attention." Charlotte's voice sharpened. "I think it's time to shut down."

"Why?"

"Because you're going to crash soon. It's one thing to push yourself to the limit. The worst that can happen is that you exhaust your senses for a while. But this is about controlling your talent."

Control. That was the critical thing, he thought. Above all he had to stay in control.

Reluctantly, he lowered his talent. The thunderstorm of energy dissipated quickly. He shut down his psychic senses altogether and sank back into his normal senses. But the intoxicating mix of soaring exhilaration, relief, and euphoria was still sweeping through him. He was in the grip of the biggest post-burn buzz he had ever experienced in his life. He was also more physically aroused than he had been since last night. He would crash soon but not yet.

He looked at Charlotte.

"Down, Big Boy," she said firmly.

"What?" He could not take his eyes off her. It was all he could do not to sweep her up in his arms and race down the short hall to the bedroom. No, forget the bedroom; he wanted to take her right here on the floor or up against the wall.

"There's no reason to pretend you don't know what I'm talking about," she said. "Just so you know, your eyes are still hot. I'm not naïve. I get panic attacks if I run flat-out for a while but most folks, most *men*, get a different reaction."

"Yeah?"

"I've heard the jokes. I know about the para-physiology involved. The bio-cocktail created by a heavy burn results in a big surge of testosterone and adrenaline and other related hormones related to physical arousal. Forget it. We're trying to conduct a scientific experiment here."

A tide of urgent need swelled through him.

"I said, forget it," she added for good measure.

"Okay," he said.

"Stop looking at me like that."

"Okay," he said again. But he could not look away.

"Let's talk about what just happened," Charlotte said.

She spoke in a calm, matter-of-fact way that was no doubt meant to de-escalate the prowling tension in the atmosphere but it had no impact on his arousal. Control, he reminded himself.

"What just happened," he made himself say, "was that I found out that I'm not going psi-blind. What just happened is that I have a whole new level of talent."

"I understand. But what can you do with it that you couldn't do before?"

"I have no idea in hell what I have become," he said quietly.

"Don't talk as if you've developed a new talent. You're just stronger now."

"Maybe. Whatever it is, I know that I can handle it. That's what I learned tonight."

"I see." She drummed her fingers on the arm of the chair. Her brows crinkled together above the frames of her glasses. "I suppose it may take a while to understand intuitively how to focus all that energy in a useful way."

"I'll figure it out some other time." The deep hunger was eating him alive. He got to his feet and went to the window.

"Are you okay?" Charlotte asked quietly.

"Sure. I just need to work off this edge," he said. "I'm going to take a run."

"All right but please be careful. It won't be long before you need to sleep. Be sure you make it home to your own bed before you go down. People might get the wrong impression of the town's new police chief if you're found sleeping on the side of the road."

He ignored her attempt at humor. He was not in a humorous mood. "I've got time."

He had to get out of here, he thought. He pivoted and went to the door, careful not to look at her. He got the door open.

"Slade," Charlotte said softly.

That was all she said but it was enough. He turned and looked at her. She was on her feet. He saw that she had replaced the pendant around her neck. The mirror no longer glowed. The yearning inside him became a howl of need. He gripped the doorknob so tightly it was a wonder that he did not crush the knob.

"I have to go," he said.

"No. I want you to stay here with me tonight."

"You're sure?"

She smiled and walked toward him through the shadows. When she was directly in front of him she put her arms around his neck.

"I'm sure," she said.

The door closed with a solid and very final-sounding *chunk*. Slade stopped trying to suppress the all-consuming fire inside him. He locked his hands around Charlotte and lifted her into the air. She clung to his shoulders and wrapped her legs around his waist.

"Oh, my," she whispered.

He did not try to speak because he knew that he was incapable of being coherent. He kissed her instead, letting her feel all of the lightning-hot passion that was flooding his veins.

And then he carried her down the hall to the bedroom.

CHAPTER 23

She opened her eyes a long time later, vaguely aware that it was still dark outside and that some faint sound had awakened her. Her pulse beat a little faster.

It took a few seconds for her to orient herself. The unfamiliar weight beside her was Slade. He had fallen asleep almost immediately after the fast, hot sex. It could take a strong talent a few hours to recover from a heavy burn, she thought. If there was something wrong, she would have to deal with it.

The sound came again, a faint, muffled chortle. Rex.

Reluctantly she shoved aside the covers and got out of bed. Slade stirred but he did not awaken. She pulled on a robe and went down the cold hall. When she reached the living room she paused to twitch the curtain aside and peer out the window.

Rex was sitting on the porch staring

302

intently at the door as if trying to will it open. She dropped the curtain and unlocked the door.

Rex sauntered across the threshold, chortling a greeting. He still had the clutch purse but it did not look as full as it had earlier.

"You gave away the paperclips, didn't you?" she asked softly. "Trying to impress some new friends in the Preserve?"

Rex chattered happily and headed for the kitchen.

"Where do you think you're going?" she said.

She followed him into the kitchen and flipped on the light. Rex was sitting on the floor, his gaze fixed on another door, the one that opened the refrigerator.

"What? You expect me to feed you again? You just came back from a hunting expedition, didn't you?"

Rex did not take his attention off the refrigerator door. She gave up and opened it. Together they both studied the glowing interior.

"Oh, look," she said. "You're in luck. There's some leftover zucchini bread."

Rex bounced a little and chortled.

She took the foil-wrapped bread out of the refrigerator and set it on the counter. She found a knife in a drawer and cut off a hefty slice of the bread. She put the slice on a plate and set the plate on top of the refrigerator. Rex bounded up to the top of the appliance and fell to his late-night snack with his usual enthusiasm.

Charlotte rewrapped the remaining loaf of zucchini bread and put it back in the refrigerator. She was about to close the door when she realized that she was hungry, too. She took out a wedge of cheddar cheese and cut off a hunk for herself.

She leaned back against the counter and studied Rex while she ate her cheese.

"What's going on with you and the guy in my bed?" she asked softly. "You've bonded with him somehow, we know that much. Is it because you're both hunters at heart?"

Rex concentrated on his bread.

"Now that he has his talent back, Slade will probably return to his old job at the Bureau. Or maybe he'll decide to go ahead with his new security business. Either way, he'll be leaving in a few months."

Rex finished his snack and bounded down to the floor. He fluttered out of the kitchen and disappeared.

"I'm going to miss you both," she said softly to the empty kitchen. "I'm really not much good at this rez-with-the-frequency thing."

She finished her cheese and went back out into the shadowed living room. She moved cautiously through the dark space, afraid of tripping over Rex but there was no sign of him.

She made her way down the hall to the doorway of the bedroom. A pair of glowing blue eyes watched her from the vicinity of her pillow. Rex was not asleep in the living room. He was curled up on her side of the bed.

"Oh, no you don't," she hissed softly. She made shooing motions with her hand. "Off you go. There isn't room for three of us."

Rex did not stir. His second pair of eyes opened, revealing amber coals. She hesitated, not sure how to proceed. This was no ordinary animal. Regardless of his strange attachment to Slade, Rex was a feral creature. She had read somewhere that truly wild animals could never be successfully tamed. She could try moving him forcefully off the bed but she was not sure how he would react. He might decide to defend his position. She knew enough about dust bunnies to know that they could be dangerous if cornered. And even if she was successful there would probably be dust bunny fur all over her pillow.

The only other option was to try to wake

Slade and ask him to get Rex off the bed. But that was probably not doable, not unless she managed to trigger his survival instincts. In a heavy post-burn sleep that was the only thing strong enough to bring a person back to a wakeful state. The problem was that Slade was a hunter-talent of some kind, a very powerful one. If his core instincts kicked in he would no doubt slam to the surface prepared to do battle. He might accidentally hurt her before he realized who she was.

She was doomed to spend the night on the couch.

"You win," she said to Rex. "But the three of us will have a long talk in the morning. This sleeping arrangement is not going to become a regular habit."

She could have sworn that Slade stirred a little at the sound of her voice but he did not awaken. Rex closed all four eyes.

She left the two hunters sleeping in her bed and stalked back down the hall to the closet. She found a spare sheet, blanket, and pillow and hauled the lot into the front room. The couch was not going to be comfortable but she wouldn't have to endure it for long. Dawn was not that far off.

A short time later she settled down on the cushions. When she pulled the blanket up over her shoulders moonlight glinted on her pendant. She touched the silvery metal and thought about what she had seen earlier when Slade had pushed into the higher regions of his talent.

During that time the room had been awash in waves of energy, *Slade's* energy. The hot, dangerous currents had stirred her senses and heated her blood. She'd had to concentrate hard to read the ultralight rainbow cast by her pendant. Her objective had been to make certain that the reflecting bands of energy created by his aura were strong and steady.

The colors and the clarity had been right, she thought. The dark rainbow had been fierce and brilliant. It had also been extremely powerful and quite unlike any rainbow she had ever viewed before.

Slade said he did not yet know what he could do with the new aspect of his talent, but one thing was certain. Whatever the nature of his ability, it would be based on his core talent. He was a hunter.

He had been dangerous before he had been hit with the mysterious vapors from the exploding gas canisters during his last assignment. He was even more lethal now.

CHAPTER 24

Slade awoke to the first light of dawn and the realization that he was not alone in the bed. That was the good news, he decided. The bad news was that there was something very wrong about the size and shape of the other occupant. He put out a hand and touched a warm body covered in fur.

"Rex," he said into the pillow. "What did you do with Charlotte?"

Rex nuzzled his arm, rumbled a greeting, and then jumped briskly down to the floor. Slade opened his eyes in time to watch him flutter through the bedroom doorway. A moment later the front door opened.

Charlotte's voice floated down the hall. "Take your time. No need to hurry back. I'm about out of zucchini bread, anyway."

Slade groaned and sat up on the side of the bed. Charlotte appeared in the doorway. She wore a pink terrycloth robe and a pair of matching slippers. Her hair stood out in a variety of interesting angles. She looked like she had spent a less than restful night.

"Hi," he said.

"Hi, yourself. How do you feel?"

He thought about the question. "Good. Real good."

"Lucky you. I'm stiff and sore from sleeping a goodly portion of the night on the couch."

He winced. "Rex?"

"He came back late, made me feed him, and then took over my side of the bed."

"You should have shoved him out."

"Easy for you to say. Personally, I try not to get into arguments with anything that has more teeth and sharper claws than I do."

"Rex wouldn't hurt you."

"Are you sure of that? I saw his hunting eyes. They tell me that is not a good sign when it comes to dust bunnies."

He looked down and was reassured to notice that he was wearing his briefs. He got to his feet.

"Pretty sure," he said.

"He's a feral animal, Slade. He appears to have formed some kind of psychic bond with you but I don't think you or anyone else can predict how he'd react if someone else tried to push him around."

She had a point, he realized. He rubbed

his jaw. He needed a shave.

"I apologize for Rex's behavior," he said. "Would you mind if I took a shower before we finish this conversation?"

"You can have the bathroom after me. I'm the one who had to sleep on the couch."

"You know, we could shower at the same time. That way we wouldn't have to worry about running out of hot water."

She gave him one of her radiant smiles and for a couple of seconds his hopes soared.

"It's a very small shower and I'm not worried about using up all the hot water because I'm going first," she said sweetly. "By the way, would you mind stripping the bed while I'm in the shower? I want to wash the sheets."

For some obscure reason, that hurt. He reminded himself that the sex had been hot and wet. The sheets probably did need washing.

"Sure," he said.

"There will be dust bunny hair on my side of the bed," she explained. "And on my pillow."

He relaxed. It was Rex she wanted to wash out of her sheets, not him. Rex could take care of himself.

"No problem," he said. "I'll get right on it."

She turned on her heel, went halfway down the short hall, and vanished into the bathroom. A moment later he heard the shower running.

He looked at Charlotte's pillow. There were a few scruffy gray hairs but the damage didn't look all that bad to him. Still, he knew enough about women to know that they could be picky about that sort of thing.

He bundled up the quilt, tossed it onto a chair and went to work stripping the sheets off the bed.

The energizing aroma of brewing coffee greeted him when he emerged from the bathroom sometime later. He followed it into the kitchen and found Charlotte at the stove. She drew a long-handled spatula slowly through a large pan of creamy-looking scrambled eggs.

For a moment Slade stood in the doorway, allowing himself the luxury of watching Charlotte make breakfast for the two of them. She was dressed in black trousers and a deep blue pullover that skimmed her gently rounded breasts. Her hair, still damp from the shower, was tucked behind her ears and secured with a thin black head-band.

It felt good just being here with her, he thought. She probably didn't feel the same way about him, though. He'd seen his face in the steamed-up mirror a few minutes ago. He looked like he had just walked out of a disaster movie. True, he had showered but he'd had no way to shave and the clothes he had on were the ones he'd worn last night.

He made a note to bring a fresh shirt, a change of underwear, and a razor the next time he came to dinner at Charlotte's. The fact that he hadn't remembered to bring a few necessities last night only went to show how long he had been out of the dating world.

Charlotte raised the spatula in greeting and smiled. "Ready for breakfast?"

"Sure," he said. He looked around. "Did Rex come back?"

"Not yet. Just as well. There aren't enough eggs for all three of us."

He glanced at the small table. It was neatly set with two green placemats, silverware, and mugs. Butter and a jar of marmalade were arranged in the center.

"Can I do something?" he asked.

"You can pour the orange juice and the coffee."

"I should be able to handle that." He opened the refrigerator and took out the bottled juice. "We need to talk."

"I thought you wanted to rez with the frequency," she said lightly.

He tried not to let the touch of frost in her voice bother him.

"Not about us," he said. He closed the refrigerator door and looked at her. "About my talent."

"Oh, right, your talent." She hefted the pan off the stove and spooned the eggs onto two plates. "Well? What about it?"

"I'd appreciate it if you wouldn't say anything about it to anyone else, especially the members of your family."

She glanced at him, brows lifted. "Why not?"

"Because your family is well-connected with Arcane and I don't want J&J or anyone else getting curious about the effects that gas had on me."

"Got it." She set the pan down. "I understand and I agree."

"You do?"

"My family may be well-connected within the Society but that doesn't mean that I don't know how things work in the organization. I'm well aware that rare and unusual talents make some members of the Society uneasy. That goes double if those talents are powerful. I don't think there's any doubt but that you are now off the charts. Level Ten with a very large asterisk."

"Off the charts with an unknown talent," he added quietly.

"A heretofore unknown aspect of your core talent," she corrected.

"Doesn't matter." He poured the juice into two glasses. "Arcane gets nervous when the words *unknown* and *off the charts* appear in the same sentence. The same is true in the Guilds and at the Bureau."

"I'm aware of that. Don't worry, I have no intention of discussing your talent with anyone else, including the members of my own family."

He was glad she was not going to argue with him. He put the bottle of orange juice back into the refrigerator and picked up the coffeepot.

"You were right about one thing, I'm going to need time to figure out just what has changed in my talent," he said.

She carried the plates to the table and sat down. "You probably won't figure it out until the first time you use it intuitively. We both know that's how psychic abilities manifest themselves."

He sat down across from her. "And sometimes people find out the hard way."

She picked up a fork. "Don't worry, you know now that you've got the control you'll need to handle the energy you're capable of generating."

"You're sure of that?"

"Absolutely."

He ate some eggs, thinking. "What was it like for you?"

She gave him a wicked smile. "Are we talking about last night or my talent?"

He grinned. "I was thinking about your talent but if you'd rather discuss last night —"

"Forget last night. I spent a good portion of it on a lumpy sofa because there was a dust bunny on my side of the bed."

He groaned. "Don't remind me. It won't happen again. By the way, I left your sheets on top of the washing machine."

"Thanks. I'll take care of them before I go to Looking Glass."

"I don't know why Rex took over your side of the bed last night. At my place, he never sleeps on the bed. In fact, he's usually gone most of the night. Shows up around breakfast time."

"Got a hunch he was guarding you," she

315

said, very thoughtful now.

"From you?"

"No." She paused. "I think he was watching over you while you slept off the burn. Somehow he understood that you weren't in a normal sleep state. He must have sensed that you were vulnerable until you woke up. He's your buddy. He was watching your back."

"You know, they say we shouldn't anthropomorphize animals."

"True. But Rex's relationship with you is certainly odd."

"I can't argue that." He slathered butter on a slice of toast. "You were going to tell me what it was like coming into your talent."

"When I was thirteen, I started seeing faint rainbows in various reflective surfaces but only whenever there was someone else in the vicinity. I didn't realize what was happening for the first few months, although I soon discovered that if I concentrated hard, the rainbows got brighter."

"You didn't realize you were seeing ultralight rainbows?"

"Not for some time. And neither did anyone else because it is not only a low-rent talent it is generally a very weak talent. A lot of people with the ability never realize

316

what they're seeing. They catch a glimpse of an ultralight rainbow in a mirror or a window and assume it's just a trick of the light. Also, because the talent is not exactly impressive, it hasn't been studied. It is poorly understood and not adequately described in the literature."

"So how did you figure out what was going on and what you could do with your ability?"

"It was a long process," she said. "When I mentioned the rainbows to my mother, the first thing she did was take me to an ophthalmologist who concluded that there was nothing wrong with my eyes. Aside from the fact that I needed glasses, that is."

"But you kept seeing rainbows."

"Of course. And they got increasingly vivid. My parents finally started to wonder if there was a link to my psychic senses because I certainly wasn't showing signs of developing any other kind of talent. Everyone in my family has some talent, you see."

"They say there's a strong genetic component in some families."

"Yes, but psychic genetics are extremely complicated. My talent doesn't appear anywhere on the family tree. At any rate, the next appointment Mom made for me was with some experts in rare talents at one of the Arcane labs. They ran a lot of tests on me and eventually announced that I was an unusually strong rainbow-talent." Charlotte waved one hand. "And that was the end of it, as far as everyone was concerned because, as everyone knows, the talent is just a novelty at best."

"You seem to have parlayed it into a good career as an antiques dealer."

She looked at him over the top of her mug, her eyes shadowed with darkly luminous mysteries. He felt the hair stir on the back of his neck, as it always did when he sensed secrets.

"Yes," she said. "It has worked out well for me from a financial point of view."

He looked at the mirrored pendant she wore. "Tell me about that necklace."

"This?" She touched the pendant with her fingers. "I came across it a few years ago in an estate sale. I had no idea what it was but I knew that I had to have it. Later I figured out that it works a bit like tuned amber. It helps me focus my talent more precisely."

"Interesting."

She looked hesitant. He got the feeling that she was about to tell him something else about the pendant but in the next moment she changed her mind. She glanced out the window.

"Brace yourself," she said lightly. "We have a visitor."

He followed her gaze and saw Thelma Duncan striding briskly along the drive toward the cottage. She was dressed in her standard uniform, an oversized denim shirt heavily embroidered with colorful flowers, sturdy trousers, and a pair of well-worn boots. Her gray hair was covered by a broad-brimmed straw hat. She carried a basket on one arm.

"Something tells me you're going to be eating zucchini bread for another week," Slade said. "Rex will be happy."

Charlotte set down her mug and got to her feet. "I admit I've had enough zucchini bread to last me until next summer's crop comes in but I hope she brought more of those incredible tomatoes and basil. I could eat those all year long."

Under other circumstances, her enthusiasm for the free produce would have been amusing, he thought.

"You do realize that Mrs. Duncan is going to see me here having breakfast with you," he said. "She will draw the obvious conclusions. The news will be all over town by noon."

Charlotte paused in the kitchen doorway and looked at him. "So what? Everyone assumes we're sleeping together, anyway."

"Assuming is one thing. Having the facts confirmed by a witness who actually saw us at breakfast takes the quality of the gossip to a whole new level."

Charlotte winked. "The locals will conclude that their cunning plan to keep you happy here on the island is working."

He thought about that for a beat and smiled slowly. "They'll conclude right."

She looked surprised and then she turned a delightful shade of pink and disappeared into the living room. He picked up his mug, got to his feet, and went to stand in the doorway between the two rooms.

Charlotte opened the door to a beaming Thelma Duncan.

"Good morning," Charlotte said. "Won't you come in? You're just in time to join Slade and me for coffee."

"Oh, goodness, is the chief here?" Thelma looked at Slade and managed to feign a start of surprise, as if she had not noticed him filling the kitchen doorway. "Why, so he is. Good morning, Slade. Lovely day, isn't it?"

"According to the weather report there's a storm coming in tonight," Slade said.

"Yes, well, of course there is." Thelma smiled serenely. "That's the thing about life, isn't it? Always something dark out there on the horizon. The trick is to enjoy the sunshine while you've got it." She handed the basket to Charlotte. "I brought you a few things from my garden and another loaf of the zucchini bread. I know how much you like it."

"Thank you so much." Charlotte took the basket and examined the contents with enthusiasm. "More tomatoes, oh and the peas are coming in, I see. Fabulous. The basil is absolutely gorgeous. I should display it in a flower vase."

Thelma looked pleased. "I must say the tomatoes and basil have been especially good this summer."

"I've never seen garden produce as beautiful as what you grow," Charlotte said. "You're an incredible gardener."

Thelma chuckled. "I don't know about incredible, but I do enjoy my little hobby."

"Come on into the kitchen and have some coffee," Charlotte said.

"Thank you, dear, but I really don't want to interrupt your breakfast."

"Nonsense, you're not interrupting anything," Charlotte said.

She started toward the kitchen, basket in one hand. Slade got out of her way.

"Well, if you're sure," Thelma murmured. She fixed Slade with her twinkling gray eyes.

"Where is Rex?"

"Who knows?" Slade said. "He took off at dawn. Haven't seen him since."

"I'm sure he'll be back. He seems to have adopted you. Very odd behavior, really. I didn't know dust bunnies made good pets."

"They don't," he said.

CHAPTER 25

Slade sensed Rex shortly before the dust bunny materialized out of the woods at the edge of the road.

"I knew you'd show up sooner or later," he said. "If you're going to hang with me, we're going to have to talk about some rules."

Rex chortled cheerfully and bounded up onto Slade's shoulder. He settled down with his purse.

"Rule number one," Slade said, "you don't take over the lady's side of the bed. Understood?"

Rex mumbled happily but otherwise gave no indication that he grasped the finer points of human sexual etiquette.

They turned off the main road and onto the graveled drive that wound through the trees to the cottage. The first chill of awareness trickled across Slade's senses when they emerged into the open area that surrounded the cabin. He stopped. On his shoulder, Rex growled.

They both looked hard at the cottage. Slade had no idea what was going through Rex's brain but his own hunter's intuition was flashing a warning. His first instinctive thought was, *No need to make yourself a target.*

He moved back into the trees. Rex sleeked out. They had both picked up the same bad vibes, Slade thought. There was something very wrong with the tranquil scene.

He raised his talent. He was no longer worried about being overwhelmed by the darkness at the end of the spectrum; nevertheless, he was cautious. He knew that he could control the storm of power but it was useless to him until he figured out how to focus it. He did not need the distraction just then.

It did not require a lot of energy to view the psi-prints on the ground. There were two distinct sets. The tracks came out of the trees on the right and wound around the cabin, vanishing behind it. The intruders had not wanted to chance being surprised by someone coming along the drive. They had gone in through the kitchen door.

The question now was whether the pair was still inside the house. He studied the fluorescing prints closely. There were two more sets of tracks leading away from the house and back into the trees toward the road.

He worked his way through the woods to the trail of retreating prints. Rex growled softly. When they reached the tracks, Slade crouched and took a close look. The prints were familiar. He'd seen them yesterday at Hidden Beach. The two men who had chased Devin and Nate into the Preserve had evidently concluded that the local chief of police was going to be a problem.

"I thought we'd have to go looking for them," Slade said quietly to Rex. "Maybe do some actual investigation work. But they're going to make it easy. They're coming after me. Probably disappointed last night when they found out I wasn't home. I'm sure they'll try again."

Rex rumbled.

Slade returned to the cabin. The front door was still locked. He made his way around to the back porch and went up the steps. The intruders had popped the lock on the kitchen door, as he had expected. He shook his head, disgusted.

"Looks like they weren't even trying to be subtle," he said.

He opened the door and moved into the

kitchen, rezzing his talent again. Out of long habit he stood quietly for a moment, absorbing the silence. Empty houses always had a unique vibe. He did not pick up any of the energy that indicated there was someone lurking on the premises. He went to the cupboard and opened a door.

Rex muttered. Slade understood the outrage. This was their territory. It had been invaded by intruders. That could not be allowed to stand.

"We'll get them," Slade said.

Rex tumbled down to the ground, still sleeked, and headed for the front room of the cabin.

Slade was mildly surprised to find his laptop still safely tucked away on the highest shelf of the cupboard. Not the most original of hiding places, but on the other hand, he hadn't been trying to protect Bureau secrets, just a business plan. Losing the computer would have been annoying and expensive but not a disaster.

"They didn't do a very good job of searching the place," he said.

But maybe that had not been their goal, he thought. Maybe they had just come here to kill him and had left when it turned out he wasn't home. Typical thug mentality.

Rex's low growl rumbled from the living

room. Slade went to the kitchen doorway.

Rex was standing on his hind paws, gazing intently into the short hall that led to the bath and bedroom. He had dropped his beloved purse on the floor.

"What is it?" Slade asked. He walked across the small space. "Did they screw up and leave something behind? That would be useful. More hard evidence is always good."

He heard the sound just as he reached Rex. The scrape-and-clunk iced his senses. He looked down the hall and saw a large, mechanical doll nearly three feet tall coming toward him. The gnomelike figure had long white hair and a flowing beard. There was a floppy velvet cap on its head. It was dressed in elaborately embroidered green-and-gold robes decorated with ancient alchemical symbols. The doll's glass eyes glittered with dark, malevolent energy.

"Son of a bitch," Slade said. "Sylvester Jones."

He had a vague memory of an old Arcane legend, something about a Victorian clockmaker who had created some very dangerous clockwork toys.

The blast of ice and lightning hit him before he could remember the details, threatening to freeze both his paranormal as well as his normal senses. The force of the blast drove him to his knees. Rex crouched beside him, snarling furiously. He was fully sleeked out, a tough little predator.

It took everything Slade had not to crumple to the floor. His heart started to pound. He could hardly breathe. The atmosphere was darkening around him. He was dying, murdered by a damn clockwork toy.

Charlotte, he thought. He would never see her again. He wanted to explain that it hadn't been just an island romance for him. But now there would not be time.

Rex crowded close against his thigh. Slade managed to put one hand on him. Rex was shivering, too.

The clockwork Sylvester halted a short distance away. Its glass eyes radiated a steady, sustained blast of lethal energy.

Slade grew colder. He tightened his hold on the snarling Rex and whispered the only name that mattered to him.

"Charlotte."

The flash of dread arced across Charlotte's senses just as she stepped outside onto the front porch. The chilling frisson struck along with the wind that was bringing in the storm. The sensation was so ominous, so overwhelming, it shocked her breathless.

Something awful was happening. To Slade.

She did not know how she could be certain that Slade was in danger but she did not question the knowledge. The Arcane experts claimed there was no such thing as telepathy but no one in the Society doubted the reality of intuition. She did not even try to tell herself that she was imagining things. She yanked her keys out of her purse and ran for her car.

CHAPTER 26

This would be a damn stupid way to go out, Slade thought. He could see the note in his Bureau file, *Agent Slade Attridge assassinated by large doll.*

He was still on his knees confronting Sylvester, the snarling Rex pressed close to his side. It was as if they were trying to give each other some psychical support through physical contact. And maybe that was what was happening.

Charlotte.

This time he said it in his head, not aloud, but it had the same steadying effect. It helped him focus and that was what he needed most in that moment. He summoned the full force of his will, the same will that he used to control his talent, and slammed his senses into the hot zone.

He entered the stormlight region of his talent. For an instant the gale of energy threatened to disorient him but he powered

330

through the disruptive currents until he found the eerie calm at the center.

The energy storm flashed around him in multicolored lightning strikes. It was an astonishingly simple, wholly intuitive process to identify the wavelengths he required to neutralize the energy of the Sylvester toy. The pressure of the cold, killing radiation lessened quickly but it took everything he had to maintain the dampening currents. He could not move. It was all he could do to take another breath. All of his energy had to be focused on countering the lethal currents. He knew he would not be able to hold on for long.

The clockwork device, on the other hand, seemed to be able to generate an endless stream of energy. It showed no signs of weakening. Every time he eased off the counterpoint currents, the energy from the Sylvester doll intensified immediately. He had to find a way to shut it down and quickly, before he exhausted his senses. If he did not show up at the station this morning, Myrna would send someone to look for him, Devin, maybe. Whoever walked through the front door to see what had happened to him would fall victim to Sylvester.

He tightened his grip on Rex, willing the dust bunny to understand.

"Fetch," he said. It was all he could do to get the single word past his lips.

He took his hand off Rex. The steady blast of energy from the doll got a little hotter. He responded by pulling more stormlight. He dampened the currents as far as he could to give Rex a chance.

Rex flew at the machine, moving like the sleek, fast predator he was. He bounded up toward Sylvester's throat and struck the device with a thud. The force of his momentum toppled the doll. The device crashed backward onto the floor. The mechanical arms and legs thrashed angrily but helplessly.

Slade was suddenly free from the paralyzing energy of the automaton's eyes. He could breathe easily again. His heart rate slowed.

Sylvester stared up at the ceiling, glass eyes rattling in their sockets as the doll tried to find a new focus. Rex snapped and snarled and tried to sink his teeth into the automaton's wooden throat.

"Rex, that's enough." Slade got to his feet and went forward. "He's not worth breaking a tooth."

Rex backed away from the thrashing doll, still snarling. Slade moved closer and crouched, careful to keep out of range of the glass eyes. He rolled Sylvester facedown and began searching for an access panel. There had to be some way to de-rez the gadget.

He found the panel on the back under the robes. He got it open and surveyed the elegantly engineered clockwork mechanism inside. There was a small, old-fashioned metal key. He removed it carefully. The doll went still.

He was still in the narrow hall studying the clockwork Sylvester and working through possible scenarios when he heard Charlotte's car roar down the driveway.

"Damn." He grabbed his cell phone, saw the missed call, and punched in her number.

The shades were drawn across all of his windows but he stayed low so as not to risk casting any shadows as he made his way across the living room. Rex watched him from the hallway, sensing that the hunt was not yet over.

Slade hunkered down against the wall and peered through a crack in the blinds. He watched Charlotte bring her small vehicle to a halt in the drive.

She must have been clutching the phone because she answered immediately. At the same time she popped open the car door.

"Slade," she gasped, rushing toward the

front steps. "Are you okay? I got this awful feeling a few minutes ago."

"I'm fine but I've got a situation here. I do not want you walking into it."

"Oh, my God, what's wrong?"

"Listen to me and do exactly as I say. I'm pretty sure someone is watching the house. You're here now so we'll have to make it look good. Knock on my front door. When you don't get an answer, act like you've decided I'm not home. Get back in the car and drive into town. Go to the café. Have coffee. Remain where there are people around you. Don't tell anyone what is going on. Wait until I call you and give you the all-clear. Got it?"

"I'll get Officer Wills."

"No, I don't want him going up against a couple of hunter-talents. Just do what I said. One more thing. If this doesn't work out well, get on the phone to Adam Winters, the boss of the Frequency City Guild. Got it? Tell him to call J&J. This is their problem."

"Got it. But —"

He closed down the phone, not giving her a chance to argue.

Through the crack in the blind he watched her close her own phone. She dropped it into her purse as she went up the steps. She knocked briskly and hesitated a few seconds as though waiting. Then, frowning, she went back down the steps, got into the car, and started the engine. It was a good act, he thought. But he did not breathe deeply again until she was safely out of the drive.

He made his way back into the narrow hall. With great care he picked up the lifeless Sylvester doll and carried it into the bathroom. He set it facedown in the bathtub. He was reasonably confident that the device could not be activated without the key, but when it came to old Arcane legends, you could never be certain. With luck the tub would act as a shield in the unlikely event that the mechanism somehow switched on again.

He went back out into the hall, shut the bathroom door behind him, and then closed the bedroom door. He took the mag-rez out of the holster and checked the load.

Satisfied with his preparations, he got down on his knees and crawled into the living room. Taking care not to throw any shadows on the blinds, he climbed the narrow steps to the sleeping loft. When you hunted, you had to think like your prey. For some reason he had never understood, prey rarely looked up first. People initially prepared for danger from in front, from the side and, if they were very smart, from behind. But they usually checked out the situation overhead last.

He reached the sleeping loft and flattened himself on the floor. Rex vaulted up the steps to join him. A low wooden barrier surrounded the loft but Slade could see around the edge of the staircase opening. From that vantage point he had a clear view of the front door and a portion of the kitchen. He settled down, gun in hand, and prepared to wait.

"They'll be coming back soon to retrieve Sylvester," he said to Rex. "They won't want to take a chance on anyone else getting to it first. These guys have to know that if the Bureau or Arcane or the Guilds get wind of that toy they'll have more trouble on their hands than they can possibly handle."

Rex growled a response. All four of his eyes were open.

Slade glanced at his watch. It would not be long. The killers probably had a way to deactivate the mechanism from a safe distance. It was the only explanation that worked.

Ghostly fingertips iced the back of his neck. Not the usual hunting vibes. More like the bad energy he'd picked up shortly before he'd gone into the lab on the island four months ago. His intuition was letting him know that something about the plan was about to go badly wrong. Nearby Rex muttered uneasily.

Charlotte.

Slade knew then beyond a shadow of a doubt that she was in danger. As if on cue, his cell phone rang. He grabbed it off his belt and looked at the screen. The incoming number was Charlotte's. Of course it was. He went cold.

He contemplated the phone as if it were a snake. Everything in him was urging him to answer the call. It was the only way to make sure that Charlotte was all right. But the hunter in him knew better. It was too late. They had her.

The phone rang again.

You're supposed to be dead, he reminded himself. *They're making sure. Stick to the plan.*

The phone went silent. Slade put it quietly on the floor. He listened to the wind prowling through the trees that surrounded the cabin and forced himself to think.

Charlotte was still alive. The bastards had spotted her coming from the house and decided they couldn't take any risks. They had grabbed her.

But they would not kill her until they got her into the house. He was sure of that.

They would figure that they might need her for a hostage. When they knew for certain that he was dead they would probably try to stage a murder-suicide scene. It was all they had. Given his para-psych history no one in the Bureau or Arcane would be surprised to learn that he had gone crazy and killed his lover and himself.

Rex snarled silently. He was suddenly intent on the kitchen. A few seconds later Slade heard the footsteps on the porch. Three sets, not two. They had Charlotte with them.

The kitchen door opened. Slade watched two men move cautiously into the house, pushing Charlotte ahead of them. Her glasses were gone. Her mouth was covered with a strip of tape. Her hands were bound behind her back. She looked pissed.

"Move, bitch," one of them said. He shoved her forward. She stumbled and went down on one knee.

The other man jerked her back to her feet.

Slade suppressed the rage that was setting fire to his blood. Emotion of any kind was not a good thing at a time like this. He would be of no use to Charlotte unless he stayed stone cold.

Her captors were dressed in windbreakers, trousers, and boots. One of the men had his hair pulled back into a ponytail. An earring glinted in the ear of the second man. They both wore billed caps, just as Devin and Nate had described.

Slade sincerely hoped the pair would not remove their caps. The bills would tend to block the upward view of the room. Ponytail had his mag-rez out. His gloved fingers were wrapped around Charlotte's upper arm. The other man held a large, old-fashioned gold pocket watch in one fist. The face of the watch was pointed away from him. *As if he's aiming it,* Slade thought.

"The body will be in the living room," Ponytail said. "That damned doll should have wound down by now but don't take any chances. Use the watch on it."

"If you're so worried about the doll, why don't you turn it off?" Earring snapped. "I'll handle the woman."

Now this was interesting, Slade thought. There was a lot of jittery tension in the room and it wasn't coming from Charlotte. She was scared as well as furious, but these vibes were different. Ponytail and Earring were nervous about the prospect of dealing with the Sylvester weapon.

"Shut up," Ponytail said. "We've wasted enough time because of the woman. Make sure of that damned doll and double-check to be certain the cop is dead. *Move.* We need to dump the bodies before someone else comes nosing around."

"Yeah, sure," Earring muttered.

They weren't even going to bother to set up a plausible murder-suicide scenario, Slade realized. Definitely not high-functioning thugs.

Down below the loft, Earring moved gingerly into the living room, careful to keep the watch aimed straight ahead. Two more steps brought him within range of the sleeping loft but Slade let him pass. Earring was not the one with the gun and for the moment, at least, he was completely focused on locating and deactivating the deadly toy.

"I don't see the cop," Earring called to his companion. He peeked cautiously down the hall. "Or the doll."

"Check the bedroom and the bath," Pony-tail ordered. "The cop might have made it that far before he collapsed and the doll might have kept moving for a while before it shut down."

Earring took a hesitant step into the hall. He was getting more nervous by the second. The pocket watch in his hand shook a little.

"Shit," he said, backing quickly out of the hall. "This isn't good. I can't see the cop or the doll. The door of the bathroom and the bedroom are closed. I know they were open when we set up the doll."

"Don't panic." Ponytail shoved Charlotte ahead of him and followed her out of the kitchen. "The cop probably staggered around before he collapsed. Maybe he made it into the bathroom or the bedroom. Check both rooms."

"What about the doll?"

"Listen, you idiot, do you hear it?"

"No," Earring admitted.

"Then it switched itself off like it's supposed to after a few minutes. Find the body."

Earring disappeared into the hall. Slade heard the bathroom door open slowly. The light came on inside and spilled out the opening.

There was a short, tense silence. Ponytail pushed Charlotte a couple of steps farther into the living room. He was directly under the sleeping loft now.

"We've got a problem," Earring shouted. "We need to get out of here."

"What the hell?" Ponytail said.

His attention was focused on the hall. Instinctively, he focused the gun in the same direction. Energy flared in the small space. He had jacked up his talent.

Charlotte looked up and saw Slade. She

kicked Ponytail hard in the leg. It was a slick, calculated move that caught Ponytail in the vulnerable spot at the side of his knee. He staggered violently and yelled in fury but he did not go down. His hunter-talent reflexes kept him on his feet.

"Bitch," he snarled.

He swung the gun toward Charlotte. But Slade was already falling toward him. The force of the impact took them both to the floor. Slade heard the gun clatter across the floorboards but there was no time to grab it. Ponytail was fast. He twisted with the lithe, wiry energy of a specter-cat and produced a knife.

Slade tried to grab the man's knife hand. He missed. Ponytail's eyes blazed with fury and psi. The guy was strong, Slade realized. And cat-fast.

Slade went hotter, flying straight into the stormlight at the end of the spectrum. He did not need any instruction this time. He did not have to run an experiment. With his senses running wide-open he could see the dangerous psychic currents of Ponytail's talent. He knew exactly what to do. He pulled dark energy and focused it.

Ponytail stiffened as though he had been struck by lightning. An instant later he went limp.

There was no time to comprehend what had happened. The second man was shouting.

"Get it off, get it off," Earring shrieked.

Slade rolled to his feet in time to see Rex clinging to the back of Earring's neck, small claws dug into the windbreaker and probably some skin as well.

Frantic, Earring tried to back up against the nearest wall, intending to squash Rex.

"Rex," Slade said. "That's enough. I've got him."

Rex leaped nimbly free, twisted in midair, and landed lightly on his feet. He faced Earring, snarling silently.

Earring was clearly traumatized but he produced a gun from under his windbreaker. Oblivious of Slade, he aimed the weapon at Rex.

Slade moved. He caught Earring's gun arm, jacked up his talent, and reached into the storm.

Earring went limp and collapsed to the floor.

Slade went quickly around the room, collecting weapons. He found two pairs of handcuffs in his desk drawer, FBPI issue, and used them to secure the wrists of the unconscious men.

He went to Charlotte. She watched him

with wide, psi-hot eyes as he gently pulled the tape off her mouth.

She gasped, taking in great gulps of air. He dug out his Takashima pocketknife and went to work freeing her wrists.

"Are you okay?" he demanded.

"Yes, sure, never better," she managed. "Scared to death, though. And they broke my glasses. Bastards."

"What happened?"

"They were watching the house, like you said. They blocked the entrance of the drive with their car. The creep with the ponytail made it clear he would shoot me through the windshield if I didn't get out of the car."

"I knew they would come back for the clockwork gadget," he said. "They couldn't afford to leave it at the scene of the murder too long because of the risk that someone would find it."

"They talked about it on the way down the drive. By then I figured out that you must have already run into the doll and dealt with it. I realized you were probably setting some kind of trap. I also knew that I had screwed things up for you."

"You had no way of knowing what had happened and there wasn't time to tell you." He looked around. "Do you see that gold watch the second man brought along?"

"Sorry," Charlotte said. "I can't see very well without my glasses."

Rex appeared from under the couch, muttering excitedly. He waved the gold pocket watch and rushed across the floor to his clutch bag. He pried open the purse and put the watch inside.

Charlotte squinted. "Did he just put the watch in the clutch?"

"He did," Slade said grimly.

"Good luck getting it back."

"Maybe I'll let Arcane handle that job." Slade reached for his phone. "I'll call Willis and have him pick up these two."

Charlotte frowned. "Hang on. They're hunter-talents, aren't they?"

"They were a little above midrange, I think. Not exactly the stuff of legend."

Charlotte tilted her head ever so slightly to one side. "They *were* a little above midrange?"

"They're just normal bad guys now. Willis can handle them."

Charlotte cleared her throat. "Why are they merely normal?"

He looked at her. "Remember you told me that I probably wouldn't figure out what I can do with all that stormlight energy until I found myself in a position where I needed to use it?"

"Uh-huh."

"I found out a few minutes ago what I can do with my talent."

"But what, exactly, did you do?"

"I burned out their para-senses. They're psi-blind."

Her mouth dropped open. "Permanently?"

"I think so, yes. Can't be positive because I've never done it before but it sure felt like a permanent psi-burn."

CHAPTER 27

"Leave the automaton in the bathtub," Marlowe Jones ordered over the phone. "Don't touch it. Don't let anyone else touch it. Sounds like you deactivated it successfully but the tub will provide some additional protection in case it's still capable of generating energy. You're sure it's facedown?"

"I'm sure," Slade said. He was standing in the bathroom, the phone clamped to his ear, looking down at the Sylvester doll in the tub. "But I think it's safe to handle as long as the key is out."

"Pay attention, Attridge. You are not to take any more chances with that device."

"Well, it sure as hell can't remain here in my tub for long. I need to shower occasionally."

"My assistant is on the phone to the lab people at the museum now. The removal-and-transport specialists should be there sometime tomorrow afternoon. The experts have ways of dealing with paranormal artifacts. They've got a specially equipped van."

"Good to know," Slade said. "But we've got a big storm coming in tonight. We're bracing for wind and rain damage. If there's a lot of it the ferry dock may be out of commission for a couple of days. Your lab people may have to wait until the following day to get here."

"I'll let them know. You say the automaton was made to resemble Sylvester?"

"The Old Bastard, himself." Slade walked out of the bathroom into the hall. "Sorry. Sometimes I forget that he's one of your ancestors."

"Believe me when I tell you that no one in the Jones family ever forgets that," Marlowe said. There was great depth of feeling in her tone.

"Give me some background on this clockwork weapon."

"The original clockwork curiosities were created by a brilliant clockmaker named Millicent Bridewell back in the late Nineteenth Century, Old World date. Mrs. Bridewell sold the devices to special customers who were in the market for a discreet assassination machine that would not leave any hard evidence at the scene. I gather from my ancestor, Caleb Jones's notes, that the toys caused a lot of trouble for J&J at the time."

"What happened to them?"

"Most disappeared after J&J worked a case that came to be known in the records as the Quicksilver affair. But a few showed up a couple hundred years later in the twenty-first century. That was back when Fallon Jones was running J&J."

"Which Jones?"

"Never mind, take my word for it, he was one of the legendary directors of J&J. He got all sorts of interesting cases. Rogue psychics, Nightshade, Mrs. Bridewell's curiosities."

Marlowe sounded wistful, Slade thought. He smiled. "Well, it's not like you and your fiancé haven't been busy lately. According to the press the two of you saved the whole Underworld."

"Yes, that was quite exciting," Marlowe said, brightening. "You say the device in your bathtub is still in working order?"

Slade thought about the cold energy that had almost iced his heart. "No doubt about it."

"Does the mechanism look like Old World technology?"

"No, the escapement and the other parts are all new," he said. "So is the costume. Everything about it was obviously constructed here on Harmony."

"Except for the eyes. I'll bet they're original. They are the source of the killing energy and no one has ever figured out how to re-create Mrs. Bridewell's brilliant work."

"Not that you know of."

"True. But there is absolutely no record of her work having been duplicated. Bridewell found a way to infuse powerful energy in glass and hold it in stasis until it is released by mechanical means. Her weapons-grade automatons could be used again and again, like guns. Quite unique."

"The question now is, how the hell did this thing end up on my island?"

There was the faintest of pauses on the other end of the connection.

"Your island?" Marlowe repeated neutrally. "Adam told me that as far as you were concerned, the job on Rainshadow was strictly temporary. He said you were planning to quit in a few months."

"Right," Slade said. "But I'm here now and I've got a job to do. So for the time being, this is my town and my island. Any idea how that curiosity got here?"

"No," Marlowe said. "But believe me, J&J

will be looking into the matter."

"Start with a dealer who worked the paranormal artifacts black market. The name is Jeremy Gaines."

"Okay. Tell me about Gaines."

"The first thing you should know is that he's dead," Slade said. "Murdered by paranormal means. He was in the para-arms business and it looks like he may have been killed by the two smugglers I just arrested but I'm not sure about that. I'll see what I can get out of them but they're obviously low-level muscle, not players."

"What else do you know about them?"

"Officer Willis called just before I phoned you. He did a quick background check and confirmed that they are a couple of small-time career-criminals. They're brothers, incidentally. Not the hottest amber in the drawer but they apparently had just enough hunter-talent to make them well-qualified for a life of crime. There are warrants out for their arrest from Frequency City. Most of it B and E. My next call will be to the Frequency cops. They can have both of them. I don't want them on my island."

"You said they're hunter-talents." Marlowe spoke deliberately. "Probably going to be hard to hold in a jail cell."

"Very low-rent hunters," Slade said, putting equally strong emphasis on his own words. "I don't think it will be necessary for J&J to make any special arrangements for those two."

"You're sure the system can handle them?"

Slade thought about the zones of energy that he had extinguished in the auras of the two men. Psychic canyons of night, he thought. The two men who had dared to put their hands on Charlotte would never recover their talent. He had made sure of it. But he wasn't about to explain that to the new director of the Frequency City office of J&J.

"If they get out of jail," he said, "it won't be because of their talent. Can't guarantee what a jury will do. That's always a crap-shoot."

"Okay," Marlowe said. "I'll take your word for it. Any idea why that pair of smugglers murdered Jeremy Gaines?"

"I haven't questioned them yet but I've got one scenario that fits. We know there's a market for para-weapons."

"Nobody ever went broke selling guns, paranormal or otherwise," Marlowe agreed. "It's like the drug business. There are always plenty of buyers."

"If I'm right about Jeremy Gaines being

352

involved in the psi-arms trade, he probably needed a couple of tough guys to handle shipping and receiving. That's a rough market."

"True."

"The pair I picked up knows how to operate a boat and they know enough about Rainshadow to figure out where on the island they could conceal illicit artifacts between shipments. It's obvious they've been using the island as a staging point for their products for some time."

"You're thinking this is a falling-out-among-thieves situation? The two smugglers quarreled with Gaines and decided they didn't need him anymore?"

"Maybe." But it didn't feel quite right, he thought. "I'll have more for you after they wake up and I've had a chance to question them."

"Wake up?" Marlowe's voice sharpened. "They're both asleep? You said they just got locked up. How many criminals take a nap shortly after being arrested? They should be busy calling their bail bondsmen and their lawyers."

"Turns out we don't have a lot of bail bondsmen and lawyers on the island. There was a bit of a scuffle when I took the bad guys down. I'm going to have to let you go.

I've got a lot to do here between trying to close out my case and prepare for the storm."

"What does this have to do with a storm?" Marlowe demanded.

"Big one coming in tonight. Tomorrow there will be a lot of downed trees blocking roads and causing power outages. Probably a fair amount of wind damage."

"So?"

"The local police department is the closest thing Rainshadow has to an emergency response agency. I've got one officer and a secretary. Come dawn, we're all going to be busy doing damage assessment and checking on some of the folks who live in the more remote sections of the island. Lots of our residents tend to be a bit eccentric and reclusive. Some of them don't even have phones. I'll call you when I have more information."

"I see." Marlowe cleared her throat. "How are you doing there on Rainshadow? Is the new job working out for you?"

"Working out fine," Slade said.

"Good. That's good. Glad to hear it." She paused delicately. "Are you feeling all right?"

"If you're asking me about my para-senses, which I assume is your real question, they haven't deteriorated any further."

"I'm so glad. Adam told me about what the explosion did to your senses. I'm so very sorry."

She meant well, Slade thought, but the sympathy in her voice was annoying.

"My talent has stabilized, at least for now," he said. He kept his own voice cool and even, making it clear he was not inviting any more conversation on the topic. Good-bye, Marlowe. Give my best to Adam. I'll see you both at the wedding."

"Wait, don't hang up —"

Slade closed the phone.

Adam Winters turned away from the window and watched Marlowe put down the phone. He could tell from the tightness at the edges of her eyes that she was annoyed. He loved looking at her, he thought, regardless of her mood. She never ceased to fascinate him. Her energy worked magic.

Evidently sensing that she was irritated, Gibson, Marlowe's dust bunny companion, vaulted up onto the desk and offered her a High-Rez Energy Bar from his precious stash. Gibson was a member of the High-Rez Energy Bar of the Month Club. He received a box of the treats every four weeks, courtesy of the Frequency City Ghost Hunters Guild. Gibson had helped save the Underworld but figuring out how to thank a dust bunny for service above and beyond the call of duty was no easy task. He seemed thrilled with his monthly energy bar shipments, though.

"Thanks, Gibson," Marlowe said. Her expression lightened with affection. She accepted the energy bar and switched her attention back to Adam as she started to unwrap the snack. "Slade said to give you his best. Said he'd see us at the wedding."

Adam raised his brows. "He said he would be coming to our wedding?"

"Uh-huh." Marlowe took a bite of the energy bar. "Seemed in pretty good spirits for a guy who is supposed to be going psi-blind."

"Is that so?"

"Said he was busy there on Rainshadow. Thinks he's got the clockwork curiosities case almost closed at his end. Of course, I've still got a lot of work to do. I need to find out if there are any more of those Bridewell toys floating around. One of the real problems is that none of the Arcane museums have accurate records of what artifacts were brought through the Curtain legally, let alone what collectors might have smuggled."

"You said Slade sounded good?"

"Yes."

"Did he mention the status of his talent?"

Marlowe munched reflectively for a time. "Said his talent had stabilized."

"I'm glad to hear it."

"He said a couple of other things, too. He referred to Rainshadow as his island."

Adam nodded. "He's taking his job seriously. That's Slade. He's a lawman to the bone."

Marlowe gave the foil wrapper from the energy bar to Gibson, who chortled and raced off to add it to his collection of wrappers.

"Slade said something else, too," Marlowe volunteered.

"What?"

"He told me that the two hunter-talents he has in jail won't be a problem for regular law enforcement after they wake up."

"They're *asleep?*"

"From what I can gather they fell asleep during what Slade referred to as a scuffle that occurred when he took them down."

"That would have been when they were holding Charlotte Enright hostage with the intent to kill her."

"Yes."

Adam smiled slowly. "And now he's not the least bit concerned that they may be

357

able to use their talent to escape jail."

"Nope." Marlowe ate the last of the energy bar. "Are you thinking what I'm thinking?"

"That Slade's talent has not only stabilized but that it may be of a slightly different nature than it was before he was caught in that explosion? Yes, that is exactly what I'm thinking."

"Think it's going to be a problem?"

"No," Adam said. "I know him. He got the protect-and-defend gene. It's encoded in his DNA."

"The ability to psi-blind another talent is heavy-duty stuff."

"No more heavy duty than our ability to work the Burning Lamp."

"Okay," Marlowe allowed. "I'll give you that."

"For obvious reasons we will not be making our speculations known to others," Adam said.

"Absolutely not. People would freak. I wonder if those two hunter-talents will ever figure out why they both went blind."

"If they've got any sense they'll realize they got off lightly."

Marlowe frowned. "Think so?"

"I know what I'd do to anyone who threatened to murder you," Adam said simply.

"Oh." She smiled. "Right. They're lucky to be alive, aren't they?"

"Yes," Adam said. "But, then, there's probably a reason for that, as well."

"What reason would that be?"

"Slade wants information from them."

"Ah, yes." Marlowe nodded. "Of course."

"Like I said, he's a natural-born crime fighter."

The office door opened. Rick Pratt, Marlowe's administrative assistant, put his head around the corner.

"Don't forget your appointment with the wedding planner, boss," Rick said. "You and Mr. Winters are due in her office in twenty minutes. Big decision today regarding the flowers."

Adam groaned. "You know, this would be so much simpler if we just eloped."

Rick gave him a stern look. "You can't elope. You're a Guild boss and this is a full Covenant Marriage ceremony. Your wedding to Marlowe is going to be *the* social event of the season here in Frequency."

"I've heard that," Adam said.

Marlowe laughed. "Come on, how hard can it be to choose a few flowers?"

Adam looked at her and fell in love all over again, just as he had the first time she rode into his life on the back of a motorcycle. Marlowe's love for him glowed in her eyes. He knew it would be like this all the days of their lives.

"I will do whatever it takes to marry you," he vowed. "Bring on the flowers."

CHAPTER 28

Charlotte was perched on a stool behind the sales counter, working on her computerized inventory, when the shop bell chimed. She was expecting Slade but it was Devin and Nate who blew into the shop.

They brought a rush of energy from the oncoming storm. The full force of the wind and rain wasn't expected for several hours but the sky was darkening rapidly. White, foamy crests had appeared on the choppy waves of the deep waters that surrounded the island.

"Miss Enright, we need you to help us pick out a birthday present for someone," Devin said. "A really cool present like the compass you gave me."

"Devin says you'll know just what he wants," Nate added. "But it can't be too expensive because we don't have much money. We can go as high as eight dollars and forty-three cents."

"Also, it's a secret," Devin added. "You can't tell him."

The boys crashed to a halt in front of the counter. They were aglow with urgent excitement.

"Okay, slow down," Charlotte said. "First, who is this birthday present for?"

"Chief Attridge," Devin said. "We're going to give him a birthday party."

"To thank him for getting us out of the Preserve," Nate added. "My mom says it would be a good idea because the chief doesn't have any family of his own here on the island to help him celebrate his birthday."

"My grandma said she'd help," Devin said. "She's going to make the cake."

"I see." Charlotte folded her arms on the glass counter. "And when is the chief's birthday?"

"Friday," Nate said.

"So soon?" Charlotte said. "How did you find out the date?"

It was oddly disconcerting to discover that she didn't know the date of Slade's birthday. Surely a woman should know that much about a man before she went to bed with him. But things like that weren't supposed to matter when you were just having a short-term fling. He didn't know her birth-

362

day, either. Well, maybe he did. For all she knew, he had done a background check on her after Jeremy's body had shown up in her back room. They said the person who found the body was automatically a suspect.

"Grandma told me his birthday," Devin said.

Charlotte wondered how Myrna had discovered the date. Then it occurred to her that dates of birth were everywhere, from driver's licenses to job applications. Slade's birthday no doubt appeared on some of the forms he had filled out when he had taken the job as chief.

"Not much time to plan a party," Charlotte said.

"We've got a lot of things to get organized," Devin said. "But first we wanted to make sure that we get the chief a really good present."

"One that doesn't cost any more than eight dollars and forty-three cents," Nate emphasized.

"I'll see what I can do," Charlotte promised.

Devin grinned. "Thanks, Miss Enright. I knew you would help us."

The boys dashed out of the shop. Charlotte waited until they were gone before she got up off the stool. Heightening her talent, she walked slowly across the shop, feeling her way through the sea of low-level psi currents that flooded Looking Glass. There had to be some object in the vast collection that suited Slade and his unique aura.

She stopped in front of the glass case that contained a display of objects set with crystals and amber. Something about the watch on the bottom stirred her energy.

She opened the door of the display case, reached inside, and took out the watch. The timepiece was an early Second Century antique, designed by an Arcane watchmaker. It would be a clever reminder of the case that Slade had just worked here on the island, and, perhaps, a memento of their time together.

She touched the pendant at her throat. The dark energy in the watch sang to her senses. She knew she could tune it for Slade.

The full force of the storm struck shortly after ten o'clock that night. Lightning danced in the skies. The fiercely gusting wind whipped the trees and rattled the windows. Rain pounded on the roof.

Slade stood with his arm around Charlotte. Together they watched nature's special effects through her living room window. They were both jacked. The energy of the storm had stirred their senses. He was aroused in more elemental ways as well, but he didn't think that he could blame that condition on the storm. Just being close to Charlotte had that effect. Just thinking about her was enough to make him rock hard.

Rex sat on the windowsill. He ignored the storm. He was occupied with the task of taking the gold pocket watch out of the clutch and putting it back inside. He repeated the process over and over as if it were a new game.

"I love storms," Charlotte said. She folded her arms beneath her breasts and snuggled against Slade, her head resting on his shoulder. "It's the energy. So thrilling."

He tightened his arm around her. They had turned the lights off inside the cottage. The strobelike flashes of lightning illuminated Charlotte's features in all the compelling hues and shades of feminine mystery.

He turned her slowly to face him.

"Thrilling," he said.

She smiled in the flaring shadows and he was suddenly on fire for her. He picked her up and carried her across the living room and down the hall to the darkened bedroom. There he stood her on her feet.

He used both hands to remove her glasses

and set them carefully aside on the end table. He cradled her face between his palms and kissed her.

She responded, as she always did, with a passion that warmed his very soul. She wrapped her arms around his neck and opened her mouth for him.

He stripped her clothes from her and bundled her into bed. It took him only seconds to get out of his trousers, boots, and shirt. He lowered himself slowly down on top of her, braced himself on his elbows, and bracketed her head with his arms. He kissed her deeply until she was breathless and twisting beneath him.

He made his way slowly down her soft, sleek body, glorying in the sensual curves of her breasts and the womanly fullness of her thighs. By the time he tangled his fingers in the triangle of soft hair below her belly he was desperate for her. But he wanted her to come first.

He used his hand and then his mouth on her, letting her spicy, damp heat intoxicate his senses. She was full and wet and tight. Her fingers clenched in his hair.

"Slade," she gasped.

Moments later he felt her release cascade through her. She was still pulsing when he climbed back up her body and thrust into her. He stroked once, twice and then his climax tore through him.

Outside the storm raged, setting fire to the night.

CHAPTER 29

Charlotte was on the front porch, heading toward her car, when she heard her phone ring. She fished it out and glanced at the screen. She smiled when she saw the caller's name.

"Good morning, Thelma," she said. "Is everything okay at your place?"

"Actually, it's not, dear."

"Are you all right?" Charlotte asked quickly.

"Yes, yes, of course. I didn't mean to alarm you. There was a good deal of damage to my garden and the high winds took off a section of the greenhouse roof. The power is off, of course."

"Same here. Slade said it's off in town, too."

"There's nothing that can't be repaired here at my place," Thelma said. "The problem is that there's a tree down in my front yard. It's blocking the driveway. I can't get my car out and I need to go into town to pick up a few things. I wondered if you could give me a ride?"

"Of course. I'm just about to leave to check up on Looking Glass. Slade did a quick drive-by early this morning when he went into town to assess the damage. He said everything looked fine at the shop but he didn't have time to go inside. I want to make sure that there were no leaks. I'll pick you up in about five minutes. How's that?"

"Perfect. I'll walk out to the road and meet you. There is so much debris down in the drive that I don't think you could get anywhere near the house."

Charlotte opened the car door. "I'm on my way."

"Thank you, dear."

"It's the least I can do after all the fabulous zucchini bread and the basil and tomatoes you've given me."

Thelma chuckled. "I'm just grateful to have a neighbor who appreciates good veggies. See you in a few minutes."

The phone went silent. Charlotte dropped it back into her purse and drove cautiously out to the main road. Branches, limbs, and windblown debris littered the drive and the narrow strip of pavement that wound along the top of the cliffs.

Slade had left early to organize his small staff and an assortment of volunteers. By now they were all out identifying hazards such as downed power lines and making sure those who lived alone were all right. When he had phoned earlier he had advised her that the road into town was reasonably clear.

Thelma was waiting at the junction of her drive and the road. She was bundled up in a faded windbreaker and carried a covered basket on her arm. She opened the door on the passenger side and got into the car.

"Good morning, dear," she said. She settled the basket on her lap. "My goodness, that was quite the storm, wasn't it?"

"They predicted seventy-mile-an-hour winds and I think we got them," Charlotte said.

"I expect Slade will be very busy for the rest of the day."

"Looks like it. When he called a while ago he was on his way out to Zeke Hodson's house to make sure everything was okay."

"Good. Zeke is getting on in years. He must be eighty-five or eighty-six by now and he has always kept to himself. Never had a phone. He could collapse in his house and no one would know it for weeks."

Charlotte's phone rang again. She braked

370

to a stop to answer it. A glance at the screen showed Slade's name.

"Hi," she said. "How's the recon going?"

"So far nothing serious," Slade said. "You okay?"

The urgency in his voice surprised her.

"I'm fine," she said. "I'm on the way into town. Thelma is with me. She called a few minutes ago to ask for a lift."

"Is she all right?"

"Yes, but there's a tree blocking her driveway so she couldn't get her car out."

"All right," he said. "Drive carefully. There are broken tree limbs hanging everywhere. Some of them are big. If one comes down on a windshield it would do some major damage."

"I know. I'll be careful."

"Power is out all over the island and there's some damage to the ferry dock and the marina. We won't be getting any ferry service for at least forty-eight hours. Willis said some of the B&B guests are not happy about being trapped on the island. The visitors out at the lodge don't like it, either. But aside from the whining, it shouldn't be a major problem. I'll check back with you later."

"Okay," she said. She closed the phone and dropped it into her purse.

Thelma smiled knowingly. "I do believe the town's cunning strategy to keep Chief Attridge on the job is working nicely. He seems quite concerned about you, Charlotte."

Charlotte felt the heat rise in her cheeks. "Slade and I are dating but that's all. I am not a part of the local conspiracy."

"I understand, dear," Thelma said. "But that fact only makes it all the more romantic, don't you think?"

Charlotte laughed. "You're incorrigible."

"I've lived alone for a long time but I haven't forgotten what romance and passion feel like," Thelma said. "I doubt if anyone ever forgets those things."

"No," Charlotte said. For better or worse, she was certainly going to remember Slade for the rest of her life.

The town's small central core had come through the gale in remarkably good shape. The tourist-oriented shops were all closed but the grocery, hardware, and gardening supply stores were open and doing a brisk business.

"Shall I drop you off at Spindler's Garden Supply?" Charlotte asked.

"No need for that. I'll get out at Looking Glass and walk down the street to Spindler's."

"Are you sure? It's no trouble, really."

"I'm sure."

"I'll just take a few minutes to make sure everything is okay inside my shop. Then I need to pick up a few things at the grocery store. After that I'll drive you home."

"Perfect," Thelma said. "I do appreciate this."

"You're more than welcome," Charlotte said.

She drove down the lane behind the row of shops and parked at the back door of Looking Glass. She and Thelma got out of the car. Thelma waved and started off toward the walkway that separated Looking Glass from the neighboring shop.

Charlotte went up the back steps and rezzed the lock on the door. She really was going to have to get a new lock, she reminded herself.

She opened the door and stepped inside. The interior of the shop was heavily shadowed. Automatically she rezzed the wall switch. Ice shivered down her spine when the lights did not come on.

Thelma spoke behind her. "The power is out, remember, dear?"

Charlotte turned quickly in the doorway. Thelma was coming up the steps. She held a Baroque silver-and-gold hand mirror, the glass face aimed at Charlotte. Dark crystals glittered on the frame and handle of the old looking glass. Strange alchemical markings were etched into the metal. It was impossible to focus on the face of the mirror. It was like looking into a pool of mercury. The surface seethed with energy.

"The Quicksilver Mirror," Charlotte whispered. The antiques dealer in her asked the first question that came to mind. "That's supposed to be in an Arcane museum. How did you get it?"

"This isn't the place to chitchat about such things." Thelma reached the top step. "Inside with you now. Wouldn't want anyone to see us."

"Forget it."

Charlotte moved forward, intending to shove Thelma off the step. But the Quicksilver Mirror flashed with a shocking radiance. The force of the short blast of energy jolted through Charlotte. For a heartbeat the world around her exploded with eerie ultralight lightning.

She gripped the doorjamb to steady herself and intuitively shut down her senses. It was the only move she could think of that might offer some protection. In the hands of a powerful talent, the mirror was a lethal weapon.

"That's better," Thelma said, her voice hardening. "Now go back into the shop."

Still dazed from the stunning shock, Charlotte turned slowly and moved a short distance into the darkened room. Thelma followed quickly. She closed and locked the door.

"What is this about?" Charlotte asked. It took everything she had to keep her own voice calm.

"It's about the Bridewell Engine," Thelma snapped. "What did you think it was about, you silly woman?"

"What engine?"

"According to the old lab notebook, it looks something like a snow globe."

Events came together with sickening clarity.

"You and Jeremy Gaines were working together," Charlotte said.

"We were partners for more than three years until he decided to cut me out of the biggest deal of all."

"You killed Jeremy?"

"We were going to split the profits from the Bridewell Engine. But Gaines got greedy."

"I trust that didn't come as a huge surprise," Charlotte said.

"No, but I made the mistake of thinking

that he understood that he needed me as much as I needed him." Thelma snorted. "Unfortunately, he was too shortsighted to see that. He planned to grab the engine and sell it on his own."

"Did you murder him with the Sylvester device?"

"Oh, no, I used the mirror on Gaines," Thelma said. "I had to work quickly that night, you see."

"I understand now. When I set out to find the snow globe for Jeremy I inadvertently led him to Mrs. Lambert. He realized that she was the collector who refused to sell."

"He broke into her house one night but he couldn't find the engine."

"He wouldn't have been able to find it even if he had known what it looks like because she kept it in a special vault."

"He was going to break in again to look for it but by then Lambert had already made arrangements to give her glass collection to the Arcane museum," Thelma said. "The staff packed up what we assumed were all of the objects. The glassware was taken away and stored in the museum's vaults."

"Then Mrs. Lambert suffered a heart attack and later died in the hospital," Charlotte said.

"We tried to come up with a plan to break

into the museum vaults but it looked impossible. J&J recently tightened security there. Then Gaines found a copy of the inventory of the items that Mrs. Lambert had given to the museum. There was no object resembling the Bridewell Engine on it. But he learned that some additional items had been bequeathed to you."

"But by then the bequest that was coming to me was under lock and key in a vault at Lambert's bank where it stayed until the estate was sorted out."

"Gaines and I cooled our heels until you took possession of the bequest. During that time Gaines tried to seduce you." Thelma looked disgusted. "He was accustomed to being able to charm women and everyone else. I swear, it was part of his talent. But he finally realized that you were not going to fall at his feet. So he sat back to wait for you to take possession of the Lambert bequest."

"Then I screwed up his plans again by shipping the Lambert bequest along with most of the contents of my Frequency City shop here to the island."

"He was furious," Thelma said. "But that was when he finally decided to tell me about the side deal he had made for the Bridewell Engine. The customer had offered him a huge amount of money, more than either Gaines or I had ever made on a single sale. It was enough to retire on."

"Why did he tell you about the deal he had arranged on his own?"

"When he found out the globe was here on the island, he realized that he would need my help," Thelma said. "I'm quite sure he planned to kill me afterward."

"But you murdered him first."

"I came to the same conclusion he did," Thelma said coldly. "I decided that I no longer needed a partner."

"You killed him here in my shop so that if there was any sort of investigation, I would be the most likely suspect."

"I wasn't terribly worried about the new police chief," Thelma said. "Attridge wouldn't have wound up on Rainshadow in the first place if he was a good cop. But one does have to keep an eye out for Jones & Jones. Occasionally the agency insists on meddling. But fortunately everyone involved accepted the obvious cause of death. Heart attack. They also accepted the obvious reason for Gaines's presence in your shop. He was supposedly stalking you."

"But you couldn't find the Bridewell Engine that night."

Thelma's face twisted with rage. "I work

glasslight. I was sure that the energy in the engine would be powerful enough to stand out, even amid all these objects. But I was wrong."

"Yes, you were. The engine doesn't get hot until someone fires it up."

Thelma's eyes glittered. "You found it? Where is it?"

"I unpacked it," Charlotte said soothingly. "I'll get it for you."

"If you try to trick me, I swear —"

"Do you want it or not?"

"Get it."

Charlotte walked across the room to the old safe. She rezzed the code. When the mag-steel door opened she reached inside and took out the dull gray glass object.

"That's not the Bridewell Engine," Thelma barked. "It can't be. It's just an old paperweight." She raised the mirror higher. "I warned you —"

"Watch," Charlotte said softly.

She touched her pendant and pulsed a little energy into the heart of the globe. The dome started to glow. It grew first translucent and then clear. A storm of tiny glass particles fell like snow over the miniature Victorian landscape. Powerful currents of psi swirled in the atmosphere of the shop.

"That's it," Thelma breathed. "I can feel

it now. Give it to me."

"Be careful," Charlotte said. "It's psi-hot."

"I told you, I can handle glass energy."

Thelma seized the globe in her free hand. She gazed into it, transfixed.

"It's incredible," she said. "I can feel the power in it. Absolutely incredible."

"Why is it worth murder?"

"Don't you know?" Thelma did not take her eyes off the sparkling scene. "This was Millicent Bridewell's greatest secret. According to the old notebook, this was the device she created that allowed her to infuse energy into glass in such a way that it could be used as a weapon."

"She used the globe to create her clockwork curiosities?"

"Yes."

"How do you know that?"

"What?" Thelma seemed distracted by the crystal snow inside the globe. Her face tightened in concentration.

"I just wondered how you know for certain that's the Bridewell Engine," Charlotte repeated softly.

"It's all in the notebook," Thelma said absently. "That's how I learned of the existence of the engine in the first place." A visible tremor shivered through her. She gasped in response and frowned. "It's incredibly powerful."

"Yes," Charlotte said. "How did you come by the notebook?"

"Your aunt found it for me, of course. After I deciphered it I realized that the rumors I had heard were true. One of the First Generation colonists had brought the Bridewell Engine through the Curtain. I told Gaines about it. He managed to locate the refurbished Sylvester doll but not the engine. I took a chance and asked your aunt to find a certain Nineteenth Century Old World snow globe. But she started to ask too many questions."

Another frisson of intuition sliced across Charlotte's senses.

"You killed Aunt Beatrix, didn't you?" she asked.

"As I said, she was starting to get suspicions. My sons and I ran a very profitable business here on the island for several years, selling items out of Looking Glass to mainland collectors. Beatrix never had a clue. All she cared about was her own search for some old artifact she called the Key. She never seemed to miss any of the antiques that my sons removed from her back room."

"Your sons?"

"Brody and Mack. The two men Attridge just arrested. I'll see about getting them out of jail later. Shouldn't be difficult. They're both hunters, after all. But right now the engine is my first priority."

"Jeremy handled the sale of the items you stole from my aunt, didn't he?"

"He was the one with the connections," Thelma said. "Our partnership worked well until he tried to cheat me out of the snow globe." She flinched. Her eyes tightened in pain. "It's getting too hot."

"I know," Charlotte said softly. "It's going to get hotter."

She heard the back door of the shop open. The shiver of awareness that went through her told her that Slade had arrived. He moved silently into the doorway between the two rooms. Out of the corner of her eye Charlotte saw another, much smaller shadow at his heels. Rex.

But Thelma did not notice. She was staring, transfixed, into the snow globe.

"Why didn't Brody and Mack use the Quicksilver Mirror on Slade?" Charlotte asked.

"Bah. Neither of them is strong enough to generate killing energy with the mirror. I had them use the automaton, instead. But something obviously went wrong. No matter, I'll deal with the chief later."

"I wouldn't plan on it, if I were you,"

Charlotte said.

"Nonsense. I did some research on him when he took the job. It appears that he had some talent at one time but he's just a burned-out FBPI agent now. According to his para-psych records, he's deteriorating and will continue to do so." Thelma started to shiver violently. *What's happening?*"

"Among sensitives, a talent for viewing aura rainbows isn't considered especially useful," Charlotte said quietly. "But it turns out that if you're really, really good at it you can tune the energy in certain objects to resonate with an individual's aura."

Dawning horror lit Thelma's features but she still could not look away from the engine.

"What are you talking about?" she gasped.

"As it happens, what can be tuned to resonate positively can be tuned to achieve the . . . opposite effect," Charlotte said.

"No."

Thelma struggled to unclamp her hand from around the snow globe. When that failed she smashed the object violently against a nearby table. The glass did not shatter. Inside the dome, ominous snow continued to fall over the ancient city of London.

Thelma shuddered violently. She opened

her mouth to scream but no sound came out. Her eyes rolled back into her head. She collapsed abruptly, crumpling to the floor.

The engine fell from her limp fingers, landing with a thud. The glass snow disappeared. The dome went dark.

Slade moved into the room, pistol in hand. He crouched briefly to check Thelma's throat for a pulse. Charlotte watched him, gripping the edge of a nearby table to steady herself. The shock of what she had done slammed through her. Her pulse was skidding violently.

Slade got to his feet, holstered the gun, and pulled Charlotte into his arms.

"It's all right," he said into her hair. "She's still alive, if that's what's worrying you."

Charlotte realized she was getting short of breath. "I wasn't sure what would happen. There was so much energy in that s-snow globe."

"What did you do to the globe?"

"Usually I t-tune objects so that they resonate harmoniously with a person's aura. This time I reversed the p-process. I tweaked the globe's c-currents so that they dampened Thelma's own frequencies."

He looked down at Thelma. "You flatlined her aura for a time. Long enough to make her lose consciousness."

"Something like that, y-yes." She touched the pendant. "It wasn't until I found this that I realized I might be able to do such a thing. But until now, I've never had a reason to actually try it and there was no way to run an experiment. I wasn't sure it would work."

Slade whistled softly. "I'll be damned. You could turn just about any psi-infused antique into a weapon."

"Yes."

He smiled slowly. "If word got out what you can do with antiques, it would not be good for your business."

"That thought o-occurred to me a few years ago. That's why I've never told anyone, not even my own family. You're the only one who knows."

He held her a little away from him. "And you're the only one who knows what I can do with my talent."

"D-don't worry, I can k-keep a secret," she whispered.

"So can I."

"Great. Now, if you'll excuse me, I'm going to have a panic attack."

"Breathe," Slade ordered.

"Right. I can do that."

CHAPTER 30

At nine thirty that night Slade lounged on Charlotte's sofa, phone in one hand, a beer in the other. He propped his ankles on a hassock and watched the flames leap on the hearth while he gave Marlowe Jones a summary of events.

"Brody and Mack Duncan were living under fake IDs," he said. "Took a while to find out their real names. They were picked up by the Frequency City cops this afternoon and booked on a number of charges. They're ratting out dear old Mom as fast as they can. Thelma Duncan is in a locked ward in the para-psych wing of Frequency Memorial Hospital. Looks like she had a stroke. She's confused and disoriented and no one thinks she'll make a full recovery."

"There is a detective in the Frequency Police Department who is Arcane," Marlowe said. "He's keeping an eye on things for me. He says that as far as the authorities are concerned, the Duncan boys and their mother were operating a small-time burglary ring that specialized in antiques."

"All true as far as it goes," Slade said. He caught Charlotte's eye.

"I called the museum lab people and warned them that in addition to the Sylvester curiosity they'll have two more hot objects to transport, the Quicksilver Mirror and the Bridewell Engine. They're very excited."

Slade watched Rex hop up onto the coffee table. Rex opened the clutch purse and removed the shiny, crystal-encrusted lady's compact that Charlotte had convinced him to exchange for the gold watch. He started playing with the compact. He had not yet figured out how to open it but that did not seem to bother him. He clearly considered the project a game.

"There's a fourth object," Slade said. "A gold watch that seems to be able to de-rez the automaton."

"I'll tell the transport team."

"That's it for now," Slade said. "Time to eat here."

"Dinner? It's nearly ten o'clock."

"It's been busy here on Rainshadow, what with the problem of Thelma and her boys and the poststorm cleanup. I'll talk to you tomorrow."

"Wait, don't hang up. Now that your talent has, uh, stabilized, will you be going back to work for the Bureau?"

"No," Slade said. He watched Charlotte set a plate of cheese and pickle sandwiches on the coffee table. "I won't be going back to my old job."

"Well, in that case," Marlowe said smoothly, "would you be interested in working as a contract agent for Jones & Jones? I'm getting more work now since Adam and I got all that publicity a while back. I could really use someone with your professional background." She paused a beat. "And your talent."

Charlotte sat down next to Slade and propped her slipper-clad feet on the table. He put his arm around her and allowed himself to relax into her warm, bright energy.

"I'll be staying here on Rainshadow," he said. "Nice little town. I like the job. It suits me. So if I can do you any favors from here, let me know."

"Thanks, I'll do that," Marlowe said. "But are you sure you want to stay on that hunk of rock there in the Amber Sea?"

Slade thought about the deep certainty that had been coalescing inside him ever since he had arrived on the island.

"I'm sure," he said. "Good night, Marlowe."

"See you at the wedding," she said.

"I'll be bringing a date."

"Good," Marlowe said. She sounded like she meant it. "That's wonderful."

He closed the phone and reached for a sandwich.

Charlotte watched him closely. "You told her you would be staying on Rainshadow."

"I did, yes." He took a large bite out of the sandwich.

"I'm glad," Charlotte said. "The island needs you."

He swallowed the bite of sandwich and looked at her. "Think so?"

"We both know now that there is something stirring out there in the Preserve. Someone needs to keep an eye on the situation. Who better than a former special agent of the FBPI?"

"I didn't make the decision to stay on the island because of the Preserve." He put the uneaten portion of the sandwich back on the plate. "I made it because of you."

Charlotte went very still. "Are you certain?"

"I've never been more certain of anything in my life. The day I walked off the ferry and found you waiting for me I knew it in my bones. It was as if I'd spent the past fifteen years trying to get back to you. If you leave the island, I'll leave with you. But as long as you're staying here, I'm staying, too. You're my future. I love you."

Her smile and her eyes were suddenly luminous. "Oh, Slade."

"For most of my life, home was always where I happened to be at any given time. But when I saw you at the ferry dock last week, I knew that home is where you are. The trouble was that I had nothing to offer you. I thought I was going psi-blind. The last thing I wanted from you was pity. So I tried to tell myself that I could handle a brief affair and then walk away before you realized what was happening to me." He took a deep breath. "But I don't know if I could have done that."

She touched the side of his jaw with gentle fingertips. "You would have because you would have told yourself that it was the best thing for me. And then I would have had to chase after you, which would have been very embarrassing."

"But you would have come after me?"

"In a heartbeat," she said. "I love you. I knew that we were meant for each other the day I watched you walk off the ferry. Actually, I knew it fifteen years ago but I told myself that it was just a teenage crush. Now I know better. It was the real thing."

A strange, heady sensation unfurled inside him. It took him a heartbeat to recognize it because he had kept it locked away in the deepest part of his being for so long. But now that he could set it free he could give it a name. *Joy.*

"You were always there in the back of my mind," he said. "That was why I kept the pocketknife that you gave me the morning I left town. It's the only thing I've ever hung on to in my life. And now I'm going to hang on to you. I'll never let go."

"And I'll never let go of you," she vowed.

He drew her close and kissed her. The warm, bright, abiding energy of love shimmered in the atmosphere around them.

CHAPTER 31

Randolph Sebastian took the phone call he had been dreading ever since he had taken the helm of Sebastian, Inc., and been entrusted with the family secrets.

"This is Sebastian," he said.

"Slade Attridge. I'm the new chief of police here on the island."

Randolph tightened his grip on the phone. A chill of intuition went through him. He could tell from Attridge's cold, controlled voice that the new police chief was a man to be reckoned with and, quite possibly, a problem.

"My assistant advised me of your identity when she put through the call," Randolph said. "What can I do for you, Chief Attridge?"

"According to the notes left by one of my predecessors, your family controls the Rainshadow Preserve Foundation."

"That's correct."

"Something is going on inside the Preserve," Slade said. "I need to know what is happening in there."

Alarm flashed through Randolph. After all these years the secrets of the Preserve were stirring.

"Has a section of the fence failed?" he asked. But he knew even as he asked that he was grasping at straws. "I can send out a repair crew."

"The fence is holding, at least as far as I know."

"I don't understand. Has someone gotten through it? That fence was made more secure by our security people five years ago after a couple of trespassers managed to get inside. Has there been another intrusion? Do you need a search-and-rescue team?"

"No, I need answers. What does that fence protect?"

Randolph tightened his grip on the phone. He got to his feet and walked to the window of his office. He stood looking out over the city of Cadence. The headquarters of Amber Sea Trading was a modern business tower located on the outskirts of the city's old Colonial-Era Quarter. Randolph had an excellent view of the ancient alien ruins in the heart of the city. The green quartz walls and ethereal towers sparkled in the sunlight as if they had been made of emeralds. At night the Dead City glowed with green psi, giving off enough light to illuminate the streets of the Quarter.

The time had come to make a decision, Randolph thought. He had to go with his intuition.

"The short answer to your question, Chief, is that I don't know what the fence is guarding," he said.

"That's not good enough. I've got a town to protect."

"I assure you, the people of Shadow Bay are safe as long as they refrain from trespassing inside the Preserve," Randolph said. "But it is imperative that no one goes through the fence."

"You know as well as I do that a No Trespassing sign is an irresistible attraction for some people."

"The fence is virtually impenetrable."

"No," Slade said. "It's not. Earlier this week I had to go in and pull out a couple of teenagers."

"What?" A terrible sensation swept through Randolph. It took him a second to recognize it as a flash of panic. "Two kids got in? You went in? You were able to find them? I don't believe it."

"Believe it," Slade said. "I need to know

what I'm up against here. If this requires the evacuation of the island I'm going to have to contact the authorities. And I'm going to need some real good reasons to give them."

"I can't give you any reasons," Randolph said, "because I don't know what is going on inside the Preserve. All I can tell you is that everyone is safe so long as they stay out." *I hope,* he added silently.

"I want answers."

"I will send the head of Sebastian Security to investigate and assess the situation immediately. He'll be on the island tomorrow."

"I'll be waiting for him."

The phone went dead in Randolph's hand. He stood at the window a moment longer, composing himself and trying to clarify his thoughts. After a time he rezzed a number into the phone. His grandson answered at once.

"What's wrong?" Harry Sebastian asked without preamble.

"Something's come up on Rainshadow. I don't want to talk about it over the phone. How soon can you be in my office?"

"Five minutes."

Randolph put the phone down. He had doubled the family fortune in the thirty years he had been in command of the company. That had been the easy part. The hardest part about running Sebastian, Inc., was managing the complicated dynamics of the sprawling Sebastian family. His strong intuitive talent made him a force of nature in the business world but it was not nearly so useful when it came to dealing with his willful, stubborn, intelligent, and highly talented relatives. His two grandsons were the most maddening of all. Probably because they had turned out a lot like him, he thought.

Four minutes later the door opened. Harry walked into the room. He had been named for his pirate ancestor and with his black hair, ascetic features, and cold, green eyes, he was the living image of the man in the portrait that hung on the wall of the office. But it was only much later when his unusual talent had appeared that everyone in the family realized he resembled the original Harry in more than just looks.

"We have a problem on Rainshadow?" Harry asked.

"If even a fraction of the legends concerning the secrets our ancestor buried there are true," Randolph said, "we have a very big problem on the island."

Chapter 32

On Friday evening, Charlotte stood with Rachel on the outdoor deck of the Shorebird Restaurant, glasses of lemonade in their hands. Together they contemplated the crowd. Slade was in the center of the group, a large knife in one hand. There was a vast sheet cake covered in chocolate and lemon-colored icing on the table in front of him. The words on the cake read *Happy Birthday, Chief.*

"You know, I think he actually was surprised when he walked in a few minutes ago," Rachel said.

Charlotte laughed. "Stunned speechless is more like it. Who'd have thought that you could pull off a real surprise party for a former Bureau agent who also happens to be Arcane?"

Devin and Nate were in front of the table, euphoric over the success of the party they had planned. Myrna and Kirk Willis stood nearby. Both had wide grins on their faces. All of the shopkeepers on Waterfront Street, including Fletcher Kane and Jasper Gilbert, as well as most of the permanent residents of the island had turned out. Rex was perched on the railing with his clutch. His attention was riveted on the cake.

"Being an FBPI agent doesn't mean you can see a surprise party coming," Rachel said. "And a man who hasn't done a lot of celebrating in his life wouldn't have any reason to expect a couple of kids to organize a whole town for a birthday party."

"No, probably not," Charlotte said.

Rachel smiled. "Something tells me that Slade has a lot to celebrate now, though."

Slade caught Charlotte's eye across the crowded space and winked. He put the large cake knife aside.

"This is a very special cake," he announced. "Myrna tells me that I get the first slice so that slice will be cut with a very special knife."

He reached into his pocket and took out the Takashima pocketknife. Charlotte felt tears gather in her eyes.

"Hang on," Myrna yelped. "You can't cut my beautiful cake with a dirty knife." She whipped a packet out of her purse, tore it open, and produced a sterilizing wipe.

Slade obediently wiped the gleaming blade and then he cut a neat square of the cake and slid it onto a paper plate.

Myrna bustled around to take his place behind the cake. "I'll cut the rest of the pieces, Chief. Rex gets the next slice."

Rachel looked at Charlotte. "Has anyone told Rex that the glory days of endless zucchini bread are over?"

"We're hoping he'll move on," Charlotte said. "Dust bunnies are very adaptable. They know how to rez with the frequency, unlike some of us."

Myrna used the large cake knife to cut off a big square of chocolate and lemon cake for Rex. She put the cake on a paper plate and set it on the railing. Rex chortled gleefully and set about polishing off the treat with as much enthusiasm as he had previously reserved for Thelma Duncan's zucchini bread.

"Were you really surprised by the party, Chief?" Devin demanded for the fifth or sixth time.

Slade smiled at him. "I was really surprised, trust me."

The crowd laughed.

"We made everyone promise to keep it a secret," Nate explained.

Slade looked around at the faces of the

people on the deck. "Shadow Bay could give the Bureau some lessons when it comes to keeping secrets."

There was another round of laughter. Slade made his way through the crowd and stopped near Charlotte and Rachel.

"Happy birthday, Chief," Rachel said. "If you'll excuse me, I'm going to get in line for my slice."

She hurried off.

Charlotte looked at Slade.

"How is the cake?" she asked.

"A whole lot better than Thelma Duncan's zucchini bread," Slade said. A look of soul-deep satisfaction lit his eyes. "In fact, I can state unequivocally that this is the very best cake I have ever eaten in my entire life."

Charlotte smiled.

Devin waved a small, gaily wrapped gift in the air. "Time to open your present, Chief Attridge. Nate and I got it for you. It's from Looking Glass."

Slade smiled at Charlotte. In his eyes she saw the heat and promise of a love that would last a lifetime.

"In that case, I won't have to worry about returning it to the store," Slade said. "Whatever it is, it's going to be just what I wanted."

He kissed her on the mouth there in front

of their friends and neighbors. A roar of applause went up from the crowd.

Slade raised his head and looked around.

"You're all invited to the wedding," he said.

ABOUT THE AUTHOR

Jayne Castle, the author of *Midnight Crystal, Obsidian Prey, Dark Light, Silver Master, Ghost Hunter,* and *Harmony,* is a pseudonym for Jayne Ann Krentz, the *New York Times* bestselling author of *In Too Deep, Fired Up, Running Hot, All Night Long, Falling Awake, Truth or Dare,* and other novels. She has been featured in such publications as *People* and *Entertainment Weekly,* and is also known for her historical romantic-suspense books written under the name Amanda Quick. A former librarian with a degree in history, she is also the editor of an award-winning essay collection, *Dangerous Men and Adventurous Women: Romance Writers on the Appeal of the Romance.* You can find her online at www.jayneannkrentz.com.